23

Cat & Cat

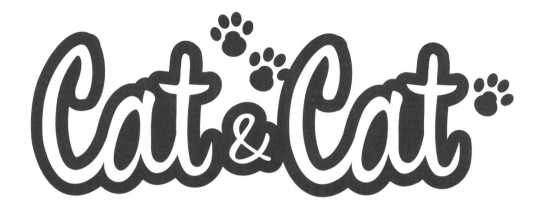

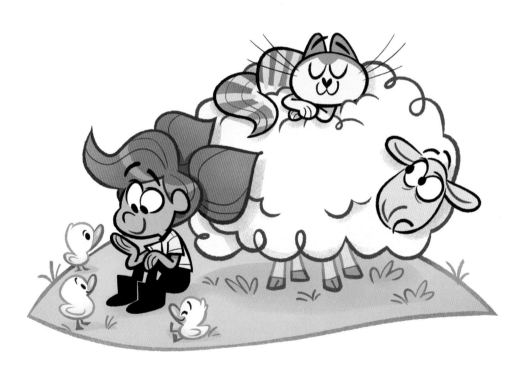

PAPERCUTZ

MORE GREAT GRAPHIC NOVEL SERIES AVAILABLE FROM PAPERCUTZ

ASTERIX

ASTRO MOUSE AND LIGHT BULB

ATTACK OF THE STUFF

BRINA THE CAT

THE CASAGRANDES

CAT & CAT

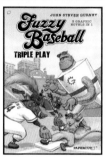
THE FLY

FUZZY BASEBALL

GEEKY F@B 5

GERONIMO STILTON REPORTER

GILLBERT

LOLA'S SUPER CLUB

THE LOUD HOUSE

MELOWY

THE MYTHICS

THE NIGHTMARE BRIGADE

THE ONLY LIVING GIRL

SCHOOL FOR EXTRATERRESTRIAL GIRLS

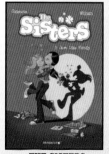
THE SISTERS

THE SMURFS TALES

PAPERCUTZ
WWW.PAPERCUTZ.COM
ALSO AVAILABLE WHERE EBOOKS ARE SOLD.

Cat & Cat

5. THE KITTY FARM

 CHRISTOPHE CAZENOVE
HERVE RICHEZ
SCRIPT

 YRGANE RAMON
ART

 YRGANE RAMON
JOÃO MOURA
COLOR

 PAPERCUTZ

To my parents,

To Inari,
To Molly Bindle, Morticia, Popeye & Arya,
To friends, readers, and all the cats who bring this series alive,
Thanks.

A huge thanks to João Moura for the coloring of characters in some
of this volume's pages.

www.joaomouraart.com

– Yrgane

& A Big
MEOW OF THANKS
to all
CAREGIVERS!

#5 "The Kitty Farm"
Christophe Cazenove &
Hervé Richez – Writers
Yrgane Ramon – Artist, Colorist
João Moura – Colorist
Joe Johnson – Translator
Emma Jensen – Letterer

Special thanks to Catherine Loiselet

Production – Mark McNabb
Editorial Intern – Taku Ward

Assistant Editor – Stephanie Brooks
Editorial Director – Rex Ogle
Jim Salicrup
Editor-in-Chief

© 2020, 2022 Bamboo Édition.
English translation and all other material © 2023 Papercutz.

Hardcover ISBN: 978-1-5458-1019-4
Paperback ISBN: 978-1-5458-1020-0

Printed in China
April 2023

First Printing

I'm home, SUSHI KITTY!

What's with the suitcases, MOM?

We're going to UNCLE XAVIER'S.

Oh, nooooooo!

Why no?

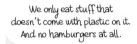

He lives on a farm with lots of weird, super scary animals like ducks and cows.

We only eat stuff that doesn't come with plastic on it. And no hamburgers at all.

Also, there are spiders all over the house. And in the barn, there are even mice!

The network is just awful, not even one bar on your smartphone. And the internet only works Sunday morning, but Xavier goes to church and we have to go with hiiiiim!

And to top it off, the toilet is outsiiiide! It's so creepy. I don't wanna go there!

Well, say something, you!

I don't want to go there either -- that's all way too scary!

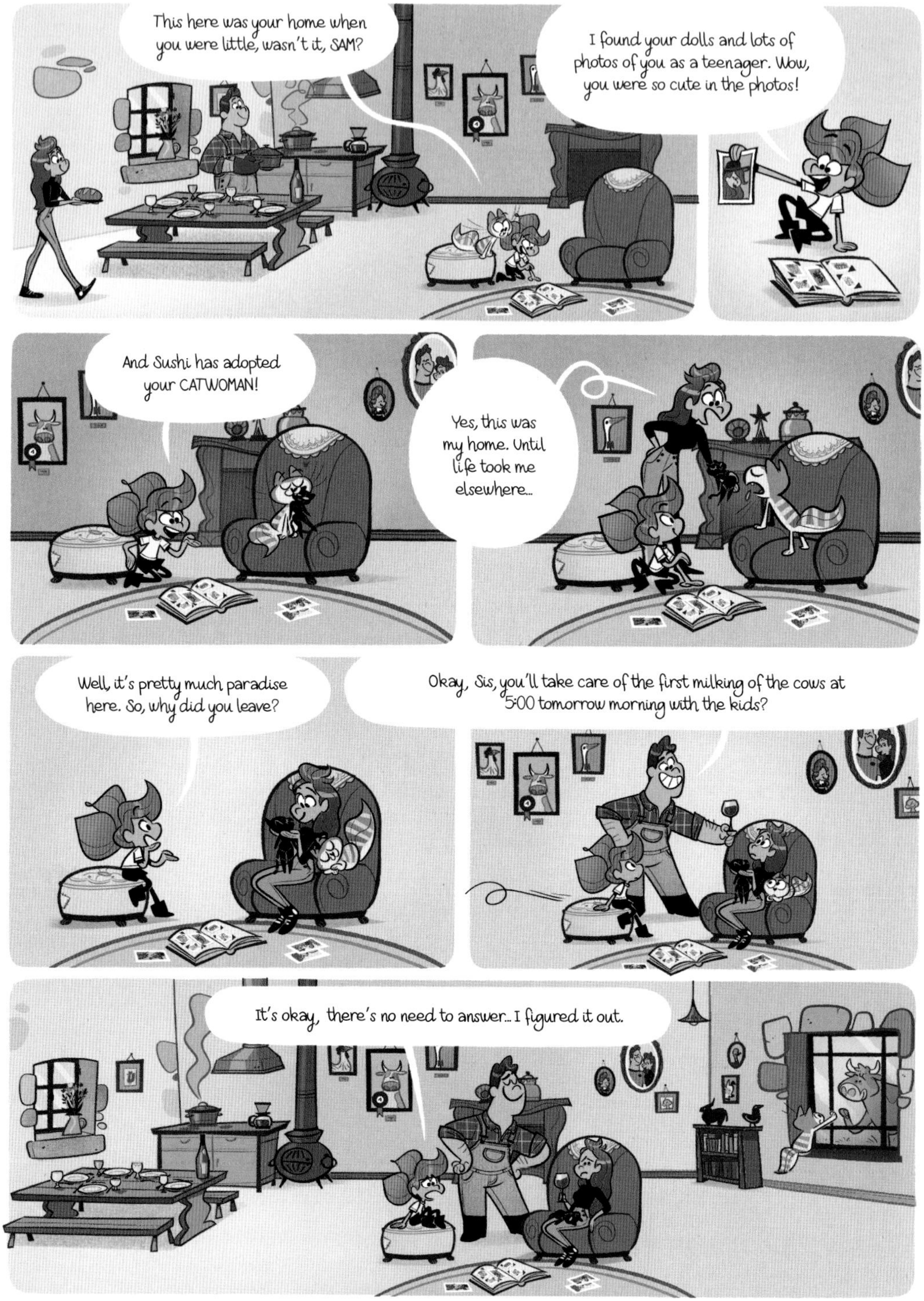
This here was your home when you were little, wasn't it, SAM?
I found your dolls and lots of photos of you as a teenager. Wow, you were so cute in the photos!
And Sushi has adopted your CATWOMAN!
Yes, this was my home. Until life took me elsewhere...
Well, it's pretty much paradise here. So, why did you leave?
Okay, Sis, you'll take care of the first milking of the cows at 5:00 tomorrow morning with the kids?
It's okay, there's no need to answer... I figured it out.

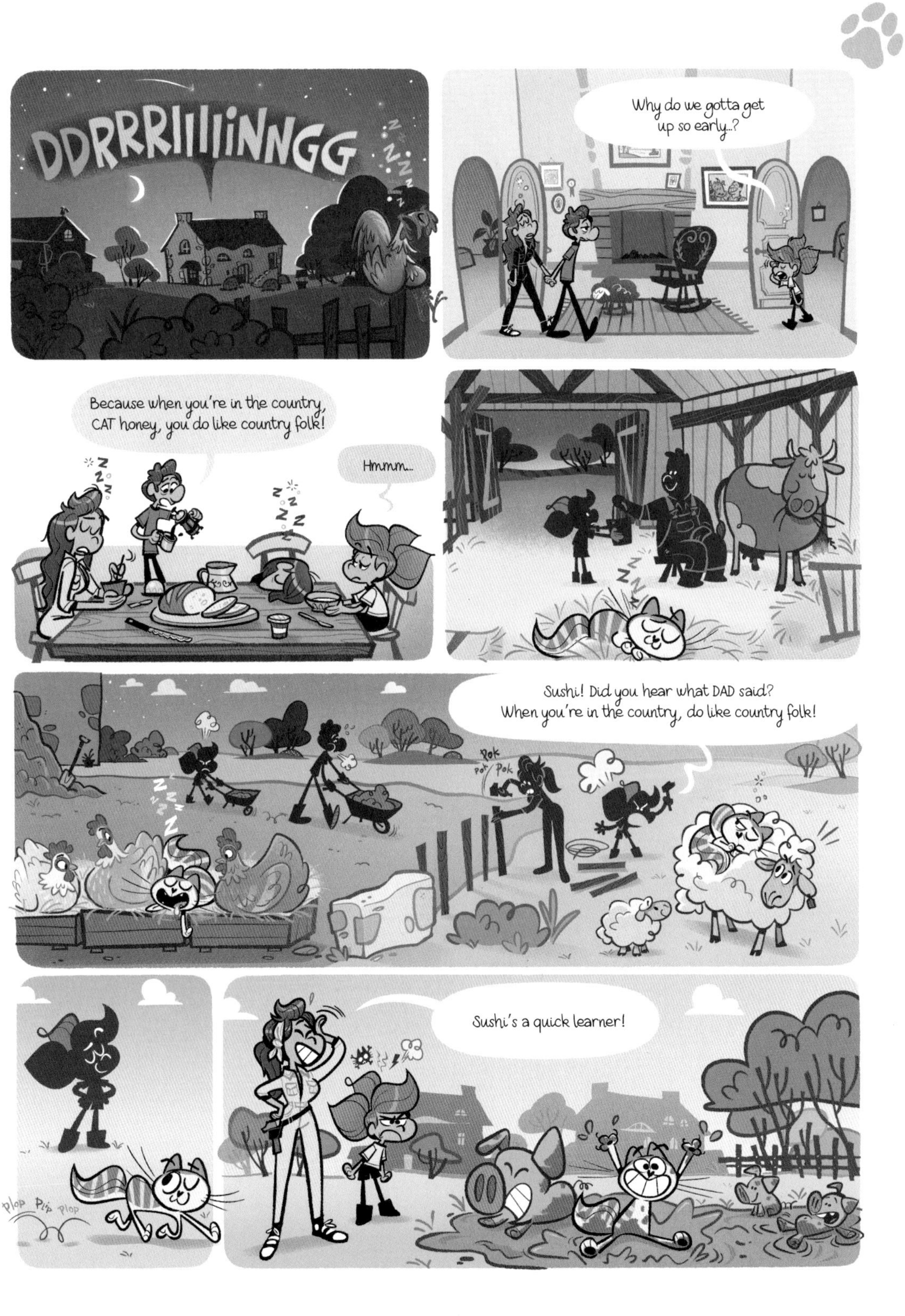
DDRRRIIIIINNGG
Z Z Z
Why do we gotta get up so early...?
Because when you're in the country, CAT honey, you do like country folk!
Hmmm...
Sushi! Did you hear what DAD said? When you're in the country, do like country folk!
Pok Pok Pok
Plop Plip Plop
Sushi's a quick learner!

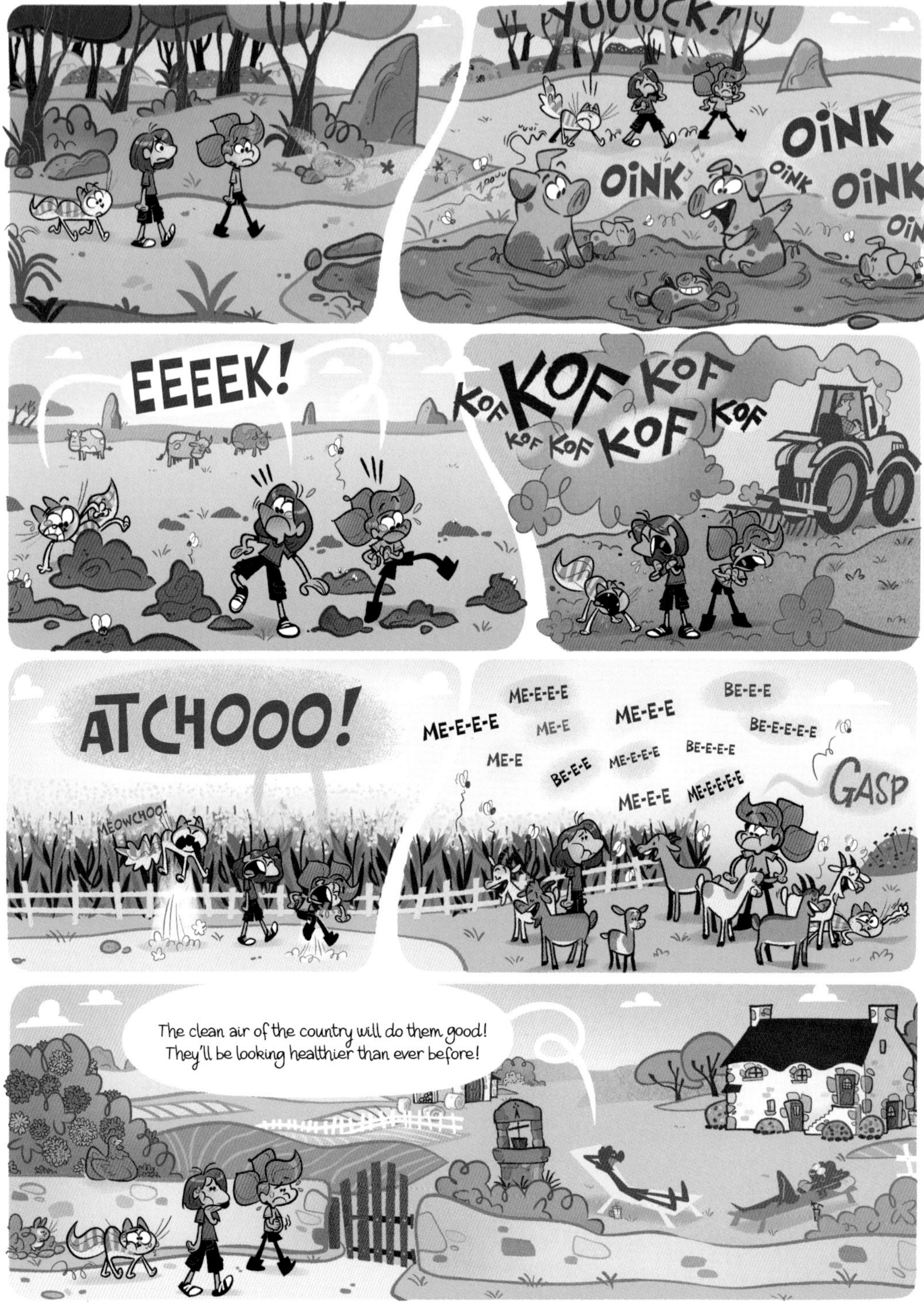
YUUUCK!
OINK
OINK
OINK
OINK
OINK
EEEEK!
KOF KOF KOF
KOF KOF KOF KOF
ATCHOOO!
MEOWCHOO!
ME-E-E-E
ME-E-E-E
ME-E
ME-E-E
ME-E
BE-E-E
ME-E-E-E
BE-E-E-E
BE-E-E
BE-E-E-E-E
ME-E-E
ME-E-E-E-E
GASP
The clean air of the country will do them good! They'll be looking healthier than ever before!

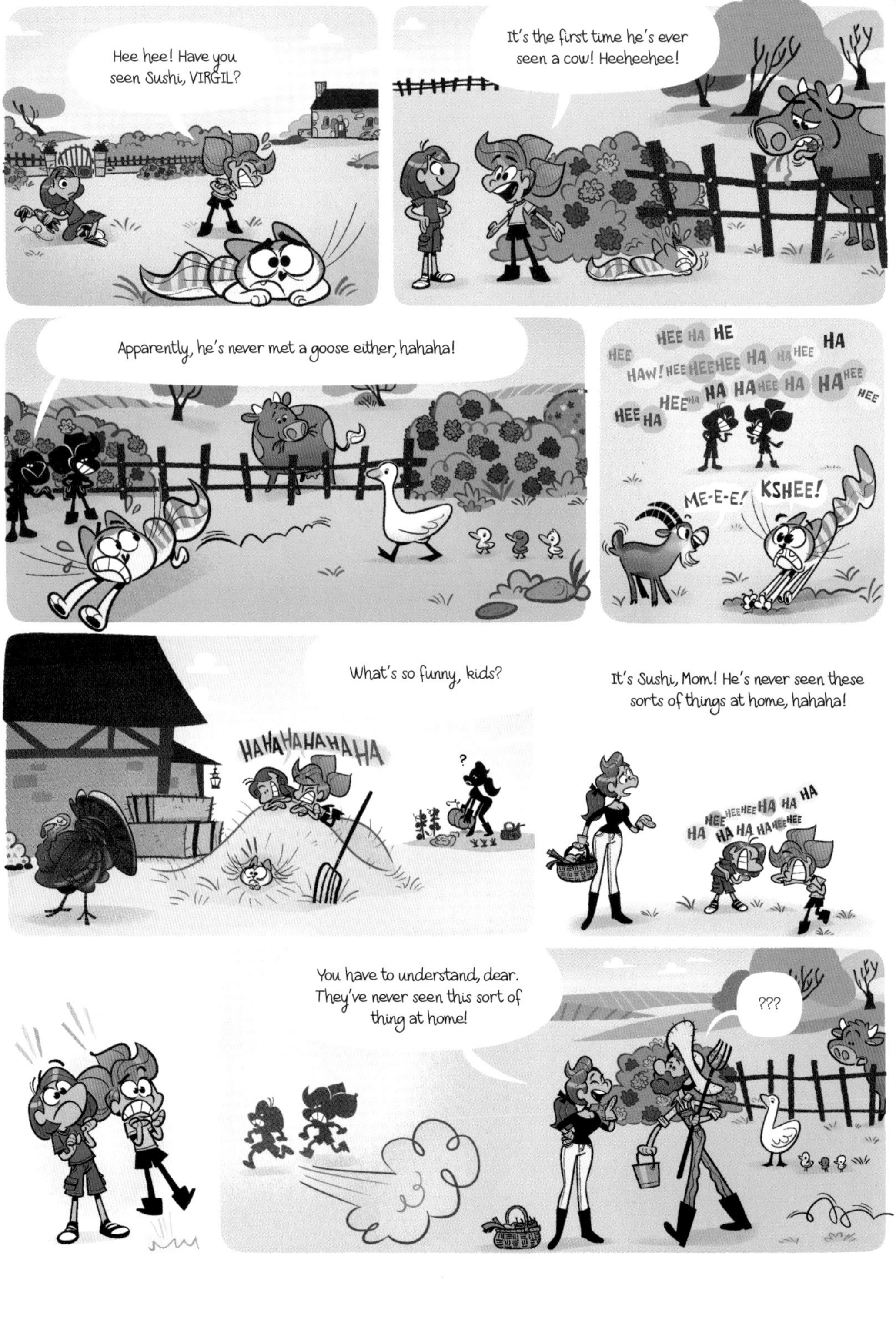

Hee hee! Have you seen Sushi, VIRGIL?
It's the first time he's ever seen a cow! Heeheehee!
Apparently, he's never met a goose either, hahaha!
HEE HA HE HEE HA HAW! HEE HEEHEE HA HA HEE HEE HA HEE HA HA HA HEE HA HA HEE HEE HA HEE
ME-E-E!
KSHEE!
What's so funny, kids?
HAHAHAHAHAHA
?
It's Sushi, Mom! He's never seen these sorts of things at home, hahaha!
HA HEE HEEHEE HA HA HA HA HA HA HEE HEE
You have to understand, dear. They've never seen this sort of thing at home!
???

We'll get your farming lives started with the basics...

You're going to milk that cow all by yourselves!

Wow! Awesome!

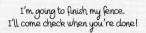

I'm going to finish my fence. I'll come check when you're done!

Okay, Uncle!

?!

BANG BANG BANG

Mooooooo?

????

So, we'll start off with the basics: what does "milking" mean?!

And if you don't know how, you ask before doing any old thing!

Hey, GLADYS, it's Cat, your buddy!

Where am I? In agony!

...Well, at my mom's brother's home. But it's still agony!

POC POC

ME-E-E-E

It's like the Middle Ages! You'd think we'd gone back in time to when Dad was a kid. Not the slightest internet connection!

We eat only organic stuff, and Sushi has put on three tons. We sleep on straw in a barn, and it itches!

!?!

PWEEK

Am I coming home soon? Two more days -- an eternity! I'll die of boredom before that! And I if don't come back, call Child Protective Services, okay?

All right, Gladys, I have to go draw 35°F water from the well to bathe myself. Smooches.

Well, now. Is being in the country as awful as all that?

It's much worse, hon. Especially for her!

HUMPH

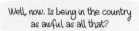

Seeing as how there's no network out in the country... there was nobody on the other end!

Whoooooa, my daughter the actress!

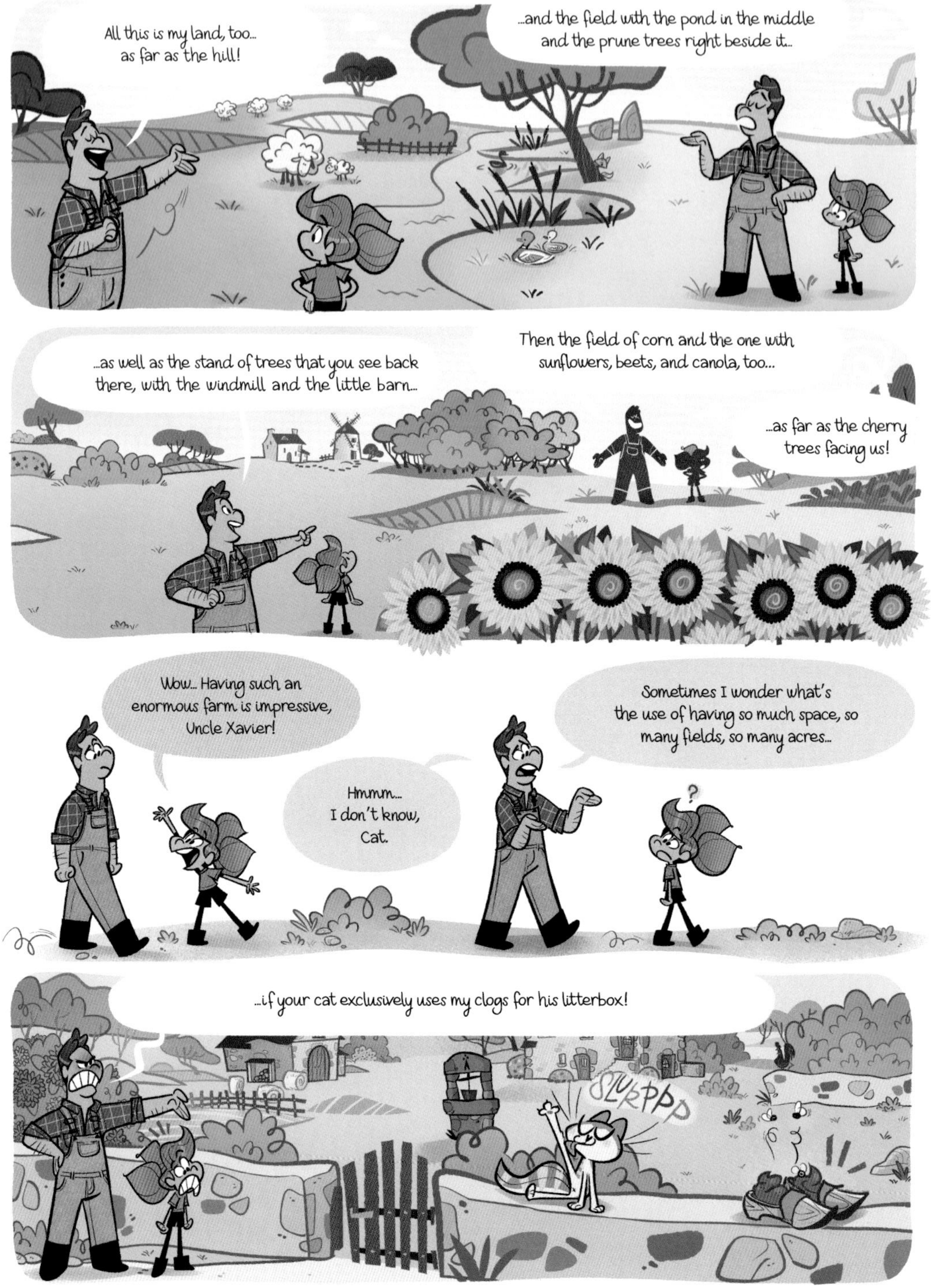
All this is my land, too... as far as the hill!
...and the field with the pond in the middle and the prune trees right beside it...
...as well as the stand of trees that you see back there, with the windmill and the little barn...
Then the field of corn and the one with sunflowers, beets, and canola, too...
...as far as the cherry trees facing us!
Wow... Having such an enormous farm is impressive, Uncle Xavier!
Hmmm... I don't know, Cat.
Sometimes I wonder what's the use of having so much space, so many fields, so many acres...
?
...if your cat exclusively uses my clogs for his litterbox!
SLURPPP

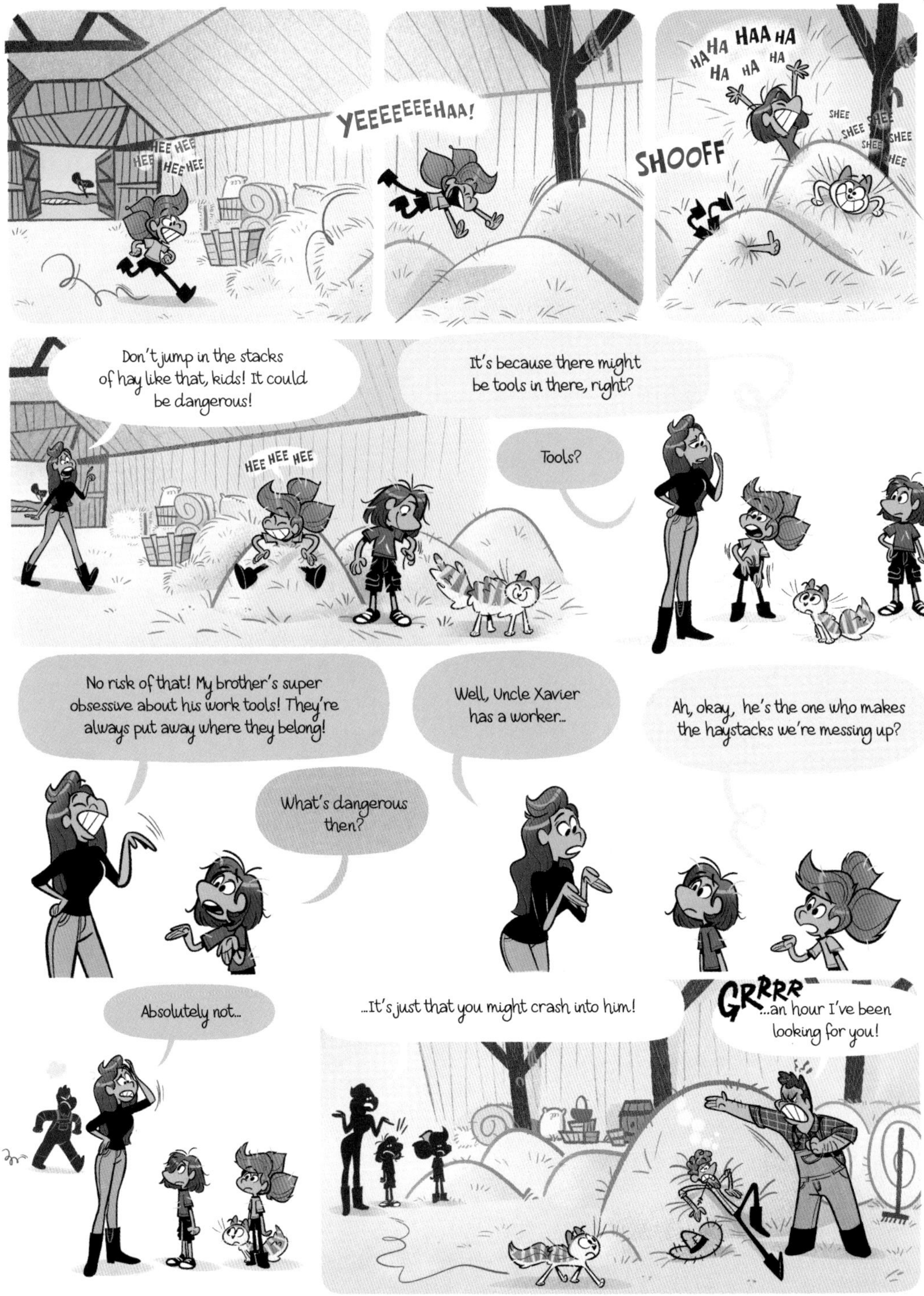
HEE HEE
HEE HEE HEE
YEEEEEEEHAA!
HA HA HAA HA
HA HA HA
SHOOFF
SHEE
SHEE SHEE
SHEE SHEE
SHEE
Don't jump in the stacks of hay like that, kids! It could be dangerous!
HEE HEE HEE
It's because there might be tools in there, right?
Tools?
No risk of that! My brother's super obsessive about his work tools! They're always put away where they belong!
What's dangerous then?
Well, Uncle Xavier has a worker...
Ah, okay, he's the one who makes the haystacks we're messing up?
Absolutely not...
...It's just that you might crash into him!
GRRRR
...an hour I've been looking for you!

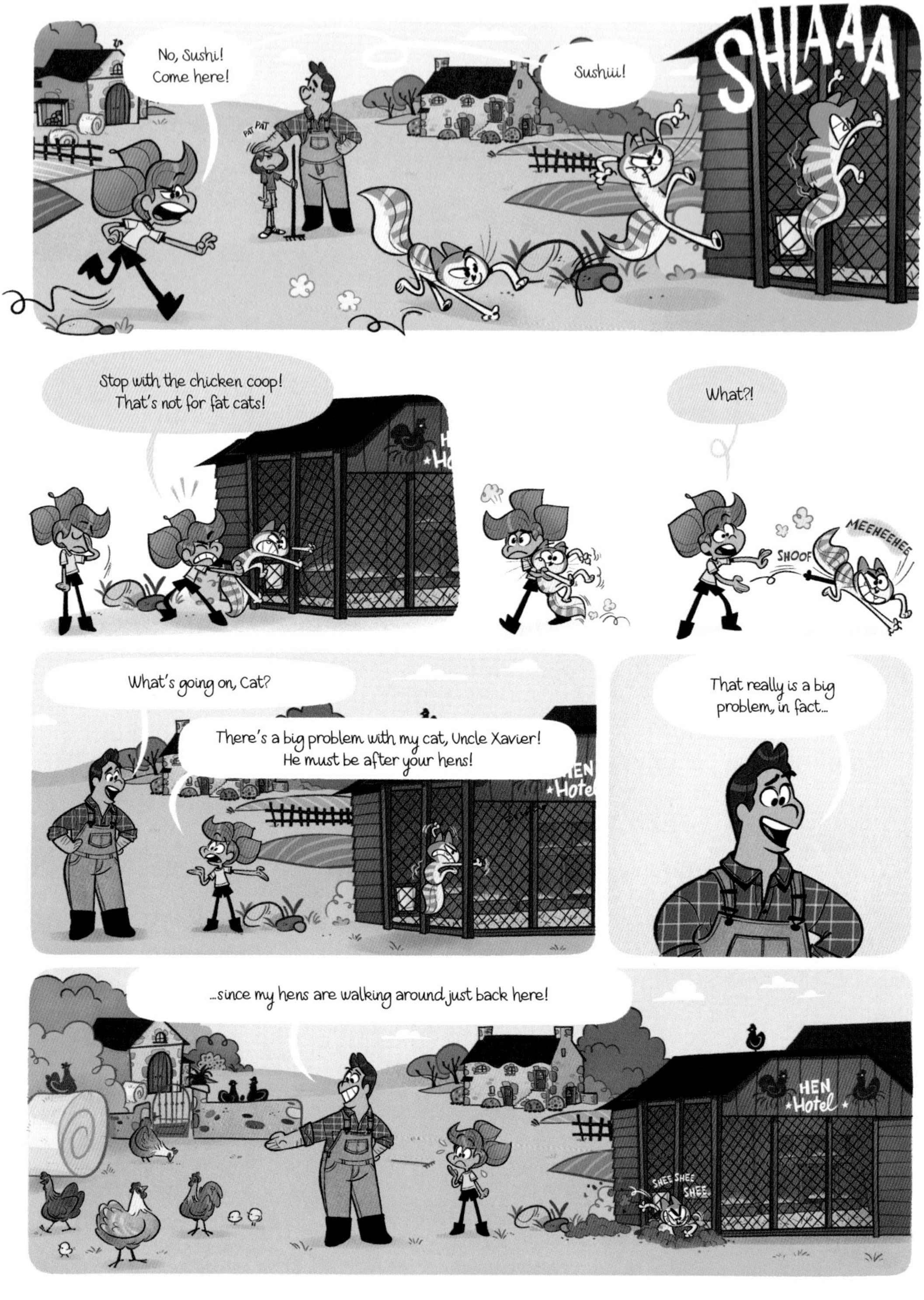
No, Sushi! Come here!
PAT PAT
Sushiii!
SHLAAA
Stop with the chicken coop! That's not for fat cats!
What?!
SHOOF
MEEHEEHEE
What's going on, Cat?
There's a big problem with my cat, Uncle Xavier! He must be after your hens!
HEN Hotel
That really is a big problem, in fact...
...since my hens are walking around just back here!
HEN Hotel
SHEE SHEE SHEE

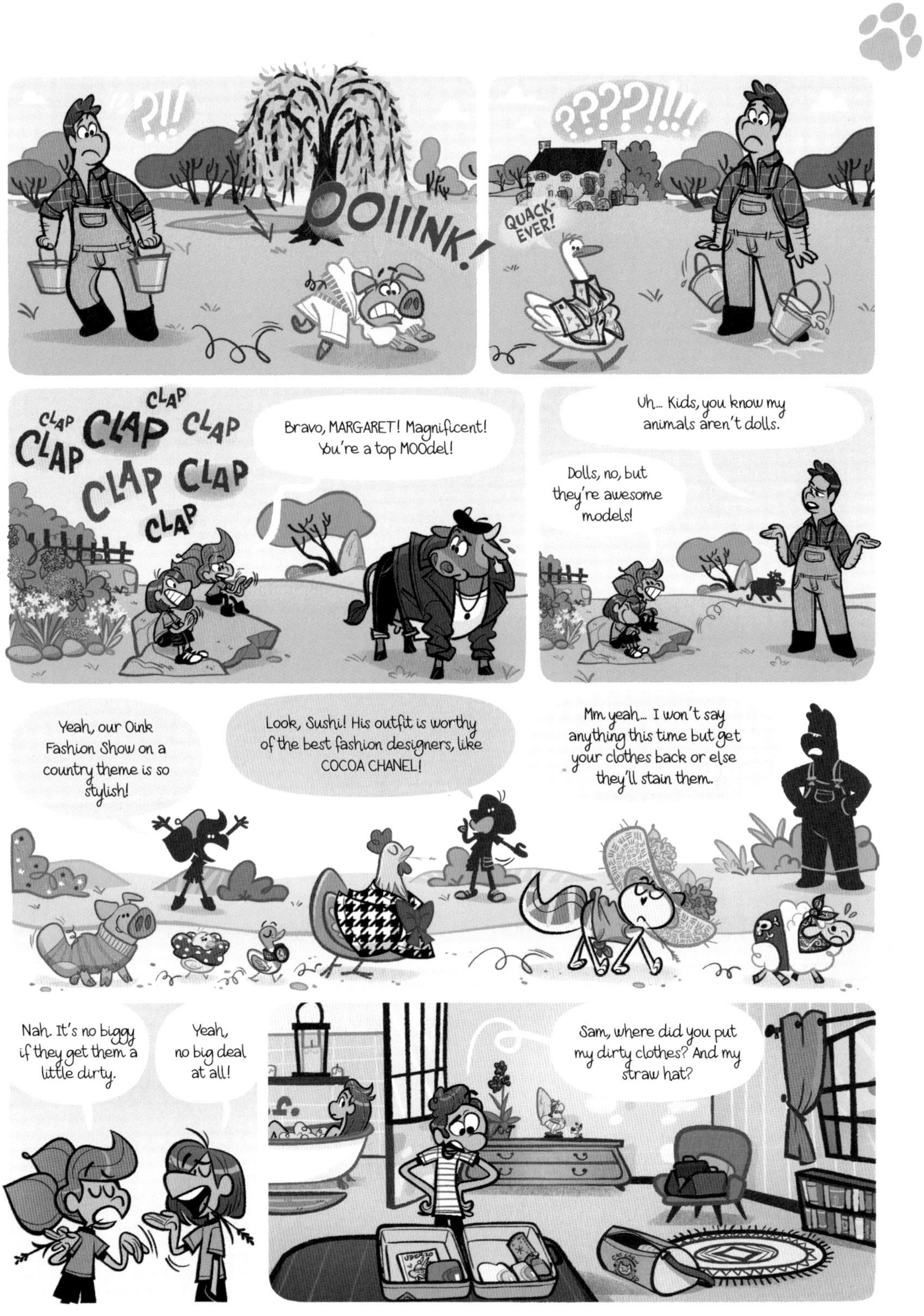
?!!
OOIIINK!
QUACK-EVER!
????!!!
CLAP CLAP CLAP CLAP CLAP CLAP CLAP CLAP
Bravo, MARGARET! Magnificent! You're a top MOOdel!
Uh... Kids, you know my animals aren't dolls.
Dolls, no, but they're awesome models!
Yeah, our Oink Fashion Show on a country theme is so stylish!
Look, Sushi! His outfit is worthy of the best fashion designers, like COCOA CHANEL!
Mm yeah... I won't say anything this time but get your clothes back or else they'll stain them.
Nah. It's no biggy if they get them a little dirty.
Yeah, no big deal at all!
Sam, where did you put my dirty clothes? And my straw hat?

COCKADOOOODLE!

:Arrr:
I can't take this anymore!

Okay! Operation "Blow the Whistle"!

What are you going to do?

Me, nothing! But Sushi is going to enjoy solving the problem!

Aren't you, kitty?

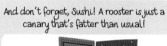

And don't forget, Sushi! A rooster is just a canary that's fatter than usual!

Dig in!

Dad, did you send Sushi out to the rooster?

SLAM

You don't think I should have, honey?

MMMEEOOOWWW

COCKADOO

? WHAT?

COCKADOOODLee
MeeeOOWWWw

Huge mistake! Now we won't get any sleep for sure!

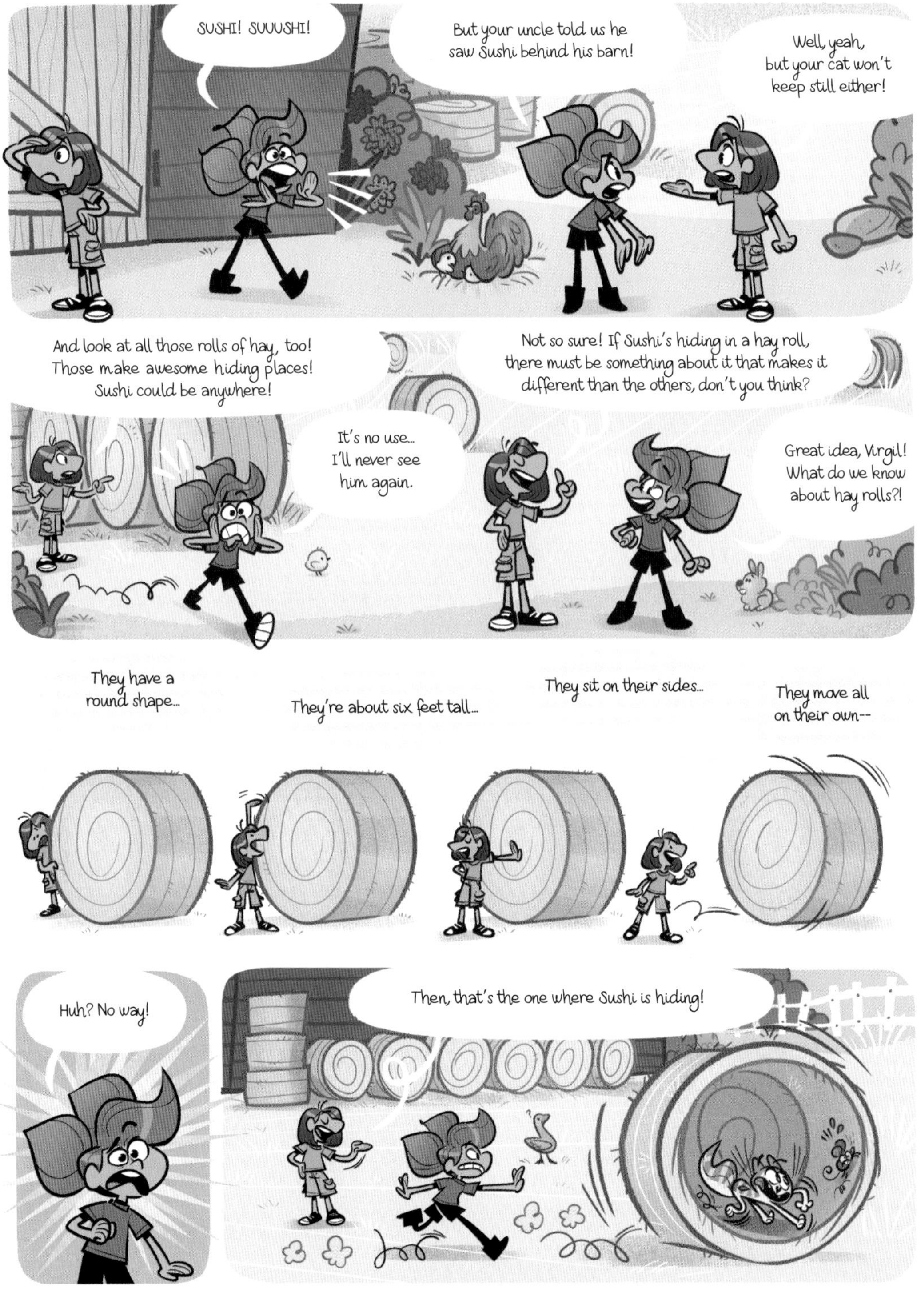
SUSHI! SUUUSHI!
But your uncle told us he saw Sushi behind his barn!
Well, yeah, but your cat won't keep still either!
And look at all those rolls of hay, too! Those make awesome hiding places! Sushi could be anywhere!
It's no use... I'll never see him again.
Not so sure! If Sushi's hiding in a hay roll, there must be something about it that makes it different than the others, don't you think?
Great idea, Virgil! What do we know about hay rolls?!
They have a round shape...
They're about six feet tall...
They sit on their sides...
They move all on their own--
Huh? No way!
Then, that's the one where Sushi is hiding!

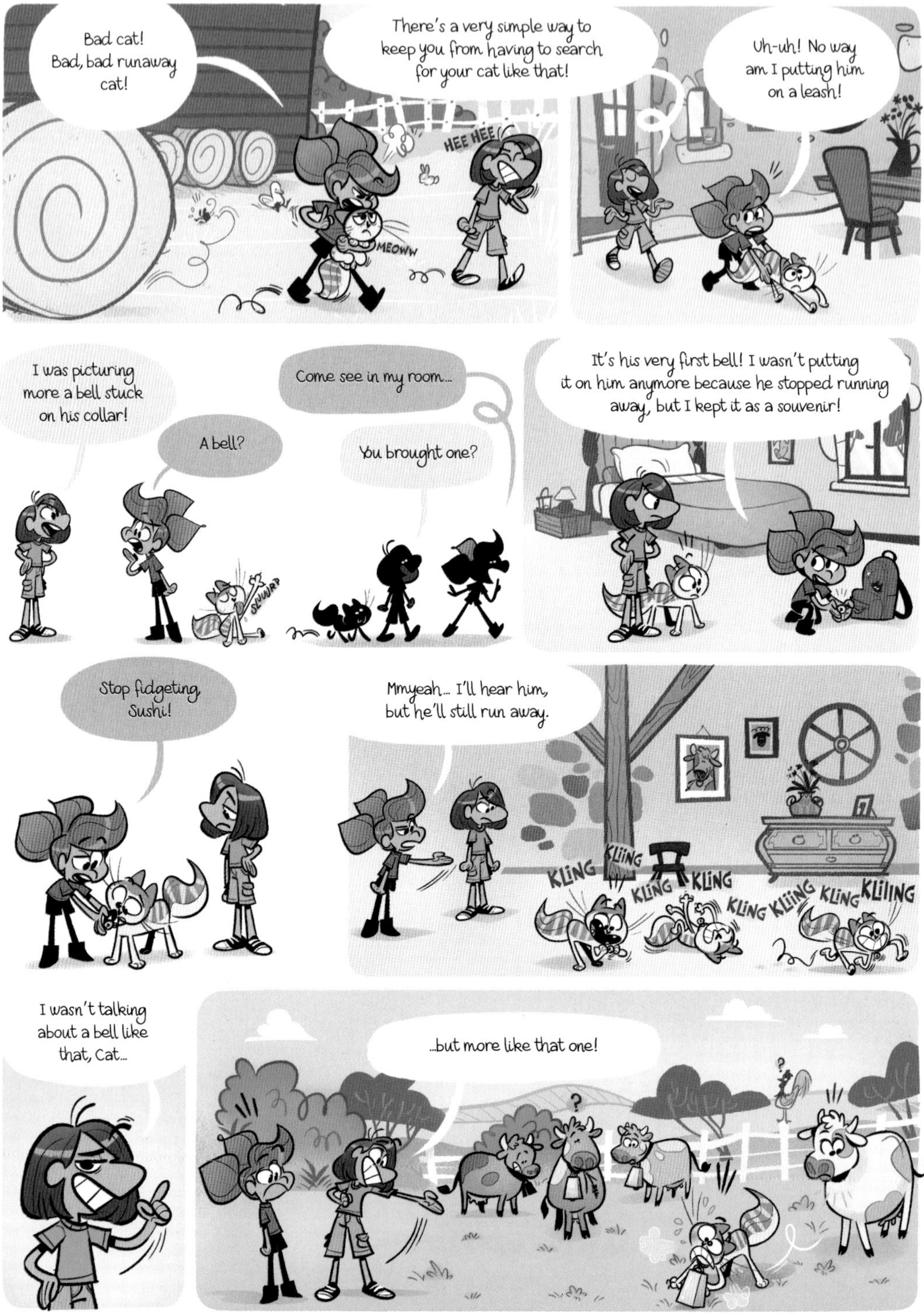
Bad cat! Bad, bad runaway cat!
There's a very simple way to keep you from having to search for your cat like that!
HEE HEE
MEOWW
Uh-uh! No way am I putting him on a leash!
I was picturing more a bell stuck on his collar!
A bell?
SLUURP
Come see in my room...
You brought one?
It's his very first bell! I wasn't putting it on him anymore because he stopped running away, but I kept it as a souvenir!
Stop fidgeting, Sushi!
Mmyeah... I'll hear him, but he'll still run away.
KLING KLING KLING KLING KLING KLING KLIING KLING KLIIING
I wasn't talking about a bell like that, Cat...
...but more like that one!

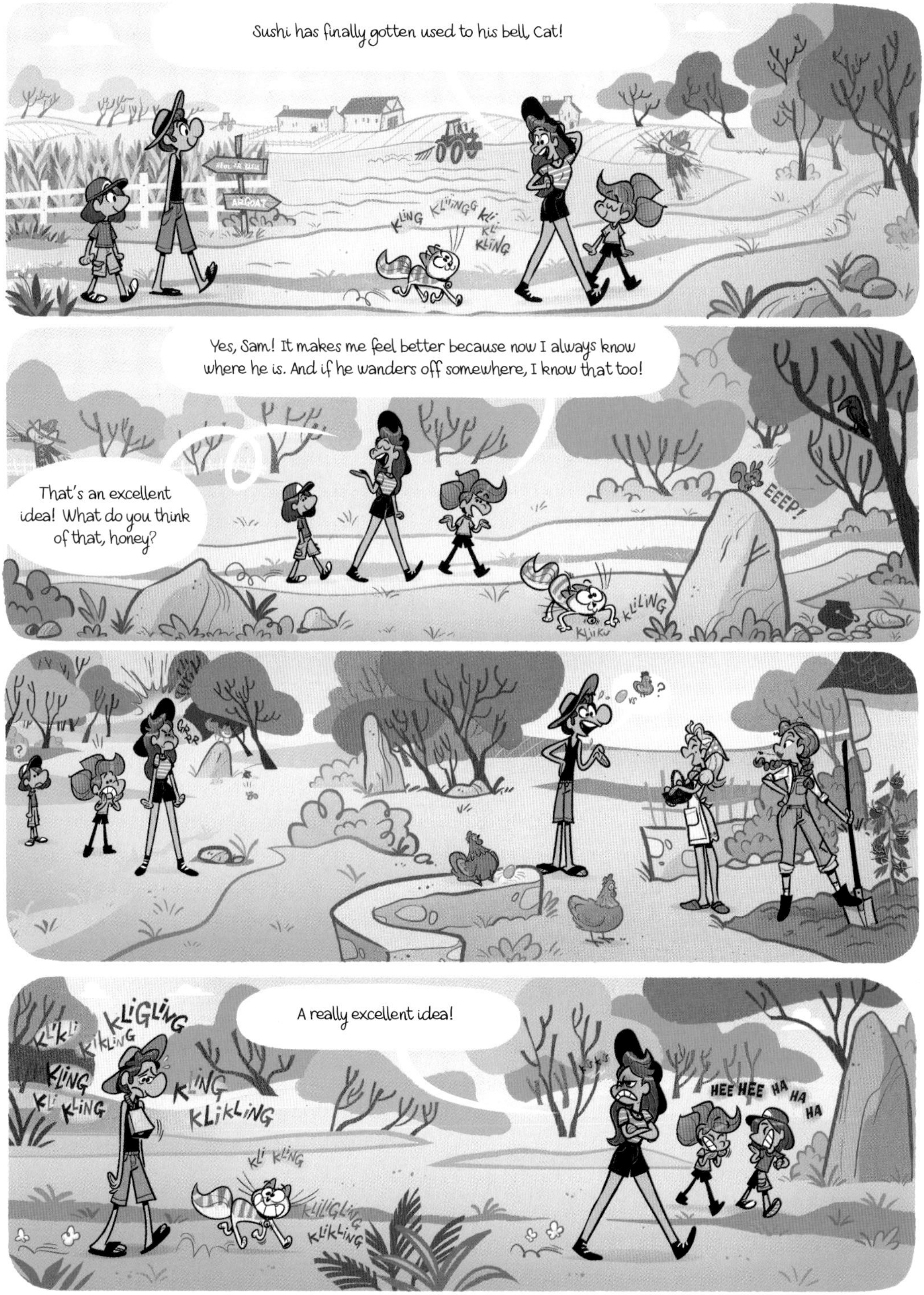
Sushi has finally gotten used to his bell, Cat!
ARGOAT
KLING KLIIINGG KLI KLI KLING
Yes, Sam! It makes me feel better because now I always know where he is. And if he wanders off somewhere, I know that too!
That's an excellent idea! What do you think of that, honey?
EEEP!
KLILING
A really excellent idea!
KLIKLI
KLIGLING
KIKLING
KLING
KLI KLING
KLING
KLIKLING
KLI KLING
KLILIGLING
KLIKLING
HEE HEE HA HA HA

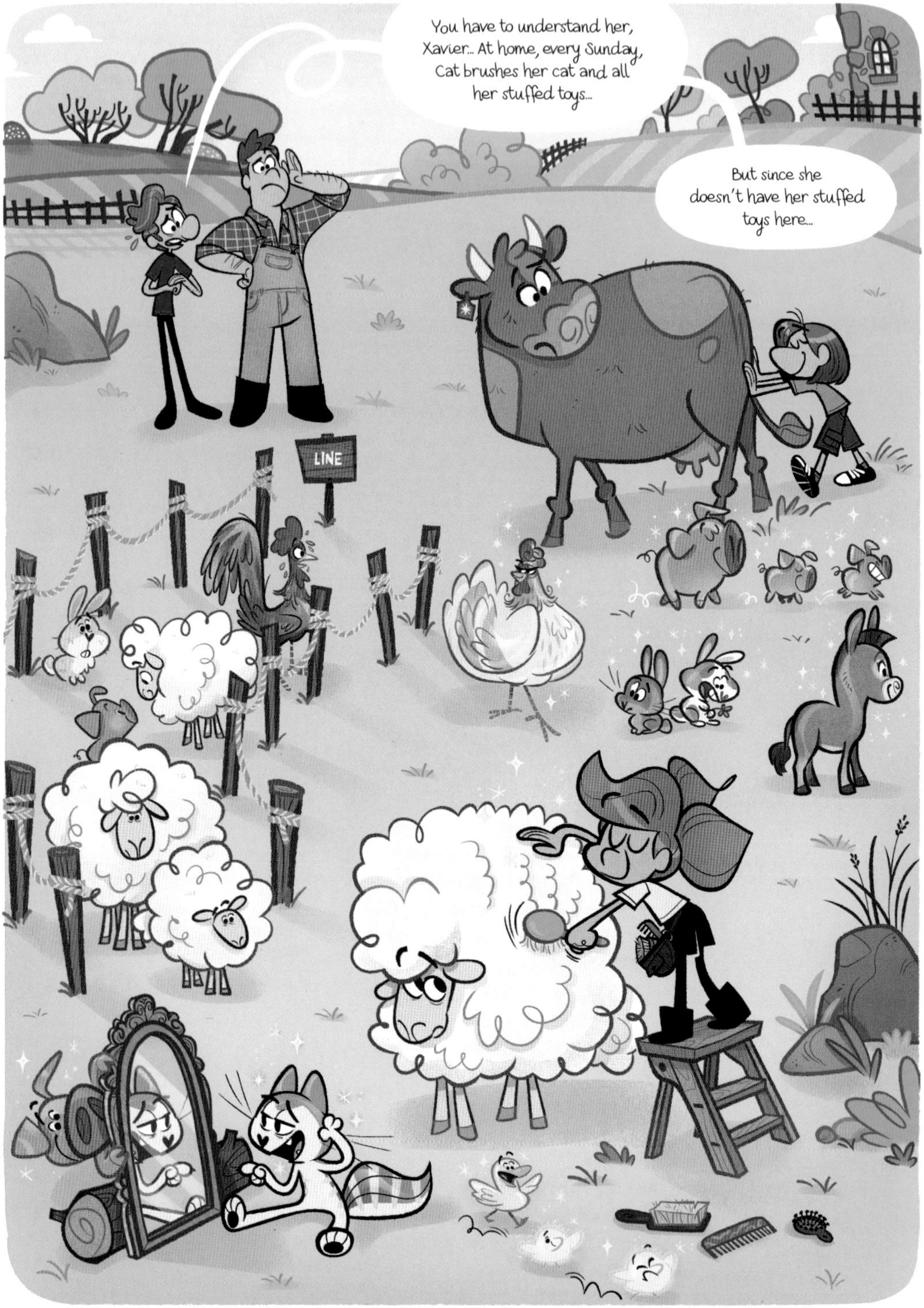
You have to understand her, Xavier... At home, every Sunday, Cat brushes her cat and all her stuffed toys...
But since she doesn't have her stuffed toys here...
LINE

YEEHAAAA!

MEOOwwYEHAAAA

A TOTAL RODEO!

Come back, SHEEP-HORSE! It's my turn!

Please, little sister! Settle them down! I don't know... Send them to play on the street!

STOP! Bedtime! You're taking a shower, brushing your teeth, and everybody in bed!

Washing up?

In the country?

MEOW MEOW?

Yes, and washing like in the country, too! Including Sushi!

There's running water in the country, you know, so there's no reason not to wash up!

But it's super coooooooooold!

...But super healthy, too! It comes straight from the spring! So go ahead and wash up. I'll be back in ten minutes.

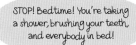

So, you figured out how to settle them down?

Yes. But I need a nice, hot shower!

RELAX

BRR BRR, IT'S SO COLD!

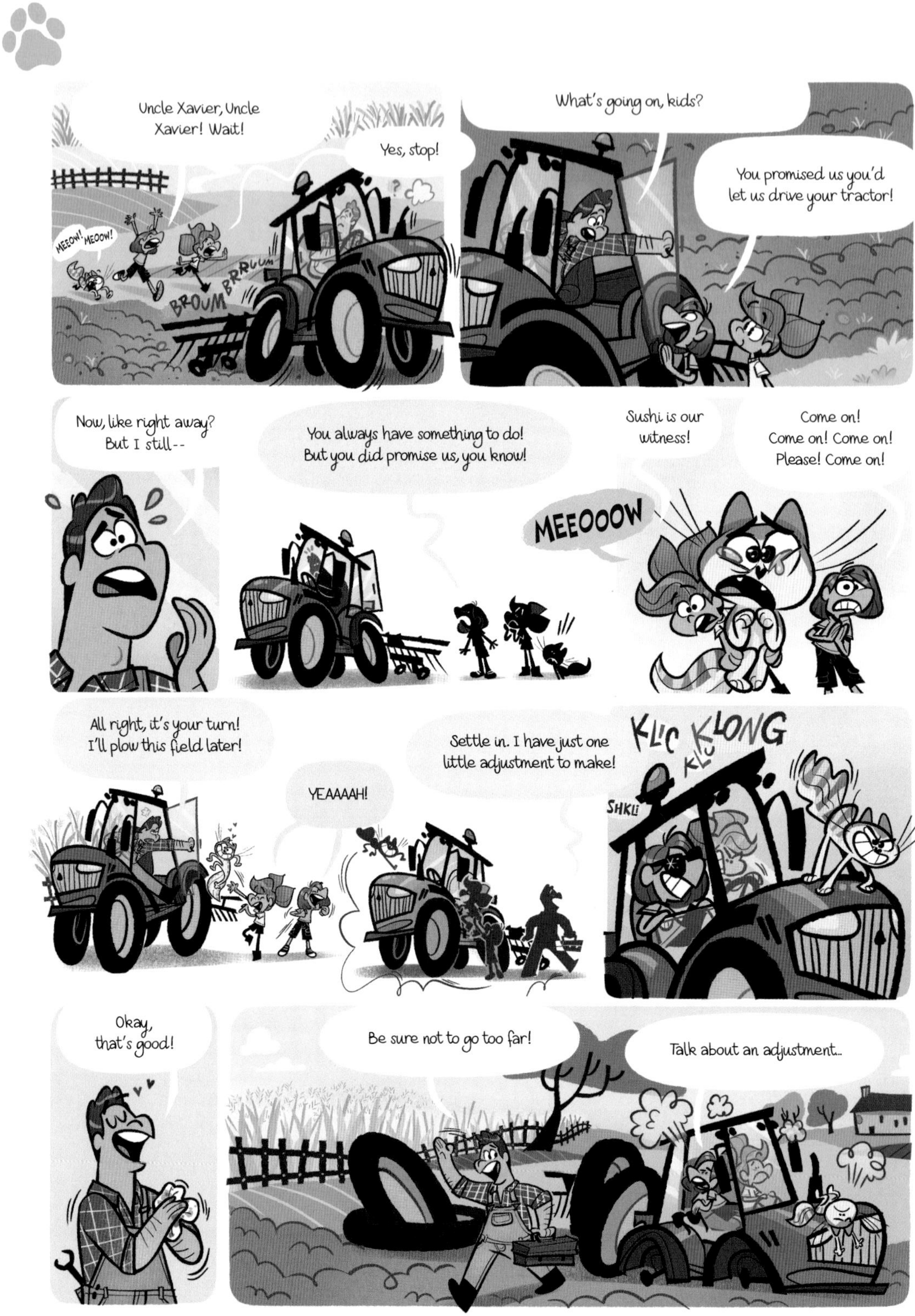

Uncle Xavier, Uncle Xavier! Wait!
Yes, stop!
MEEOW! MEOOW!
BROUM BRRUUM
What's going on, kids?
You promised us you'd let us drive your tractor!
Now, like right away? But I still--
You always have something to do! But you did promise us, you know!
Sushi is our witness!
Come on! Come on! Come on! Please! Come on!
MEEOOOW
All right, it's your turn! I'll plow this field later!
YEAAAAH!
Settle in. I have just one little adjustment to make!
KLIC KLIC KLONG
SHKLI
Okay, that's good!
Be sure not to go too far!
Talk about an adjustment...

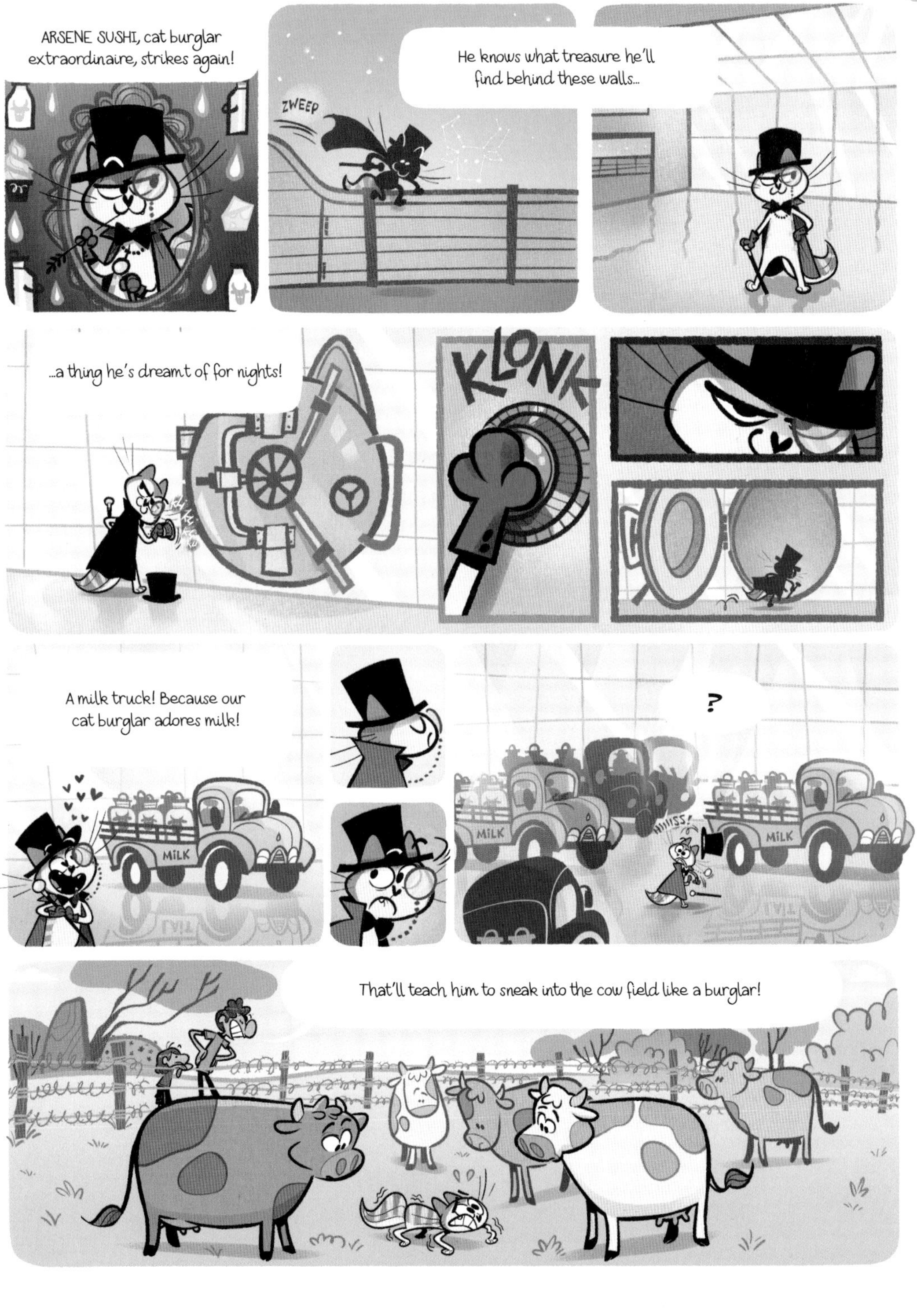
ARSENE SUSHI, cat burglar extraordinaire, strikes again!
ZWEEP
He knows what treasure he'll find behind these walls...
...a thing he's dreamt of for nights!
KLONK
A milk truck! Because our cat burglar adores milk!
MILK
?
MILK
MILK
That'll teach him to sneak into the cow field like a burglar!

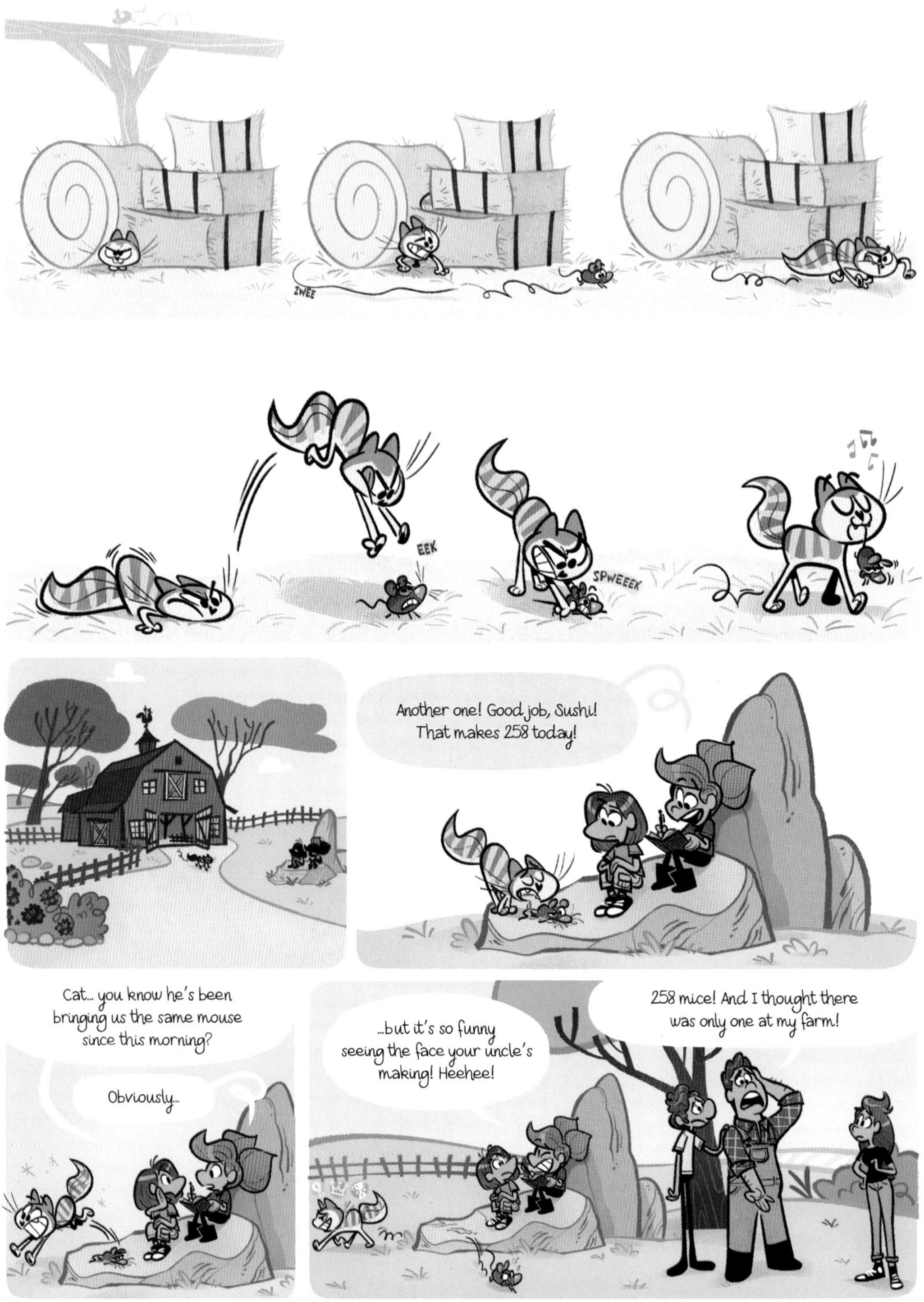
ZWEE
EEK
SPWEEEK
Another one! Good job, Sushi! That makes 258 today!
Cat... you know he's been bringing us the same mouse since this morning?
Obviously...
...but it's so funny seeing the face your uncle's making! Heehee!
258 mice! And I thought there was only one at my farm!

PURRRRR

That cat is really incredible, isn't he? He's super useful!

POF
DIF
POFF

Okay, I get it.

HUMF

ZWEEE

That darn cat...

ZWEE DOW
DOW

I don't know that moo... That's not one of my cows! One of the neighbor's must have gotten into my field!

Let's just say he's already convinced I'm stealing his tools and grain... So, if he sees one of his cows in my field, he's really going to think I'm a rustler!

Is that bad?

MMMOOOOOOOO!

Well, goodness me? Did you hear that too, Cat? Where's that cow hiding?!

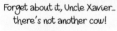

Forget about it, Uncle Xavier... there's not another cow!

It's just my cat, who has a gift for foreign languages!

OOOOOOIINK!

OOOINK

26

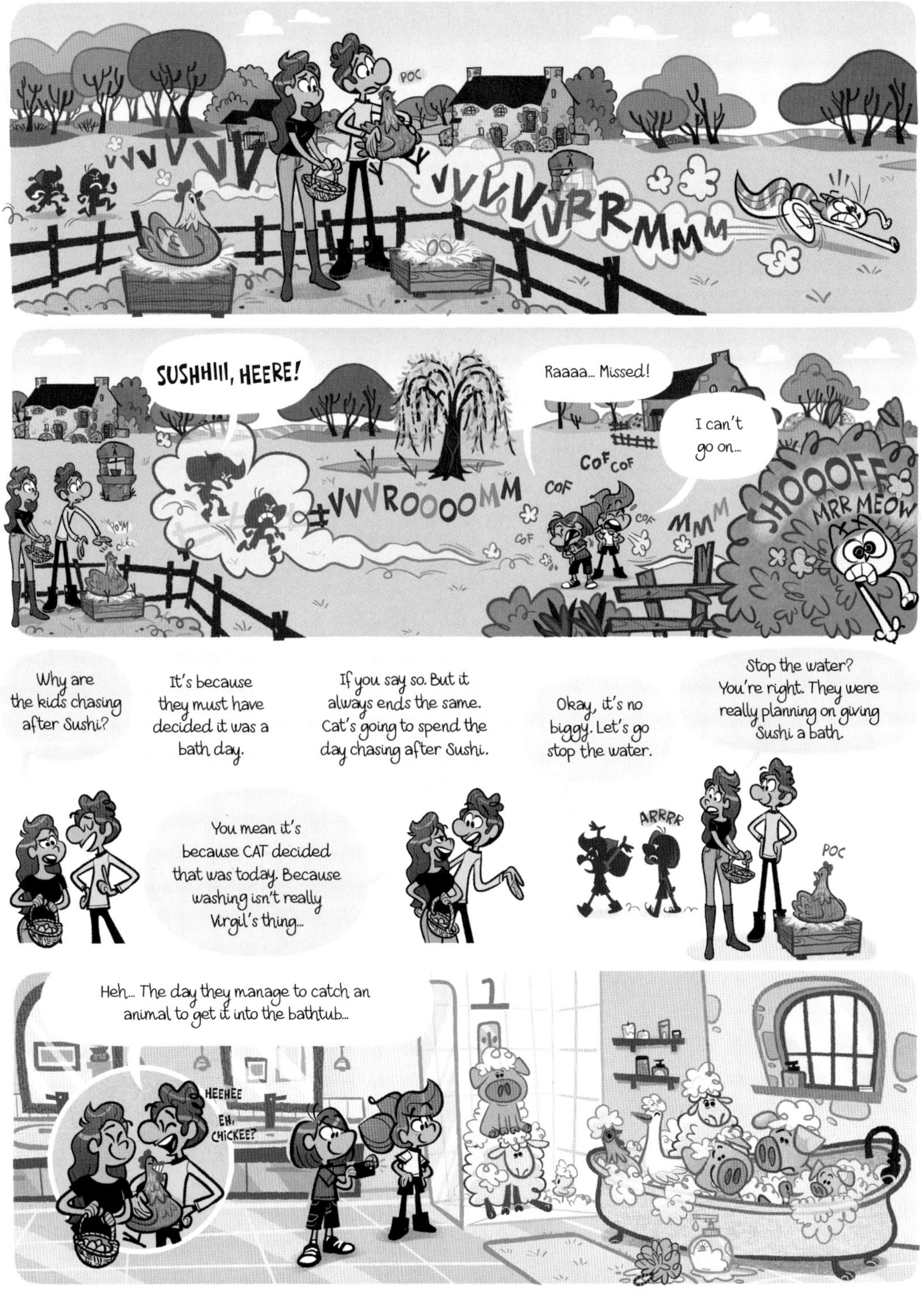
POC
SUSHIIII, HEERE!
VVVROOOOMM
Raaaa... Missed!
COF
COF COF
COF
I can't go on...
SHOOOFF
MRR MEOW
Why are the kids chasing after Sushi?
It's because they must have decided it was a bath day.
You mean it's because CAT decided that was today. Because washing isn't really Virgil's thing...
If you say so. But it always ends the same. Cat's going to spend the day chasing after Sushi.
Okay, it's no biggy. Let's go stop the water.
Stop the water? You're right. They were really planning on giving Sushi a bath.
ARRRR
POC
Heh... The day they manage to catch an animal to get it into the bathtub...
HEEHEE
EH, CHICKEE?

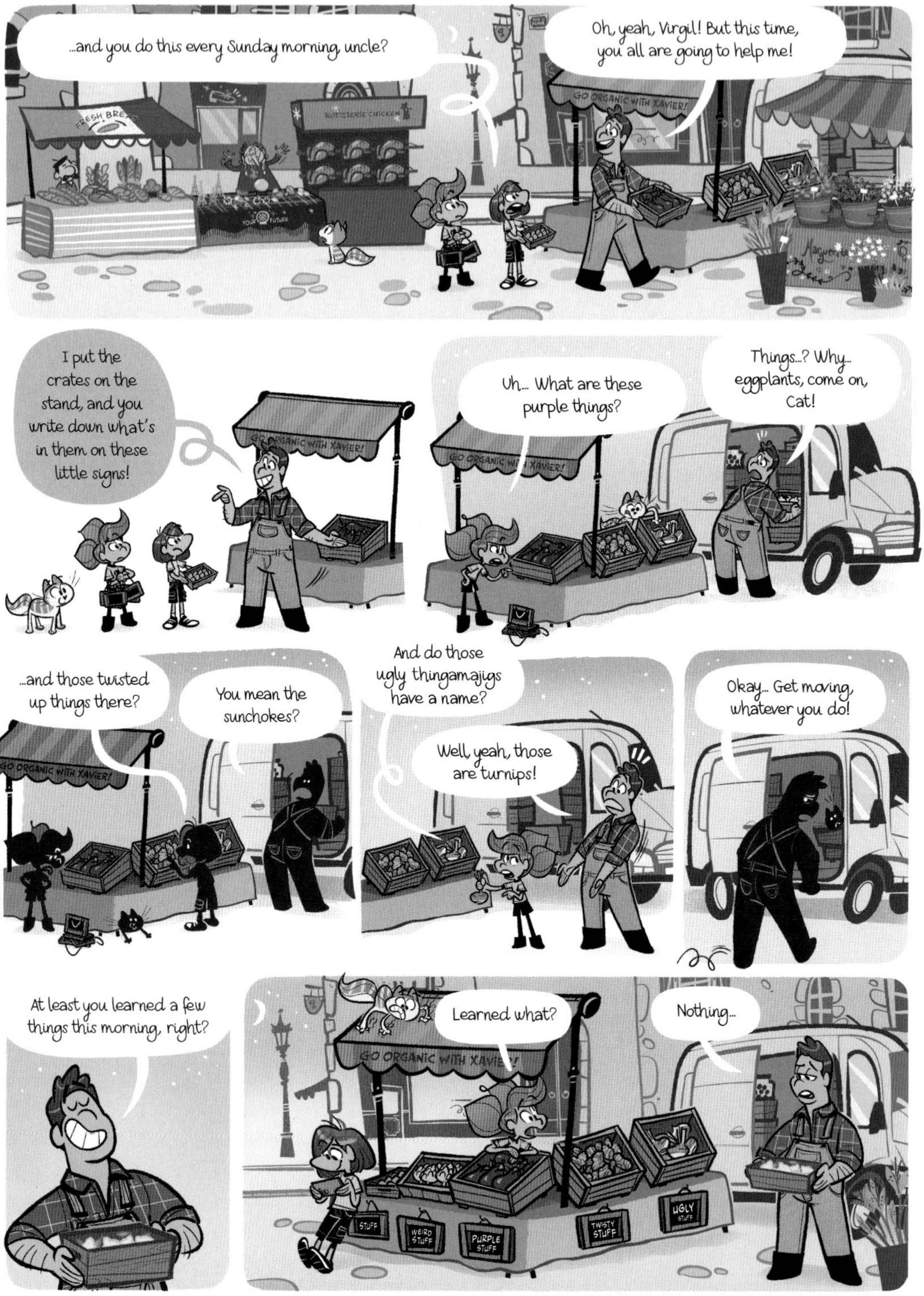

...and you do this every Sunday morning, uncle?
Oh, yeah, Virgil! But this time, you all are going to help me!
FRESH BREAD
ROTISSERIE CHICKEN
YOUR FUTURE
GO ORGANIC WITH XAVIER!
I put the crates on the stand, and you write down what's in them on these little signs!
Uh... What are these purple things?
Things...? Why... eggplants, come on, Cat!
...and those twisted up things there?
You mean the sunchokes?
And do those ugly thingamajigs have a name?
Well, yeah, those are turnips!
Okay... Get moving, whatever you do!
At least you learned a few things this morning, right?
Learned what?
Nothing...
STUFF
WEIRD STUFF
PURPLE STUFF
TWISTY STUFF
UGLY STUFF

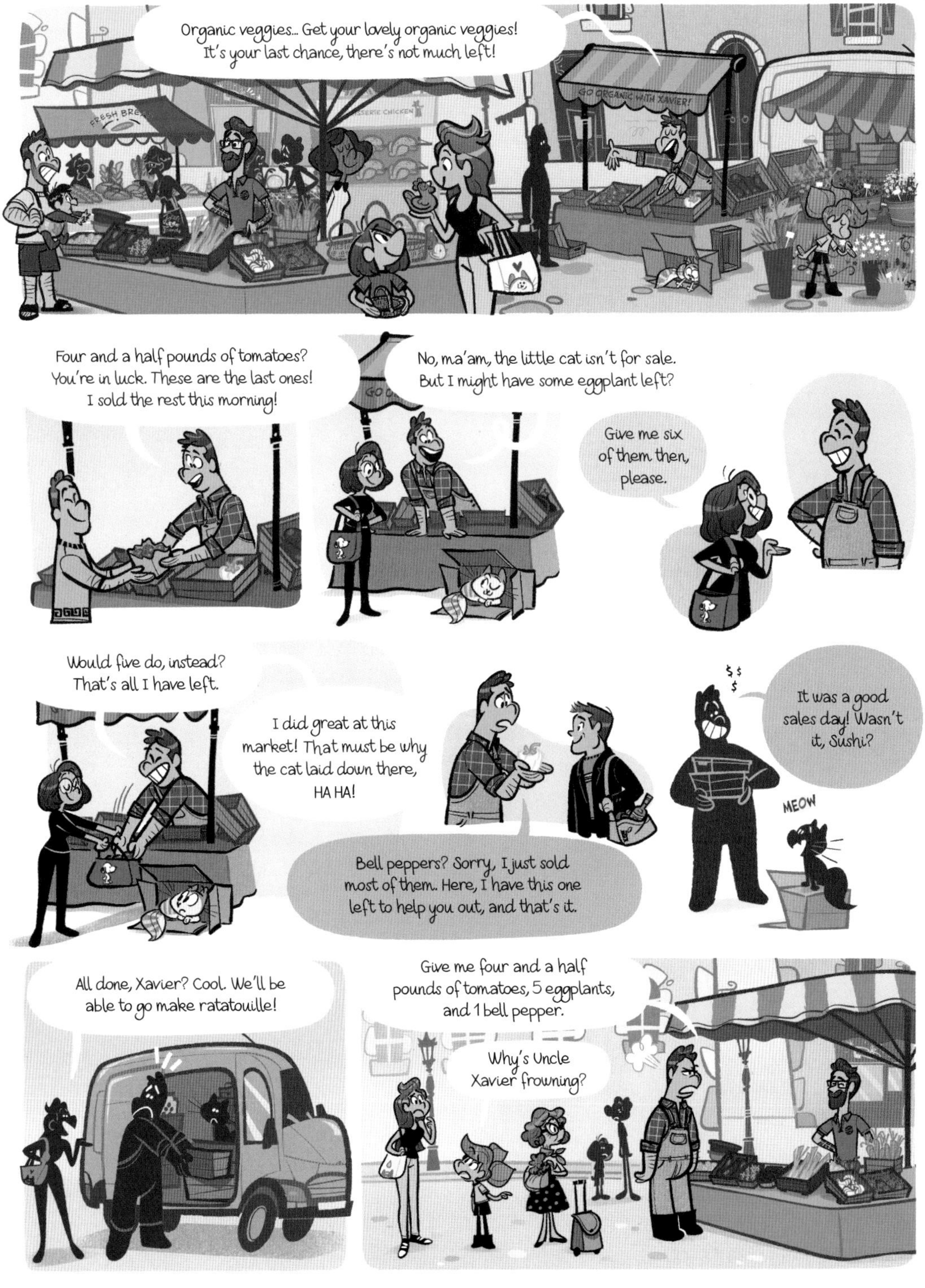
Organic veggies... Get your lovely organic veggies! It's your last chance, there's not much left!
GO ORGANIC WITH XAVIER!
Four and a half pounds of tomatoes? You're in luck. These are the last ones! I sold the rest this morning!
No, ma'am, the little cat isn't for sale. But I might have some eggplant left?
Give me six of them then, please.
Would five do, instead? That's all I have left.
I did great at this market! That must be why the cat laid down there, HA HA!
Bell peppers? Sorry, I just sold most of them. Here, I have this one left to help you out, and that's it.
It was a good sales day! Wasn't it, Sushi?
MEOW
All done, Xavier? Cool. We'll be able to go make ratatouille!
Give me four and a half pounds of tomatoes, 5 eggplants, and 1 bell pepper.
Why's Uncle Xavier frowning?

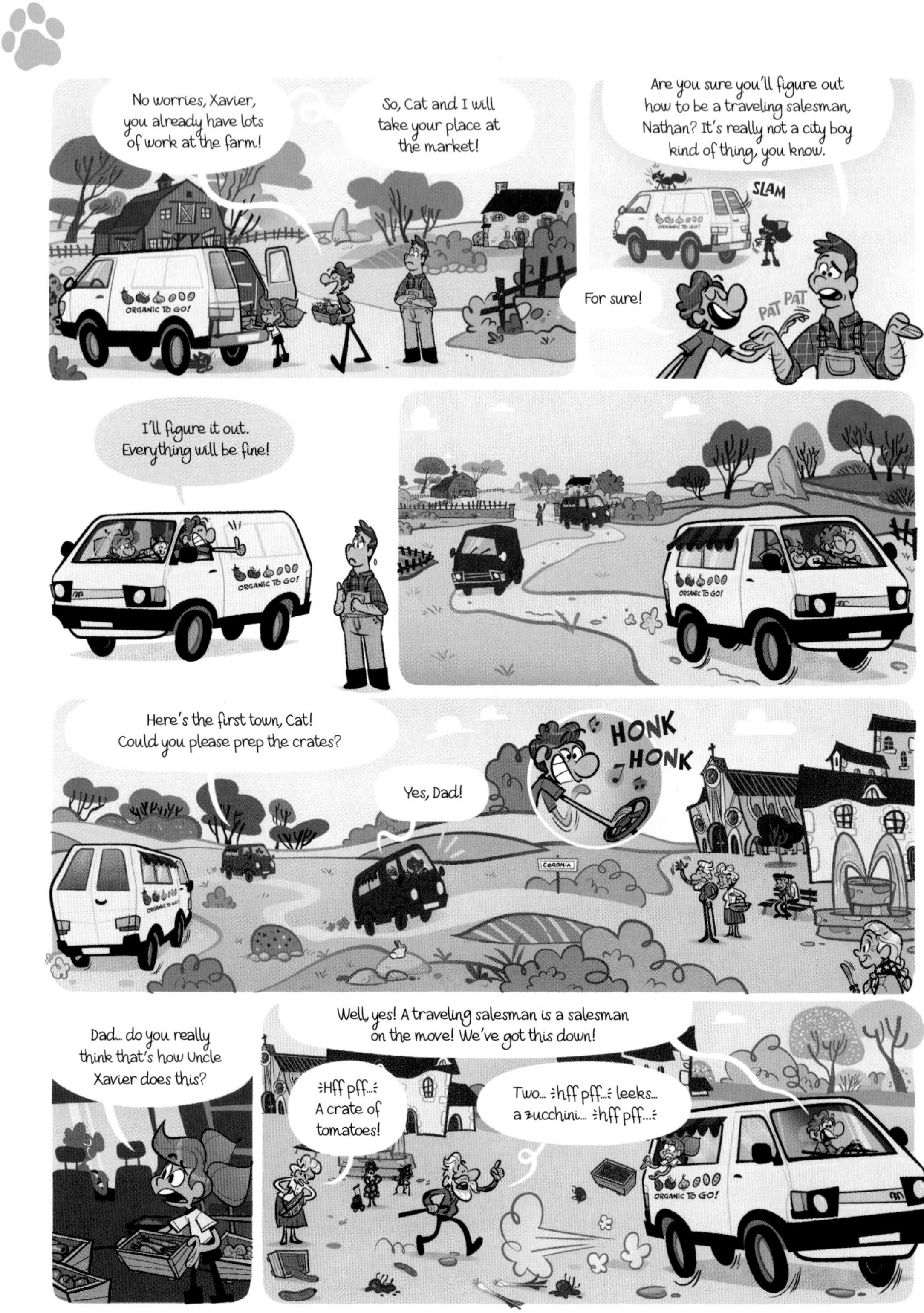
No worries, Xavier, you already have lots of work at the farm!
ORGANIC TO GO!
So, Cat and I will take your place at the market!
Are you sure you'll figure out how to be a traveling salesman, Nathan? It's really not a city boy kind of thing, you know.
SLAM
For sure!
PAT PAT
I'll figure it out. Everything will be fine!
ORGANIC TO GO!
ORGANIC TO GO!
Here's the first town, Cat! Could you please prep the crates?
Yes, Dad!
HONK
HONK
COROMIA
Dad... do you really think that's how Uncle Xavier does this?
Well, yes! A traveling salesman is a salesman on the move! We've got this down!
Hff pff... A crate of tomatoes!
Two... *hff pff...* leeks... a zucchini... *hff pff...*
ORGANIC TO GO!

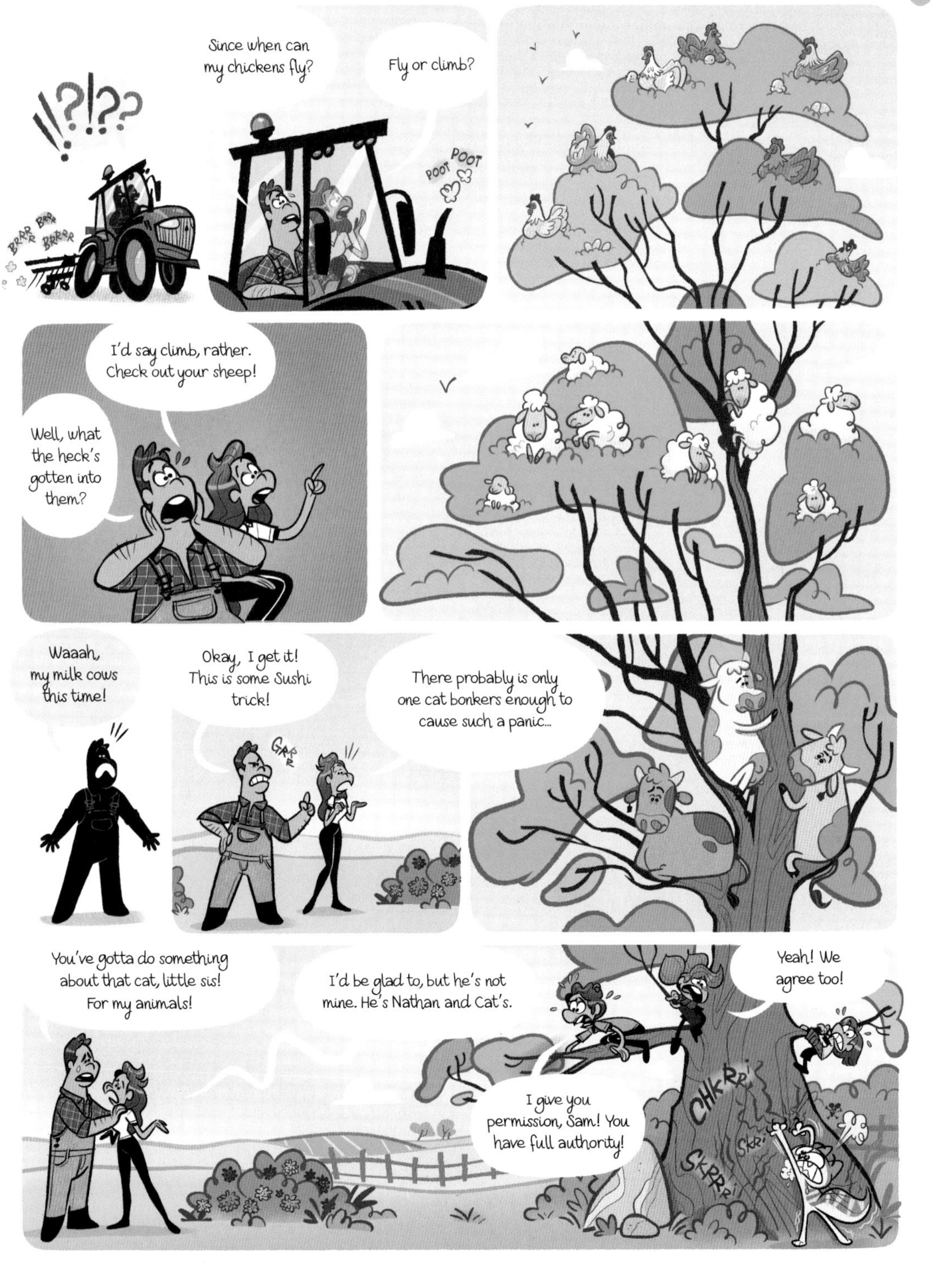
!!?!??
BRRR BRRR BRRRR
Since when can my chickens fly?
Fly or climb?
POOT POOT
I'd say climb, rather. Check out your sheep!
Well, what the heck's gotten into them?
Waaah, my milk cows this time!
Okay, I get it! This is some Sushi trick!
GRR
There probably is only one cat bonkers enough to cause such a panic...
You've gotta do something about that cat, little sis! For my animals!
I'd be glad to, but he's not mine. He's Nathan and Cat's.
Yeah! We agree too!
I give you permission, Sam! You have full authority!
CHKRRi
SKRRi
SKRi

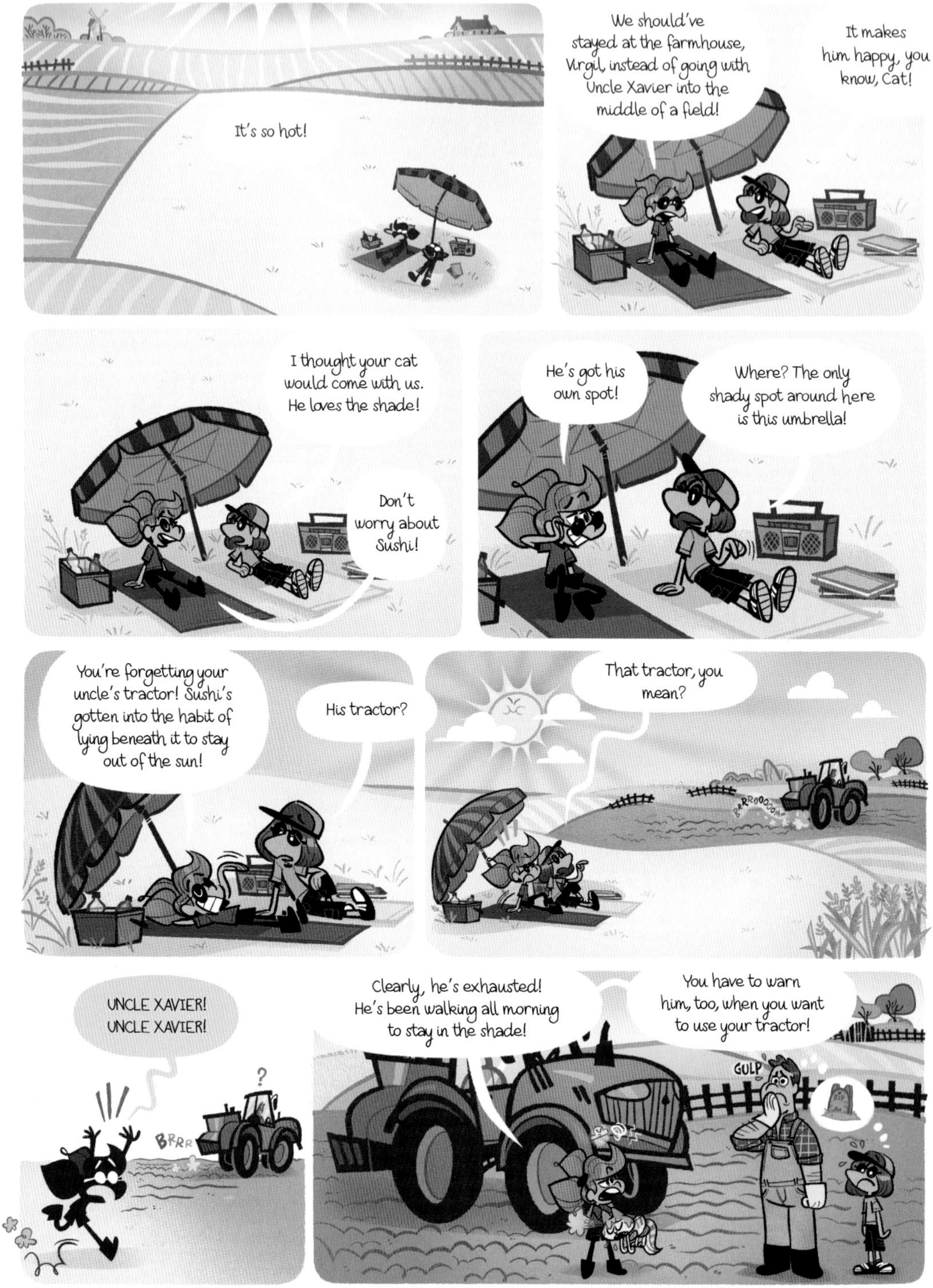
It's so hot!
We should've stayed at the farmhouse, Virgil, instead of going with Uncle Xavier into the middle of a field!
It makes him happy, you know, Cat!
I thought your cat would come with us. He loves the shade!
Don't worry about Sushi!
He's got his own spot!
Where? The only shady spot around here is this umbrella!
You're forgetting your uncle's tractor! Sushi's gotten into the habit of lying beneath it to stay out of the sun!
His tractor?
That tractor, you mean?
BRRROOOOOMM
UNCLE XAVIER!
UNCLE XAVIER!
?
BRRR
Clearly, he's exhausted! He's been walking all morning to stay in the shade!
You have to warn him, too, when you want to use your tractor!
GULP
RIP

IT'S A GOOD IDEA TO CHECK UNDER VEHICLES FOR PETS.

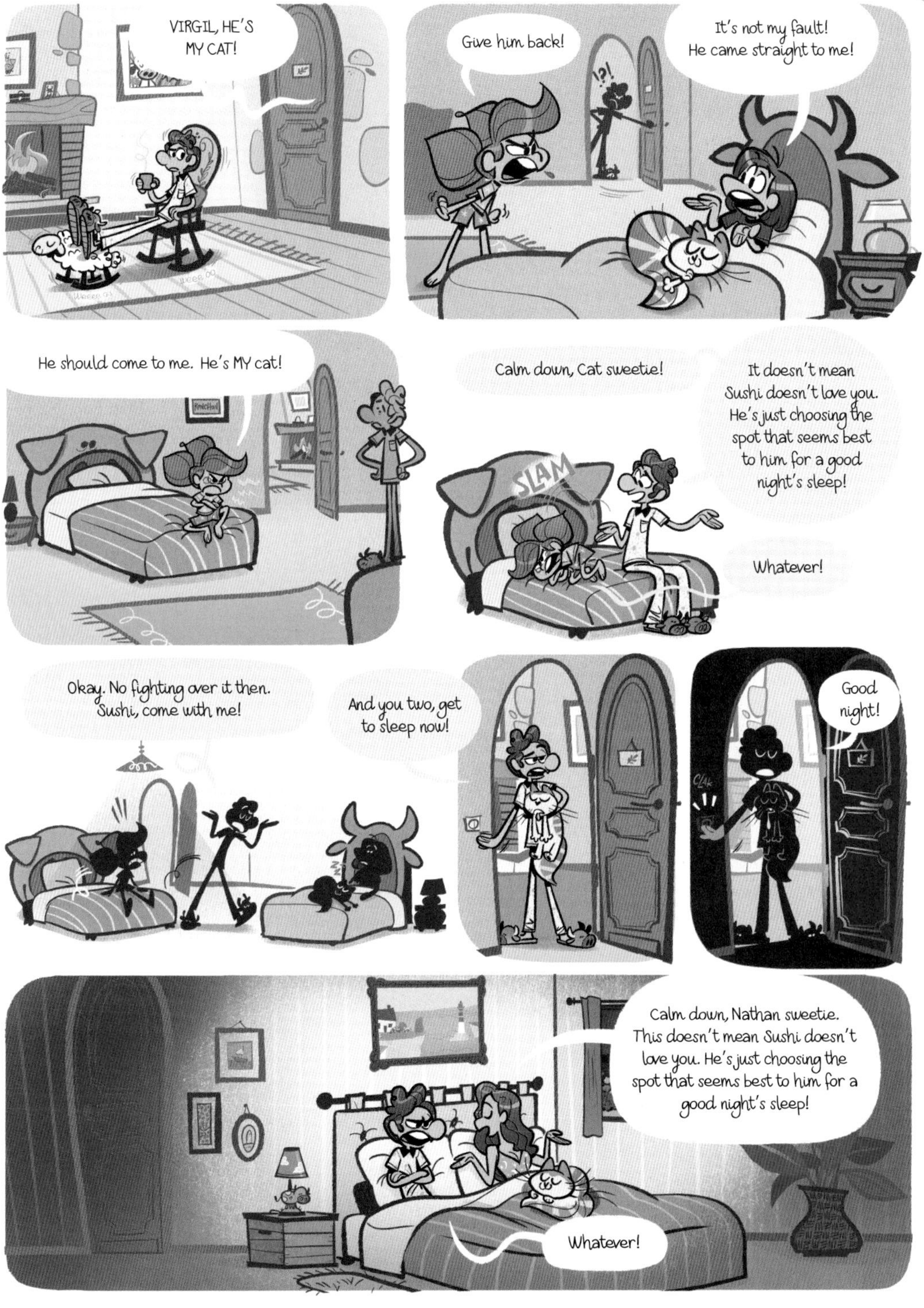
VIRGIL, HE'S MY CAT!
Give him back!
It's not my fault! He came straight to me!
He should come to me. He's MY cat!
Calm down, Cat sweetie!
It doesn't mean Sushi doesn't love you. He's just choosing the spot that seems best to him for a good night's sleep!
SLAM
Whatever!
Okay. No fighting over it then. Sushi, come with me!
And you two, get to sleep now!
Good night!
CLAK
Calm down, Nathan sweetie. This doesn't mean Sushi doesn't love you. He's just choosing the spot that seems best to him for a good night's sleep!
Whatever!

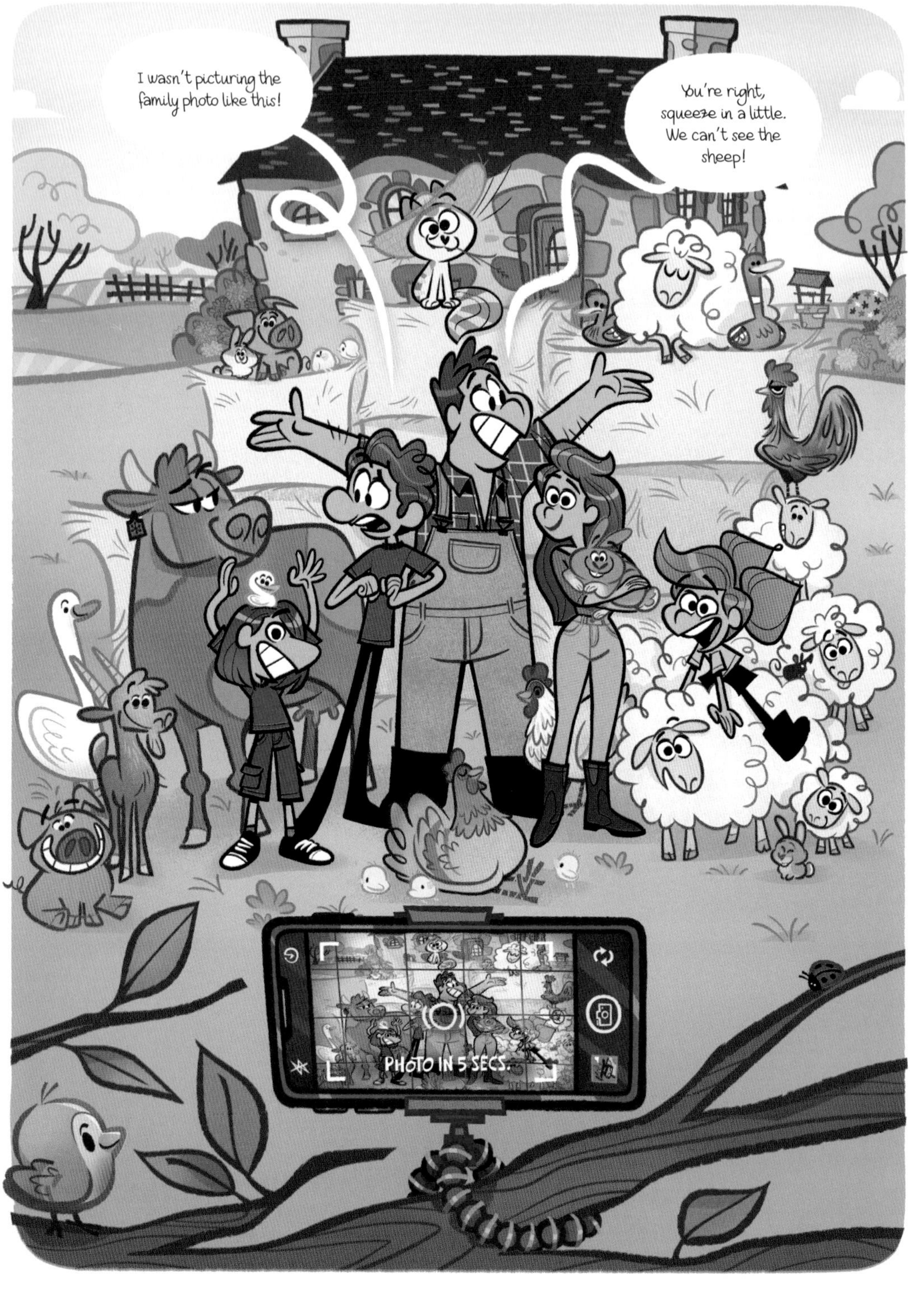
I wasn't picturing the family photo like this!
You're right, squeeze in a little. We can't see the sheep!
PHOTO IN 5 SECS.

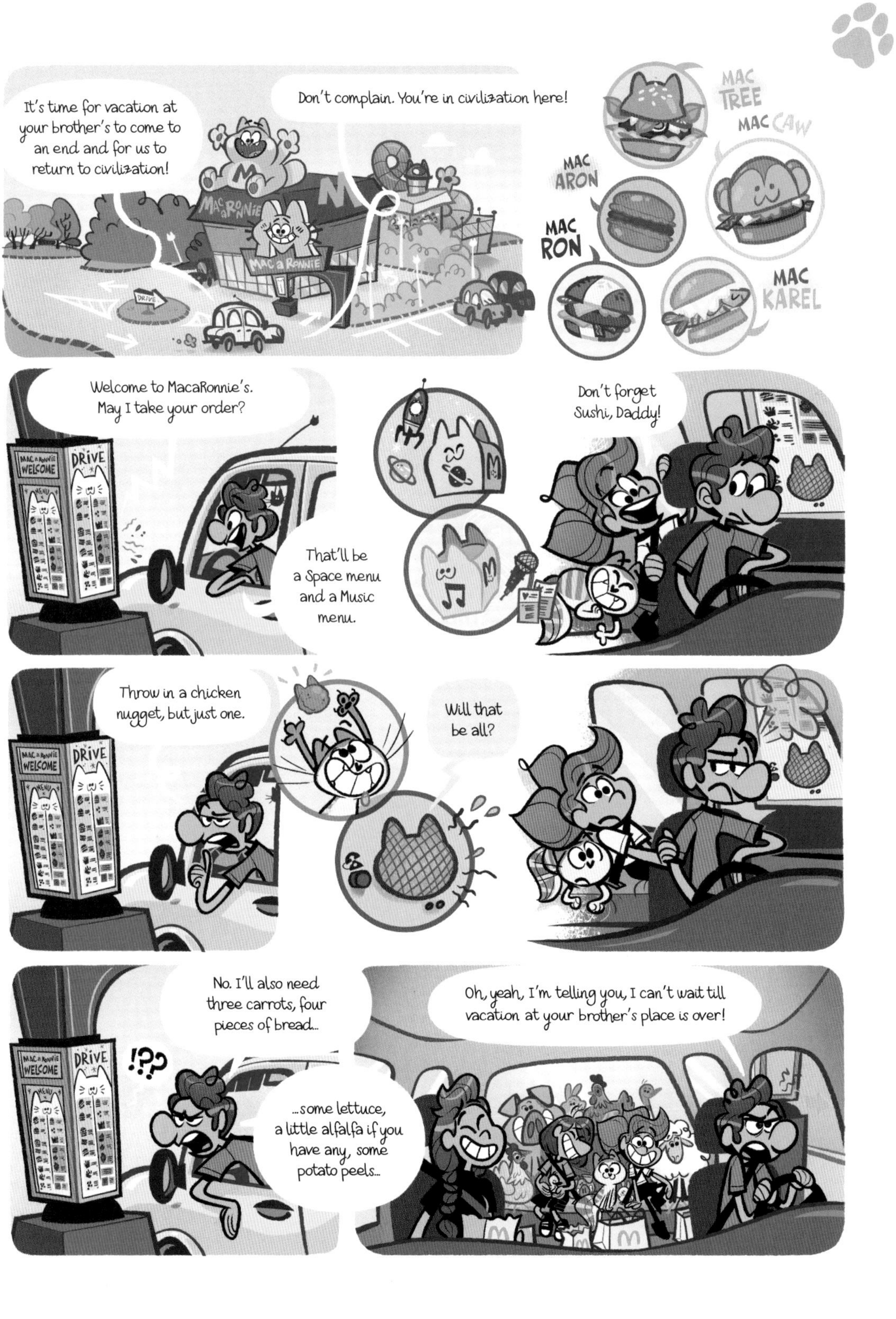
It's time for vacation at your brother's to come to an end and for us to return to civilization!
Don't complain. You're in civilization here!
MAC a RONNIE
DRIVE
MAC TREE
MAC CAW
MAC ARON
MAC RON
MAC KAREL
Welcome to MacaRonnie's. May I take your order?
MAC a RONNIE WELCOME
DRIVE
That'll be a Space menu and a Music menu.
Don't forget Sushi, Daddy!
Throw in a chicken nugget, but just one.
Will that be all?
No. I'll also need three carrots, four pieces of bread...
!??
...some lettuce, a little alfalfa if you have any, some potato peels...
Oh, yeah, I'm telling you, I can't wait till vacation at your brother's place is over!

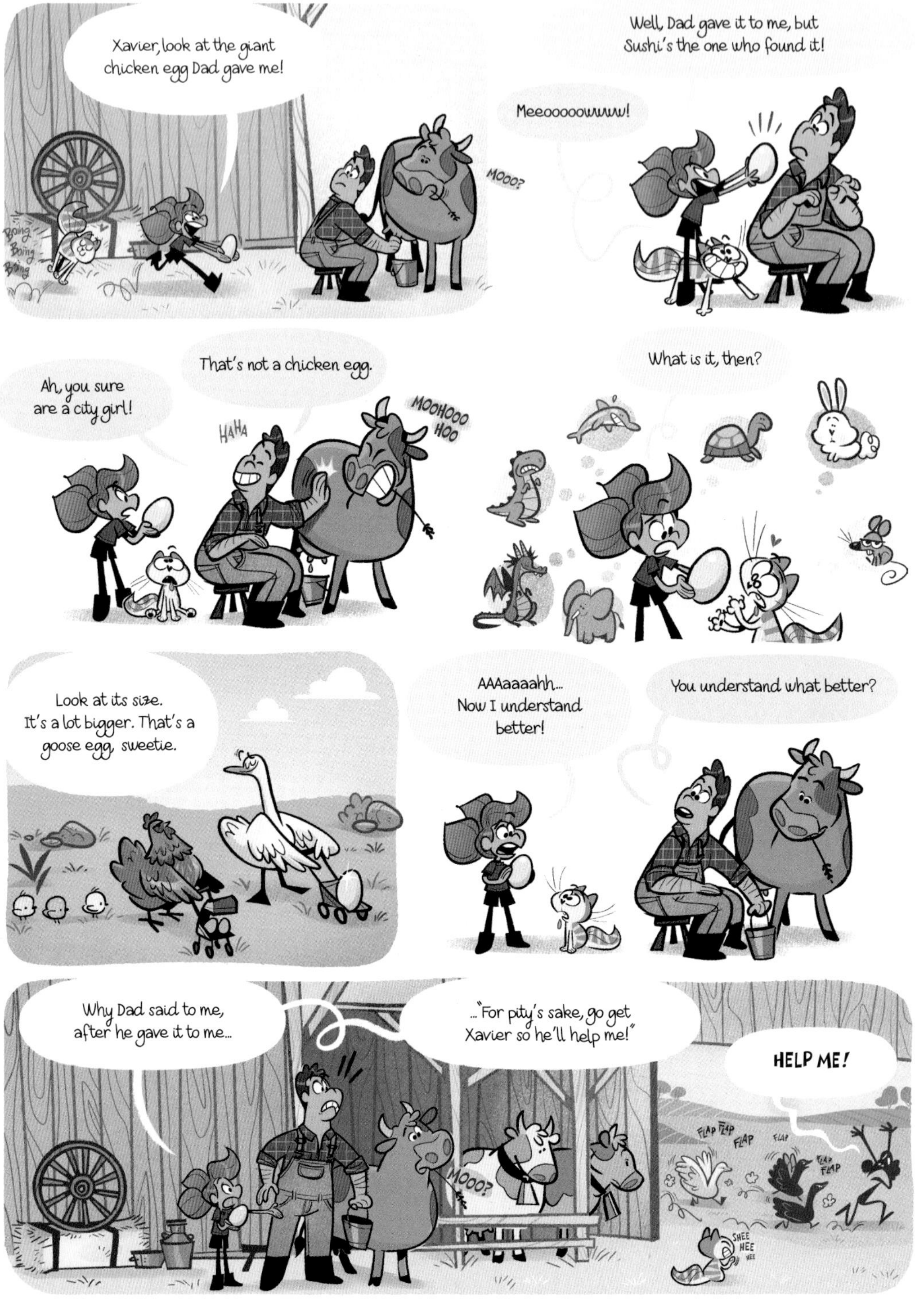
Xavier, look at the giant chicken egg Dad gave me!
Boing Boing Boing
MOOO?
Well, Dad gave it to me, but Sushi's the one who found it!
Meeooooowww!
Ah, you sure are a city girl!
That's not a chicken egg.
HAHA
MOOHOOO HOO
What is it, then?
Look at its size. It's a lot bigger. That's a goose egg, sweetie.
AAAaaaahh... Now I understand better!
You understand what better?
Why Dad said to me, after he gave it to me...
..."For pity's sake, go get Xavier so he'll help me!"
HELP ME!
MOOO?
FLAP FLAP FLAP
FLAP
FLAP FLAP
SHEE HEE HEE

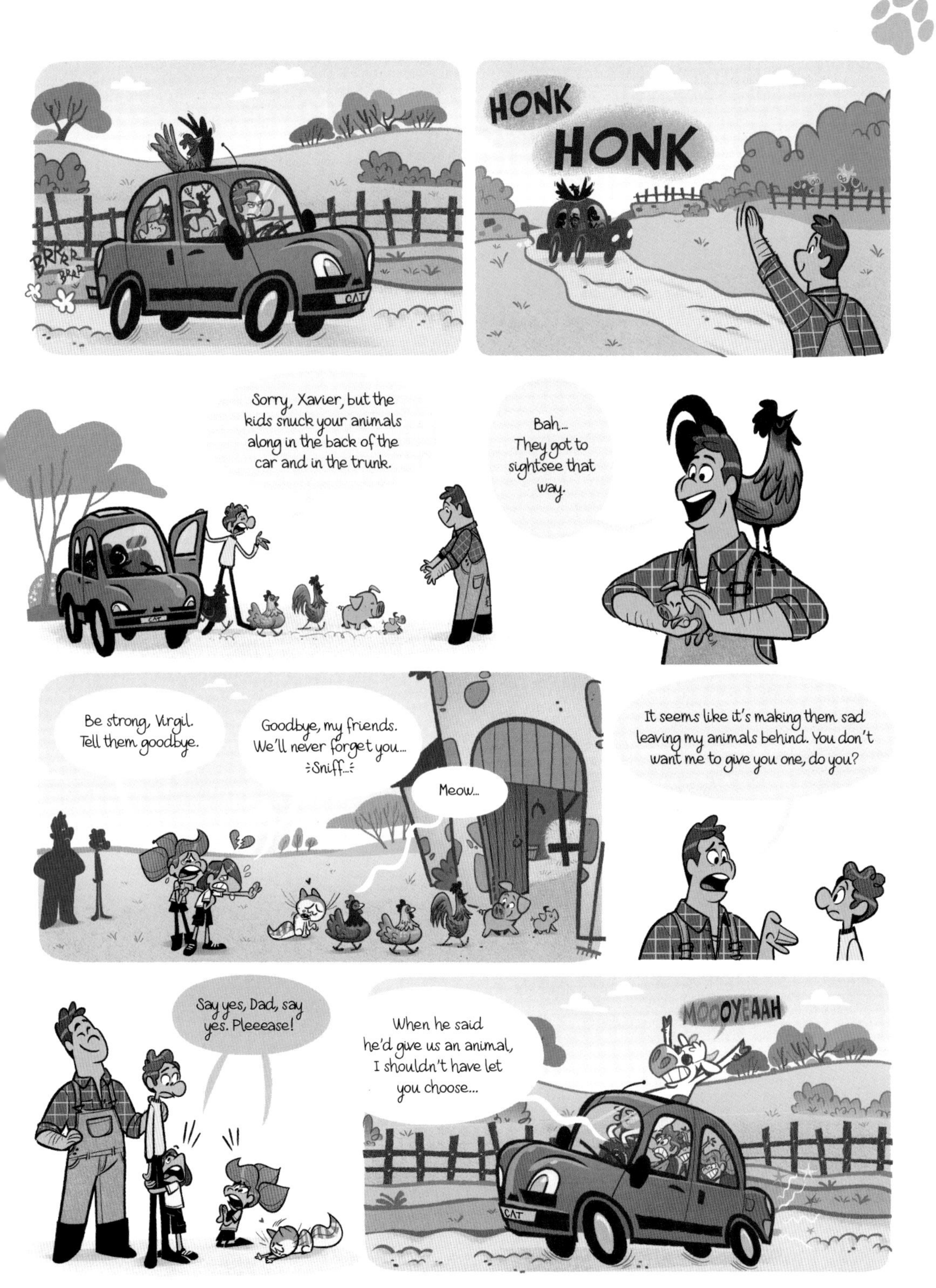
BRRRR BRAR
HONK
HONK
Sorry, Xavier, but the kids snuck your animals along in the back of the car and in the trunk.
Bah... They got to sightsee that way.
Be strong, Virgil. Tell them goodbye.
Goodbye, my friends. We'll never forget you... Sniff...
Meow...
It seems like it's making them sad leaving my animals behind. You don't want me to give you one, do you?
Say yes, Dad, say yes. Pleeease!
When he said he'd give us an animal, I shouldn't have let you choose...
MOOOYEAAH

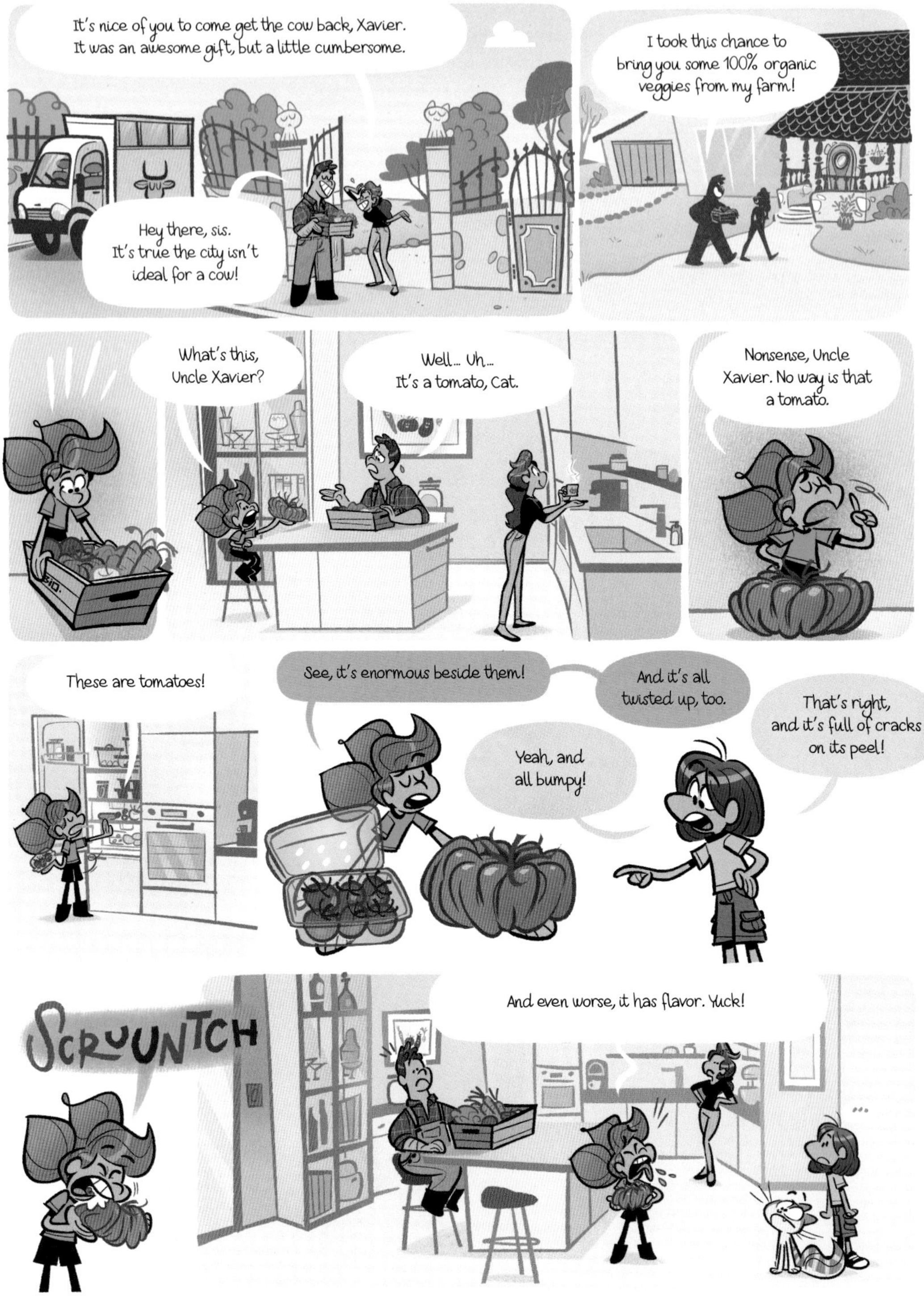

It's nice of you to come get the cow back, Xavier. It was an awesome gift, but a little cumbersome.
Hey there, sis. It's true the city isn't ideal for a cow!
I took this chance to bring you some 100% organic veggies from my farm!
What's this, Uncle Xavier?
Well... Uh... It's a tomato, Cat.
Nonsense, Uncle Xavier. No way is that a tomato.
These are tomatoes!
See, it's enormous beside them!
And it's all twisted up, too.
Yeah, and all bumpy!
That's right, and it's full of cracks on its peel!
SCRUUNTCH
And even worse, it has flavor. Yuck!

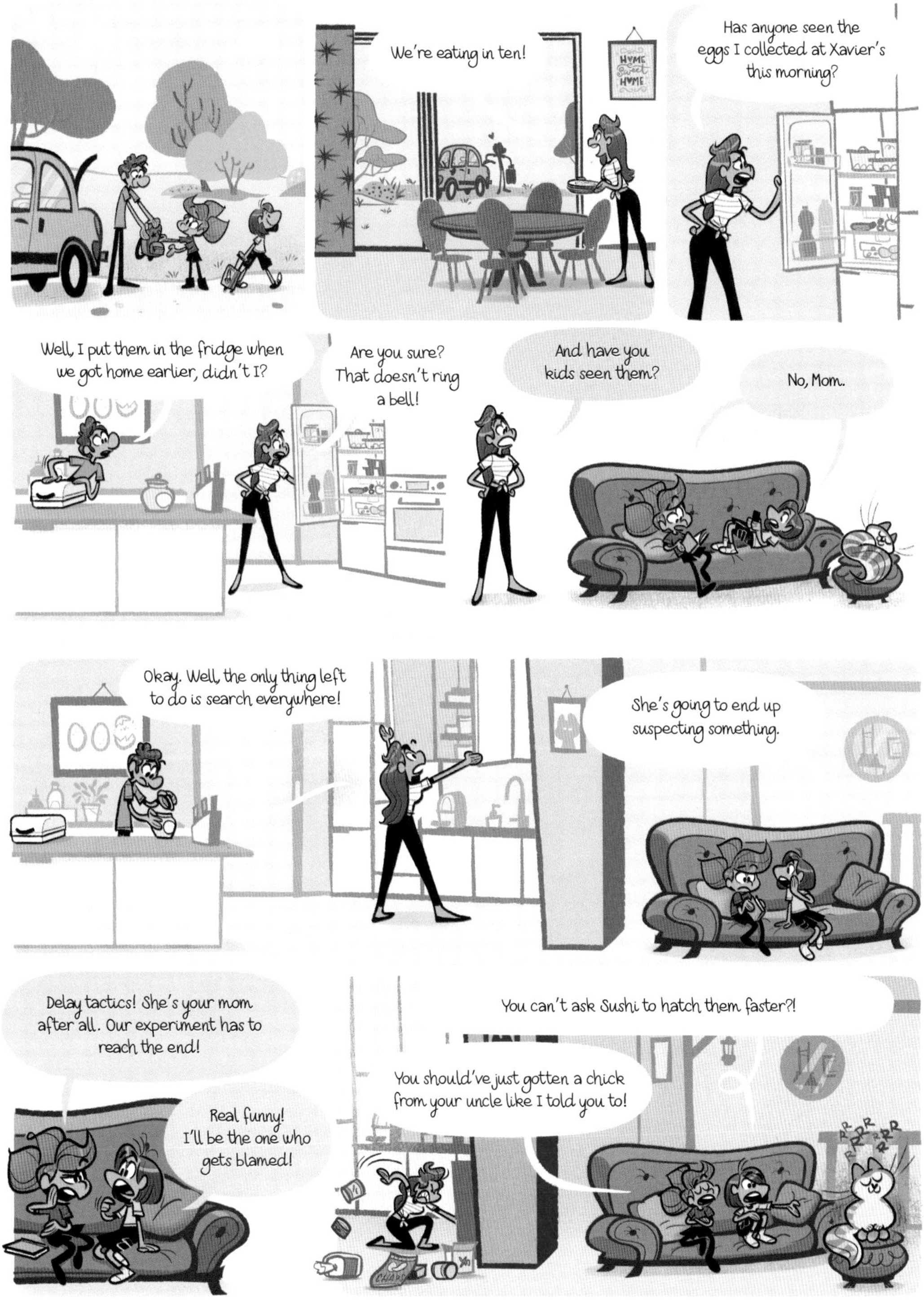
We're eating in ten!
Has anyone seen the eggs I collected at Xavier's this morning?
Well, I put them in the fridge when we got home earlier, didn't I?
Are you sure? That doesn't ring a bell!
And have you kids seen them?
No, Mom.
Okay. Well, the only thing left to do is search everywhere!
She's going to end up suspecting something.
Delay tactics! She's your mom after all. Our experiment has to reach the end!
Real funny! I'll be the one who gets blamed!
You can't ask Sushi to hatch them faster?!
You should've just gotten a chick from your uncle like I told you to!
RRRRRR

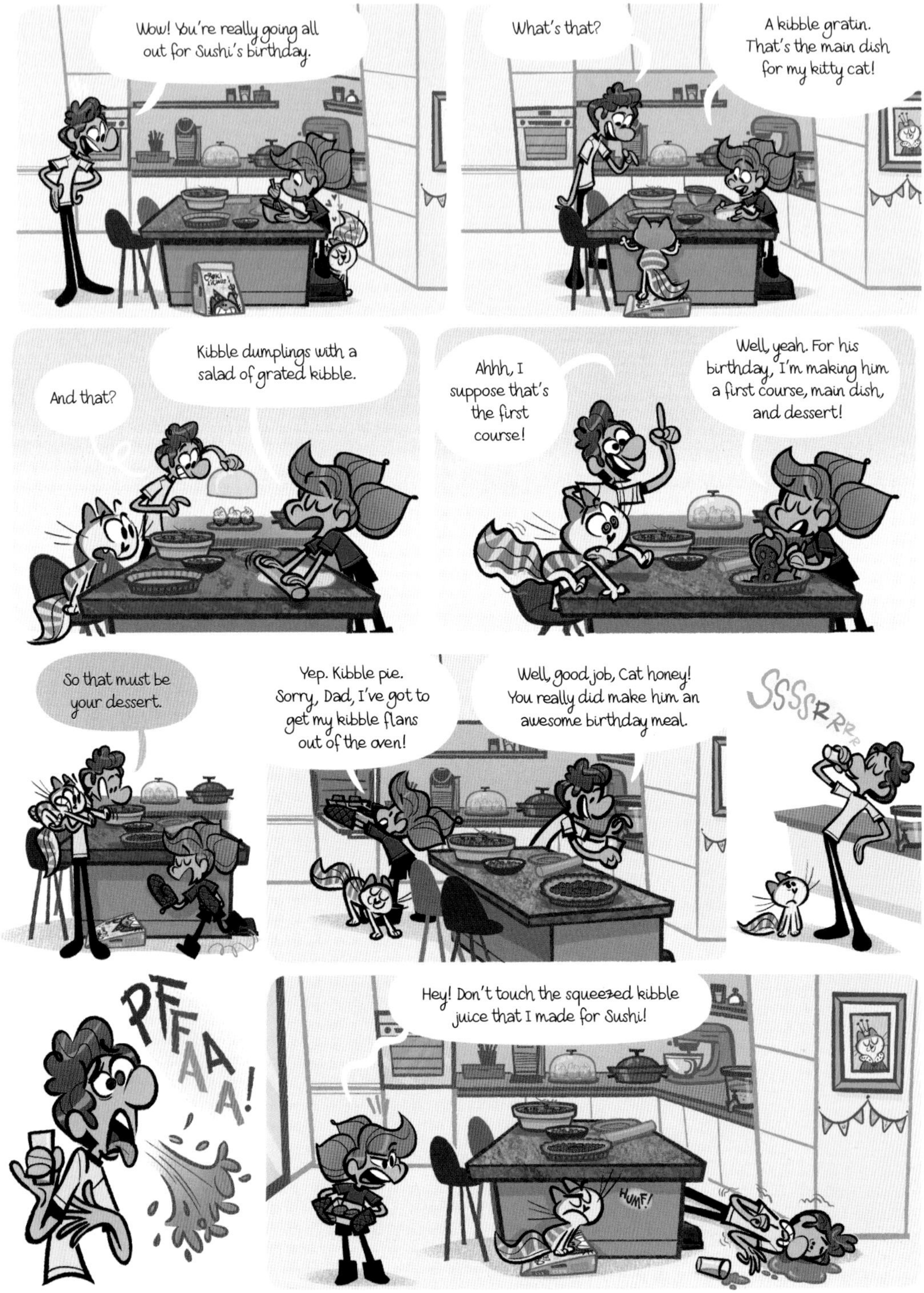
Wow! You're really going all out for Sushi's birthday.
What's that?
A kibble gratin. That's the main dish for my kitty cat!
And that?
Kibble dumplings with a salad of grated kibble.
Ahhh, I suppose that's the first course!
Well, yeah. For his birthday, I'm making him a first course, main dish, and dessert!
So that must be your dessert.
Yep. Kibble pie. Sorry, Dad, I've got to get my kibble flans out of the oven!
Well, good job, Cat honey! You really did make him an awesome birthday meal.
SSSSRRRR
PFFAAA!
Hey! Don't touch the squeezed kibble juice that I made for Sushi!
HUMF!

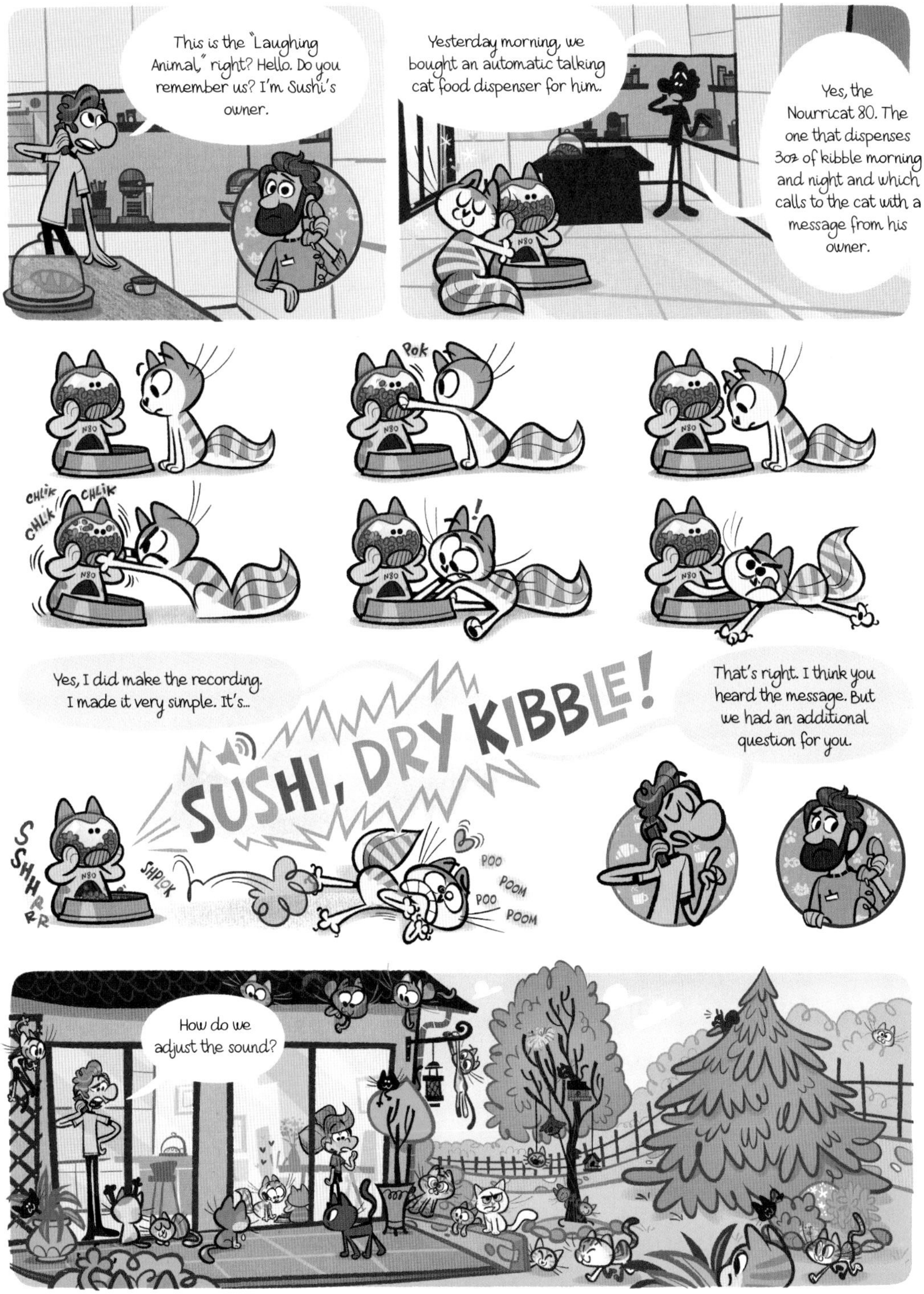

This is the "Laughing Animal," right? Hello. Do you remember us? I'm Sushi's owner.
Yesterday morning, we bought an automatic talking cat food dispenser for him.
Yes, the Nourricat 80. The one that dispenses 3oz of kibble morning and night and which calls to the cat with a message from his owner.
N80
POK
CHLIK CHLIK CHLIK
Yes, I did make the recording. I made it very simple. It's...
SUSHI, DRY KIBBLE!
That's right. I think you heard the message. But we had an additional question for you.
SSHHRRR
SHPLOK
POO POOM POO POOM
How do we adjust the sound?

It's a hi-tech cat food dispenser for our Sushi, Sam!

Of course, it does a lot more than shoot out kibble... Would you start it, Cat?

For sure!

So, to start with, it dispenses food servings at regular times.

It dispenses filtered, purified, and always fresh water.

Bip VOOM

SHPLIK SHPLOK

It has different games based on the cat's mood.

BOOP

It even does irresistible scratching between the cat's ears, and he loves that.

Basically, it's awesome, it does everything!

GLING FLOOP FLOOP BOP

PRRR PRRR PRRR

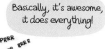

VZZZZZZ

HEE HEE!

Come on, kitty!

It sucks. It does everything!

MEAWW

42

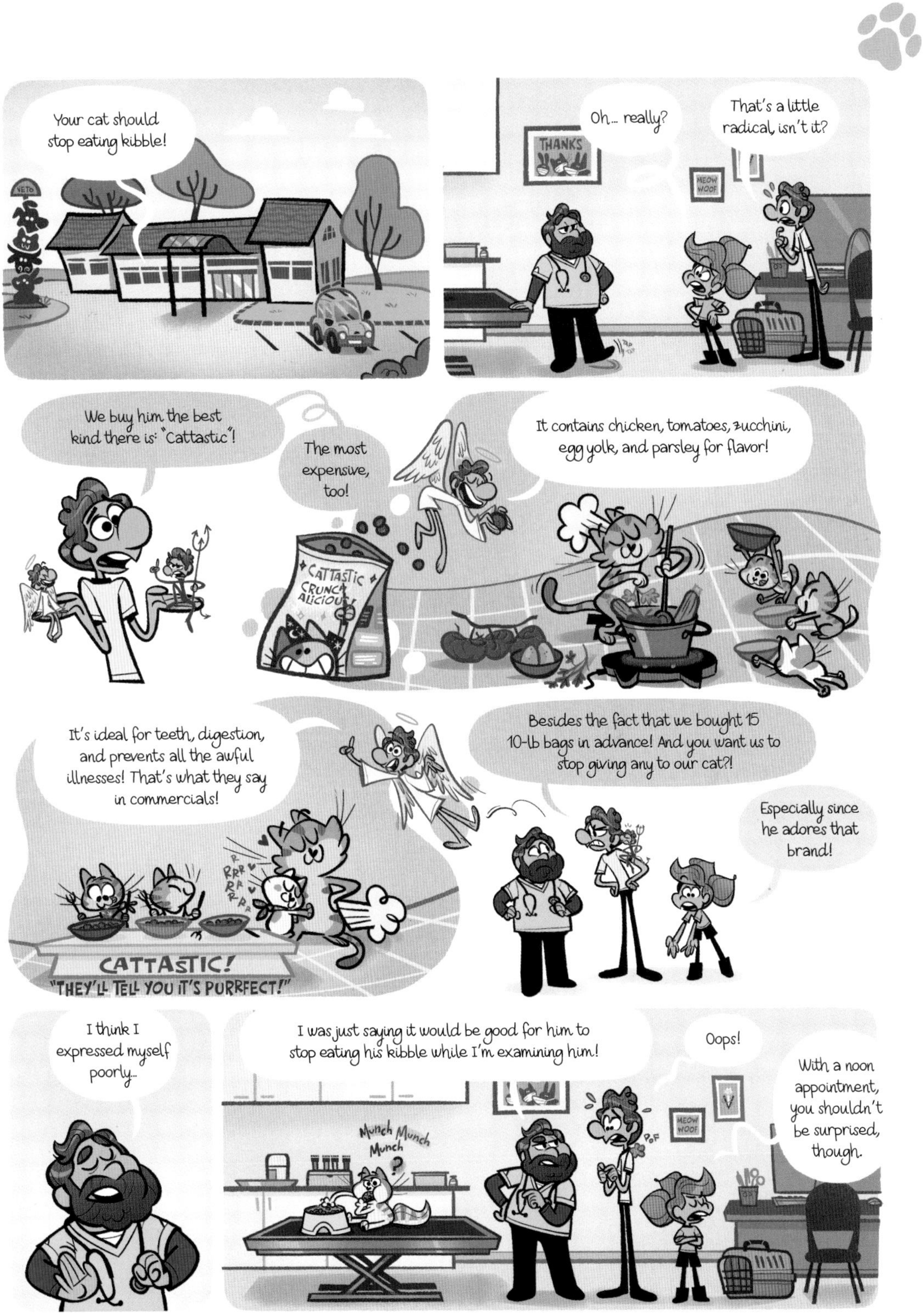
VETO
Your cat should stop eating kibble!
Oh... really?
That's a little radical, isn't it?
THANKS
MEOW WOOF
We buy him the best kind there is: "Cattastic"!
The most expensive, too!
It contains chicken, tomatoes, zucchini, egg yolk, and parsley for flavor!
CATTASTIC CRUNCH ALICIOUS
It's ideal for teeth, digestion, and prevents all the awful illnesses! That's what they say in commercials!
Besides the fact that we bought 15 10-lb bags in advance! And you want us to stop giving any to our cat?!
Especially since he adores that brand!
CATTASTIC!
"THEY'LL TELL YOU IT'S PURRFECT!"
I think I expressed myself poorly...
I was just saying it would be good for him to stop eating his kibble while I'm examining him!
Oops!
Munch Munch Munch
MEOW WOOF
POF
With a noon appointment, you shouldn't be surprised, though.

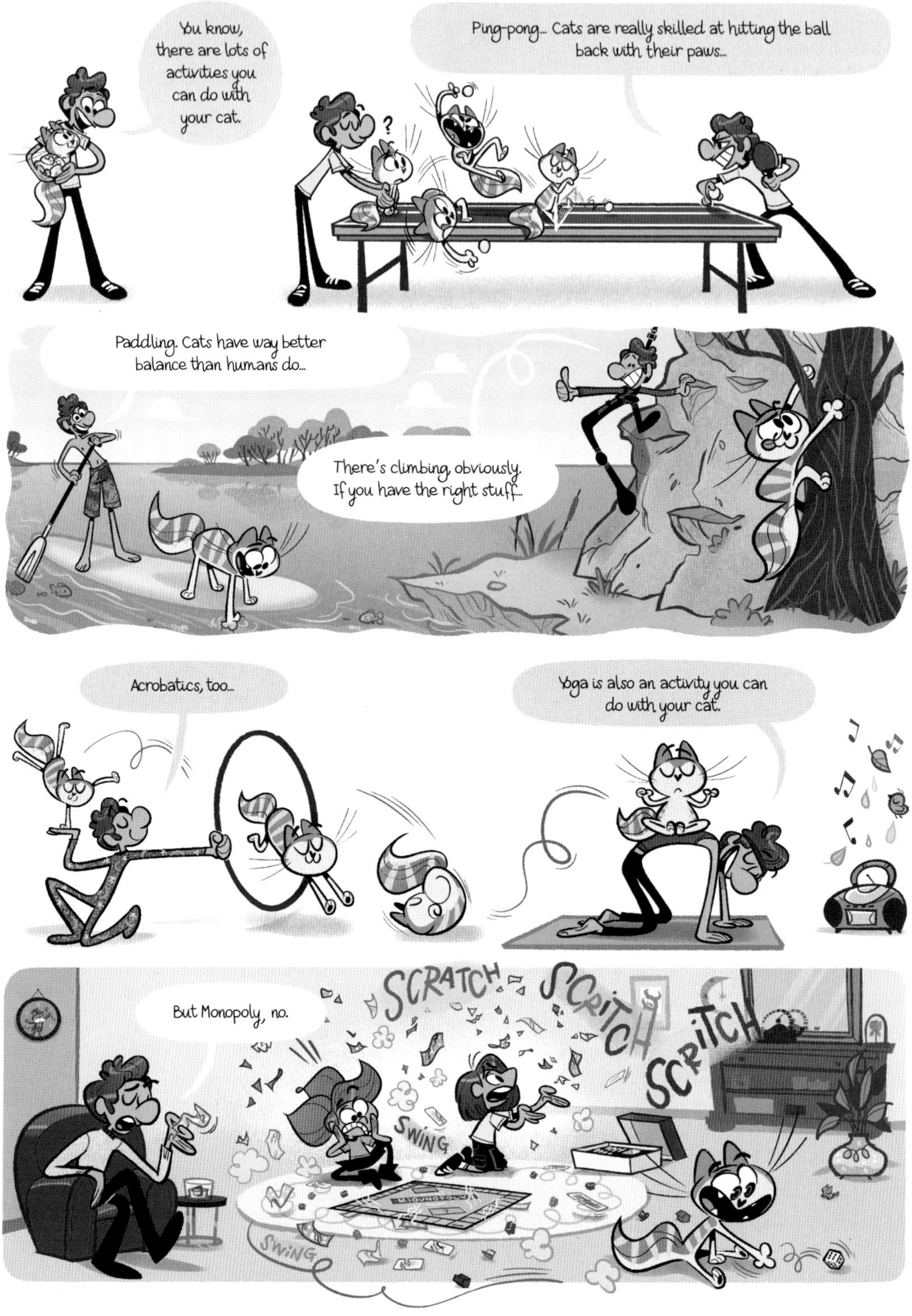

You know, there are lots of activities you can do with your cat.
Ping-pong... Cats are really skilled at hitting the ball back with their paws...
Paddling. Cats have way better balance than humans do...
There's climbing, obviously. If you have the right stuff...
Acrobatics, too...
Yoga is also an activity you can do with your cat.
But Monopoly, no.
SCRATCH
SCRITCH
SCRITCH
SWING
SWING

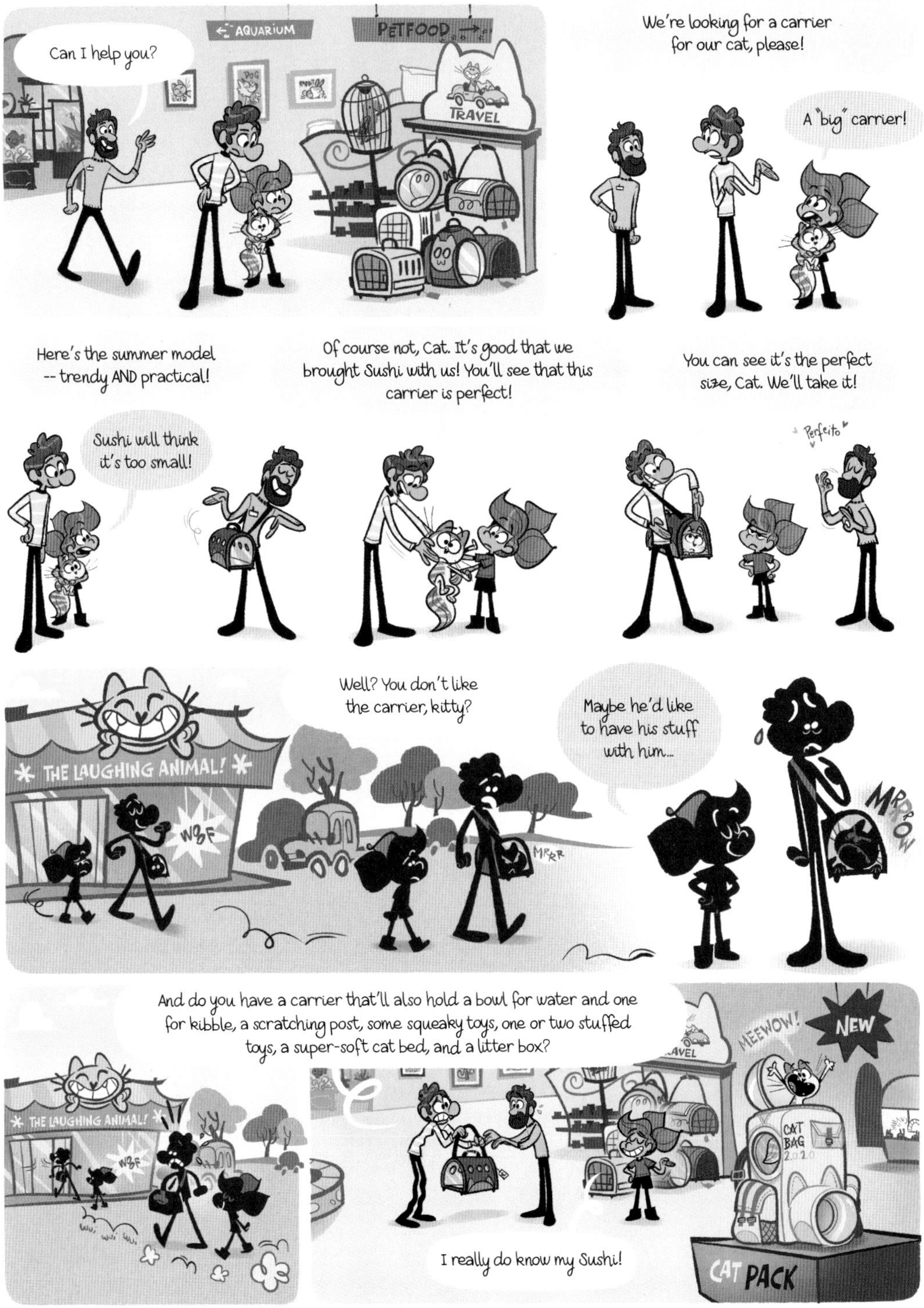

← AQUARIUM
PETFOOD →
TRAVEL
Can I help you?
We're looking for a carrier for our cat, please!
A "big" carrier!
Here's the summer model -- trendy AND practical!
Sushi will think it's too small!
Of course not, Cat. It's good that we brought Sushi with us! You'll see that this carrier is perfect.
You can see it's the perfect size, Cat. We'll take it!
Perfeito
* THE LAUGHING ANIMAL! *
WBF
Well? You don't like the carrier, kitty?
MRRR
Maybe he'd like to have his stuff with him...
MRRROW
And do you have a carrier that'll also hold a bowl for water and one for kibble, a scratching post, some squeaky toys, one or two stuffed toys, a super-soft cat bed, and a litter box?
* THE LAUGHING ANIMAL! *
WBF
MEEWOW!
NEW
CAT BAG 2.0
I really do know my Sushi!
CAT PACK

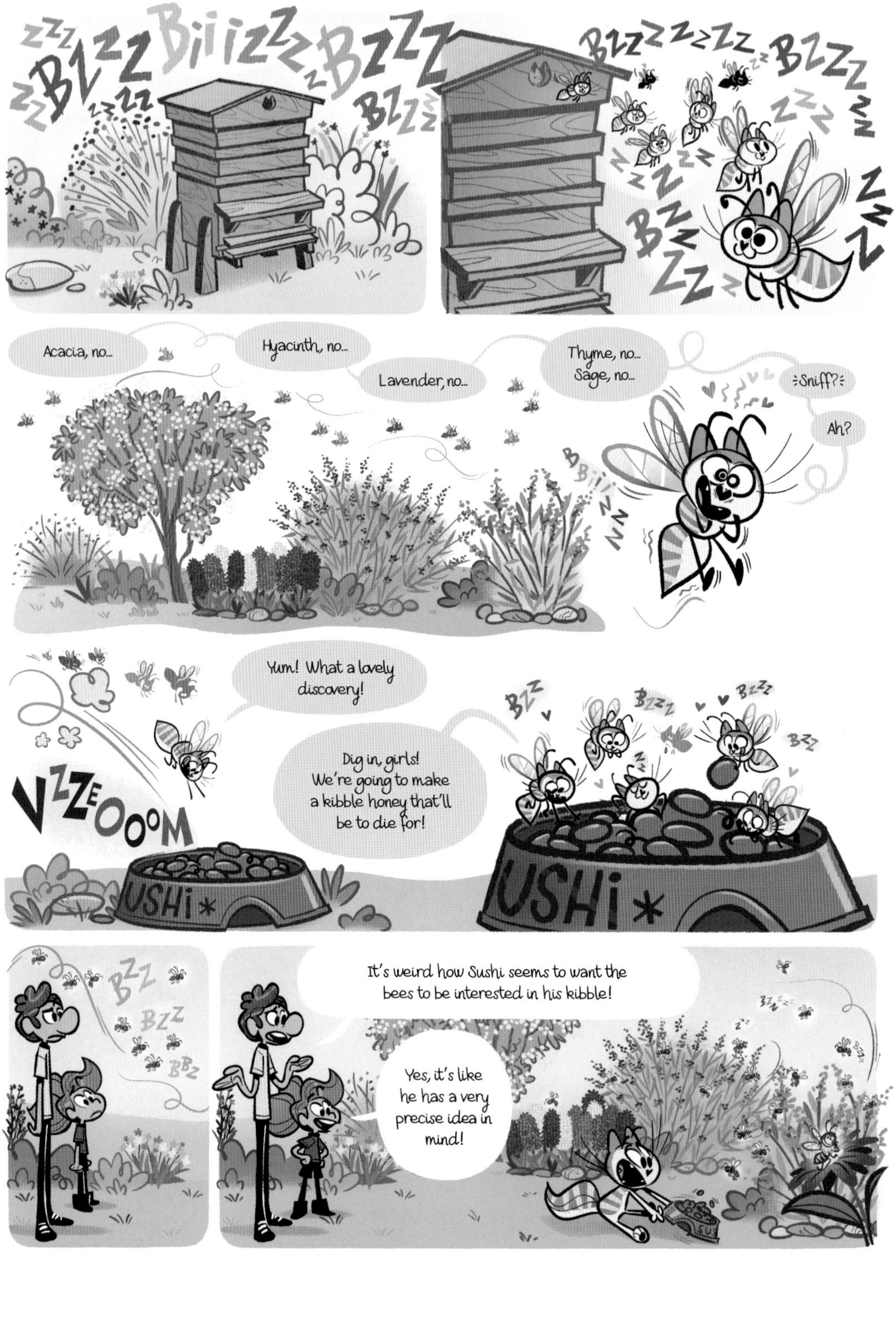
BZZ BIIIZZZ BZZZ
BZZ
BZZZZZZ BZZZ
BZZ
Acacia, no...
Hyacinth, no...
Lavender, no...
Thyme, no...
Sage, no...
Sniff?
Ah?
VZZEOOOM
Yum! What a lovely discovery!
Dig in, girls! We're going to make a kibble honey that'll be to die for!
BZZ
BZZZ
BZZZ
BZZ
USHI
USHI
BZZ
BZZ
It's weird how Sushi seems to want the bees to be interested in his kibble!
Yes, it's like he has a very precise idea in mind!

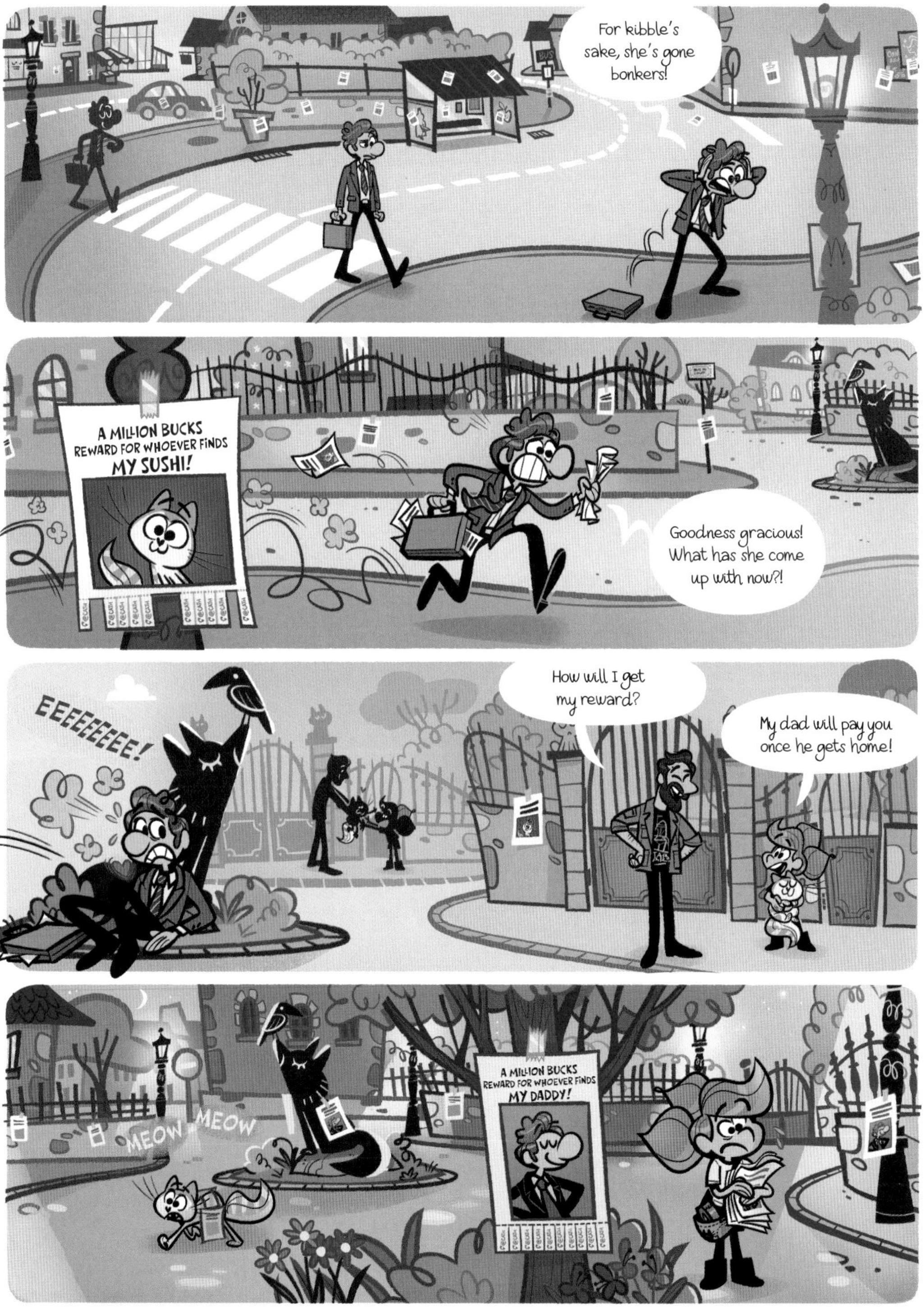
For kibble's sake, she's gone bonkers!
A MILLION BUCKS REWARD FOR WHOEVER FINDS MY SUSHI!
Goodness gracious! What has she come up with now?!
EEEEEEEEE!
How will I get my reward?
My dad will pay you once he gets home!
MEOW MEOW
A MILLION BUCKS REWARD FOR WHOEVER FINDS MY DADDY!

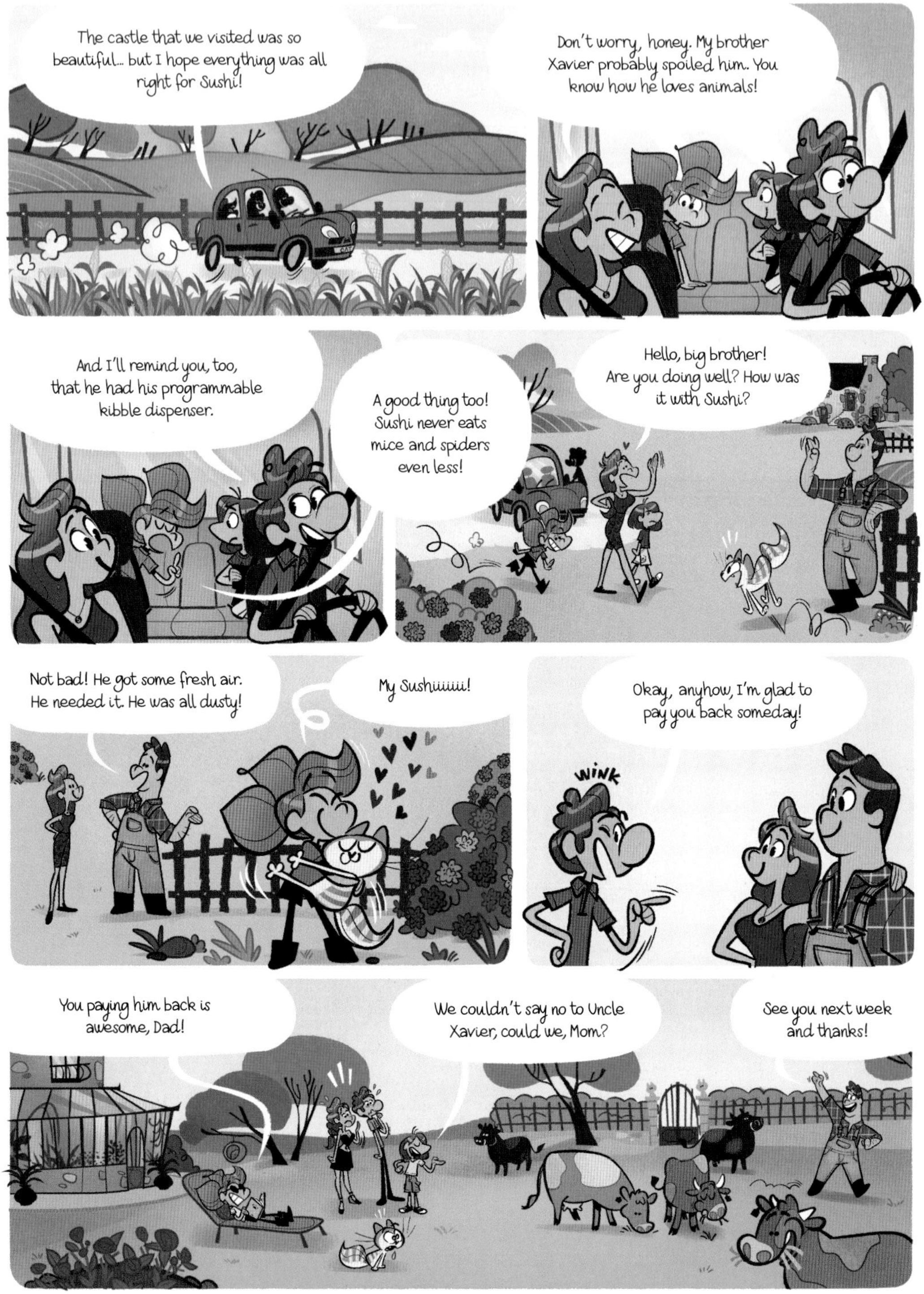
The castle that we visited was so beautiful... but I hope everything was all right for Sushi!
Don't worry, honey. My brother Xavier probably spoiled him. You know how he loves animals!
And I'll remind you, too, that he had his programmable kibble dispenser.
A good thing too! Sushi never eats mice and spiders even less!
Hello, big brother! Are you doing well? How was it with Sushi?
Not bad! He got some fresh air. He needed it. He was all dusty!
My Sushiiiiiii!
Okay, anyhow, I'm glad to pay you back someday!
WINK
You paying him back is awesome, Dad!
We couldn't say no to Uncle Xavier, could we, Mom?
See you next week and thanks!

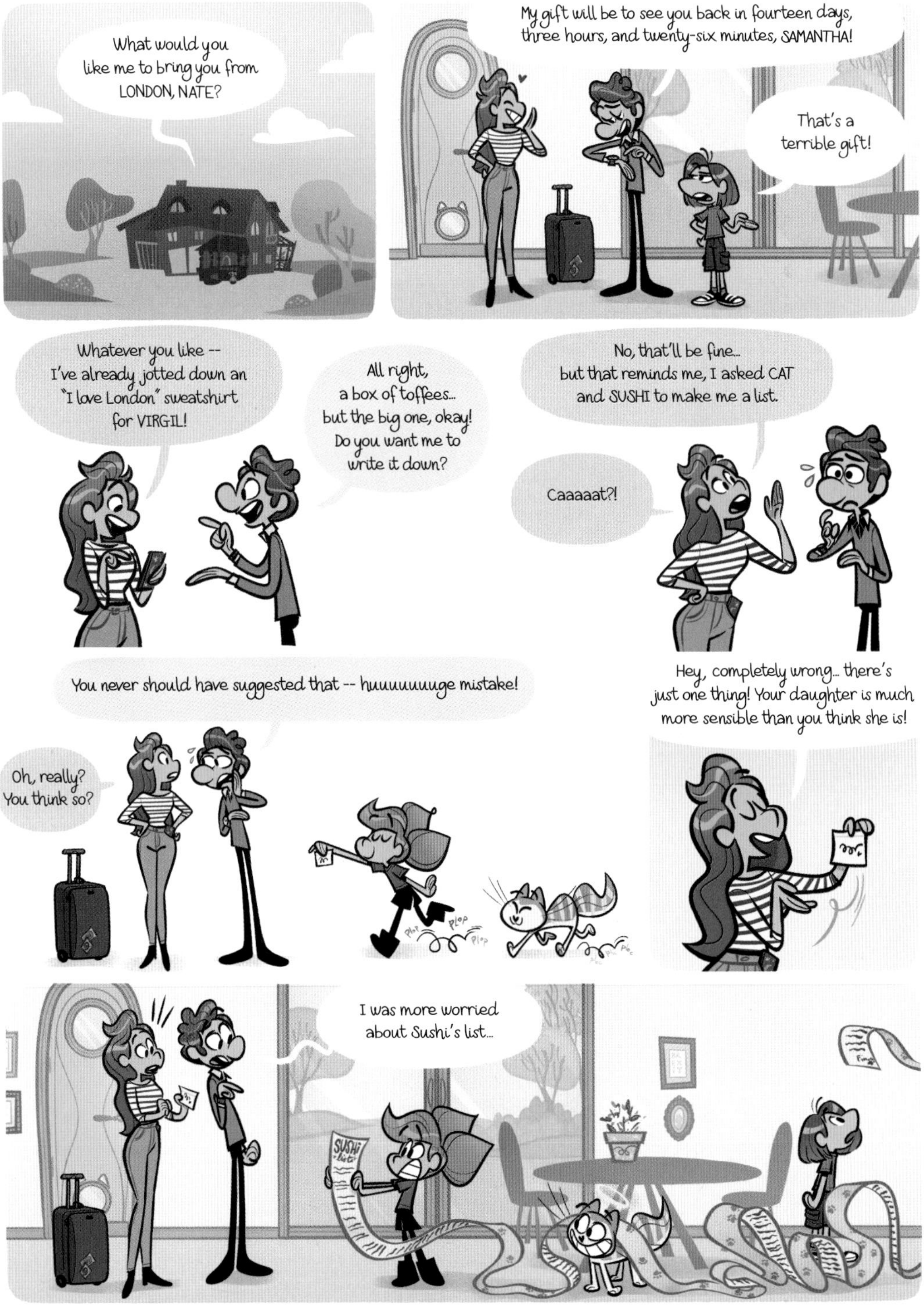
What would you like me to bring you from LONDON, NATE?
My gift will be to see you back in fourteen days, three hours, and twenty-six minutes, SAMANTHA!
That's a terrible gift!
Whatever you like -- I've already jotted down an "I love London" sweatshirt for VIRGIL!
All right, a box of toffees... but the big one, okay! Do you want me to write it down?
No, that'll be fine... but that reminds me, I asked CAT and SUSHI to make me a list.
Caaaaat?!
You never should have suggested that -- huuuuuuuge mistake!
Oh, really? You think so?
Hey, completely wrong... there's just one thing! Your daughter is much more sensible than you think she is!
I was more worried about Sushi's list...
SUSHI list

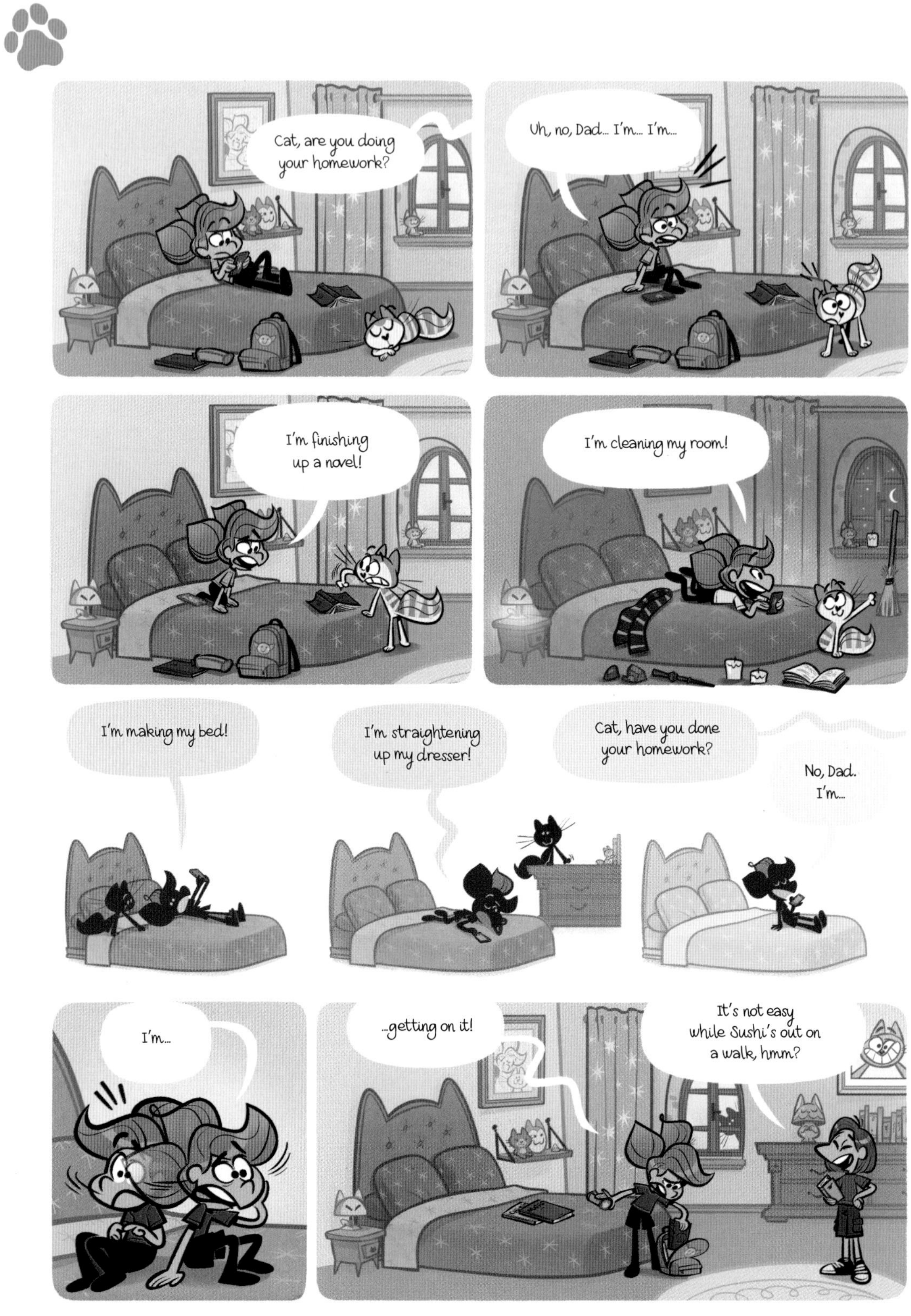
Cat, are you doing your homework?
Uh, no, Dad... I'm... I'm...
I'm finishing up a novel!
I'm cleaning my room!
I'm making my bed!
I'm straightening up my dresser!
Cat, have you done your homework?
No, Dad. I'm...
I'm...
...getting on it!
It's not easy while Sushi's out on a walk, hmm?

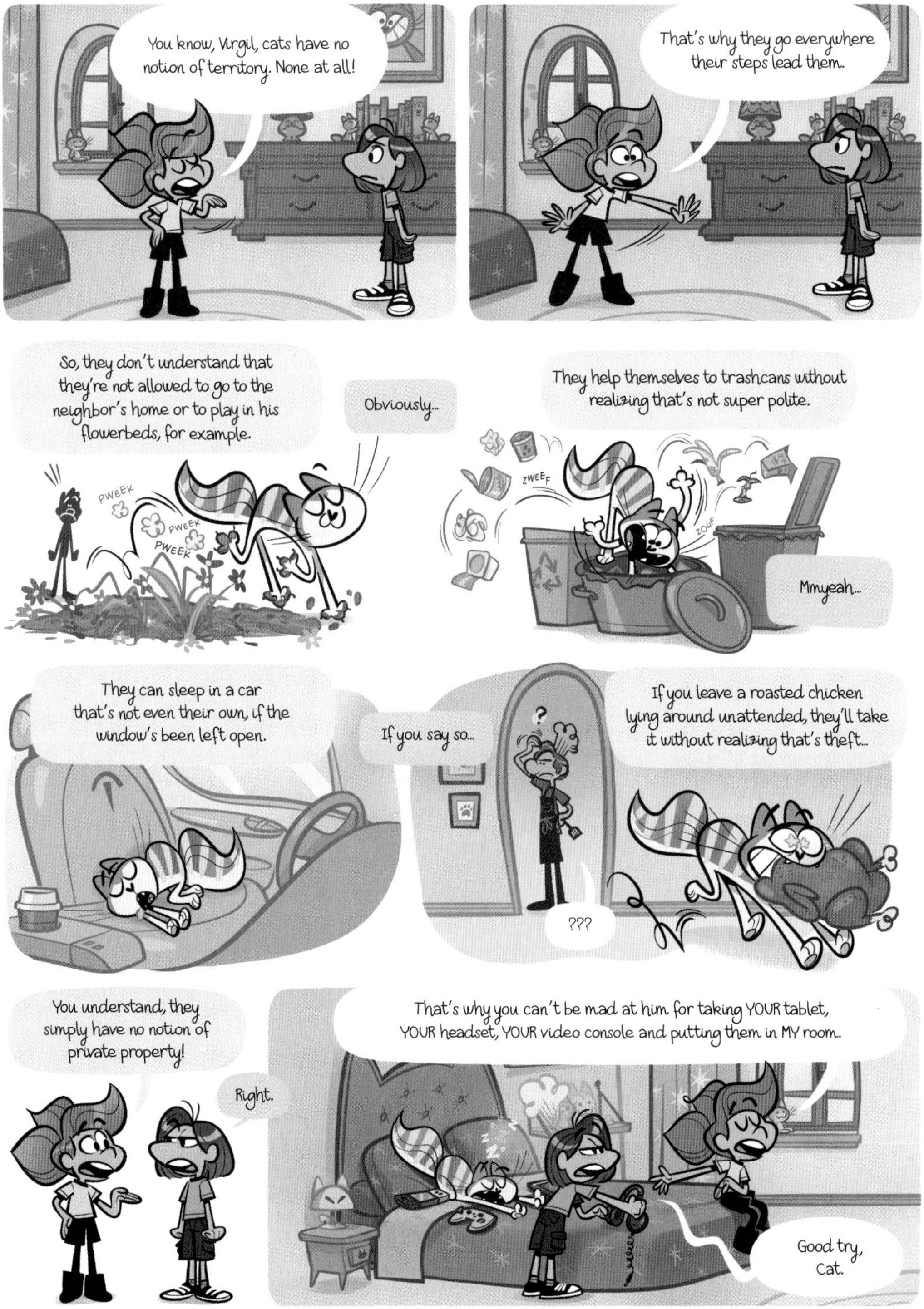
You know, Virgil, cats have no notion of territory. None at all!
That's why they go everywhere their steps lead them.
So, they don't understand that they're not allowed to go to the neighbor's home or to play in his flowerbeds, for example.
Obviously...
PWEEK
PWEEK
PWEEK
They help themselves to trashcans without realizing that's not super polite.
ZWEEF
ZOUF
Mmyeah...
They can sleep in a car that's not even their own, if the window's been left open.
If you say so...
If you leave a roasted chicken lying around unattended, they'll take it without realizing that's theft...
???
You understand, they simply have no notion of private property!
Right.
That's why you can't be mad at him for taking YOUR tablet, YOUR headset, YOUR video console and putting them in MY room.
Good try, Cat.

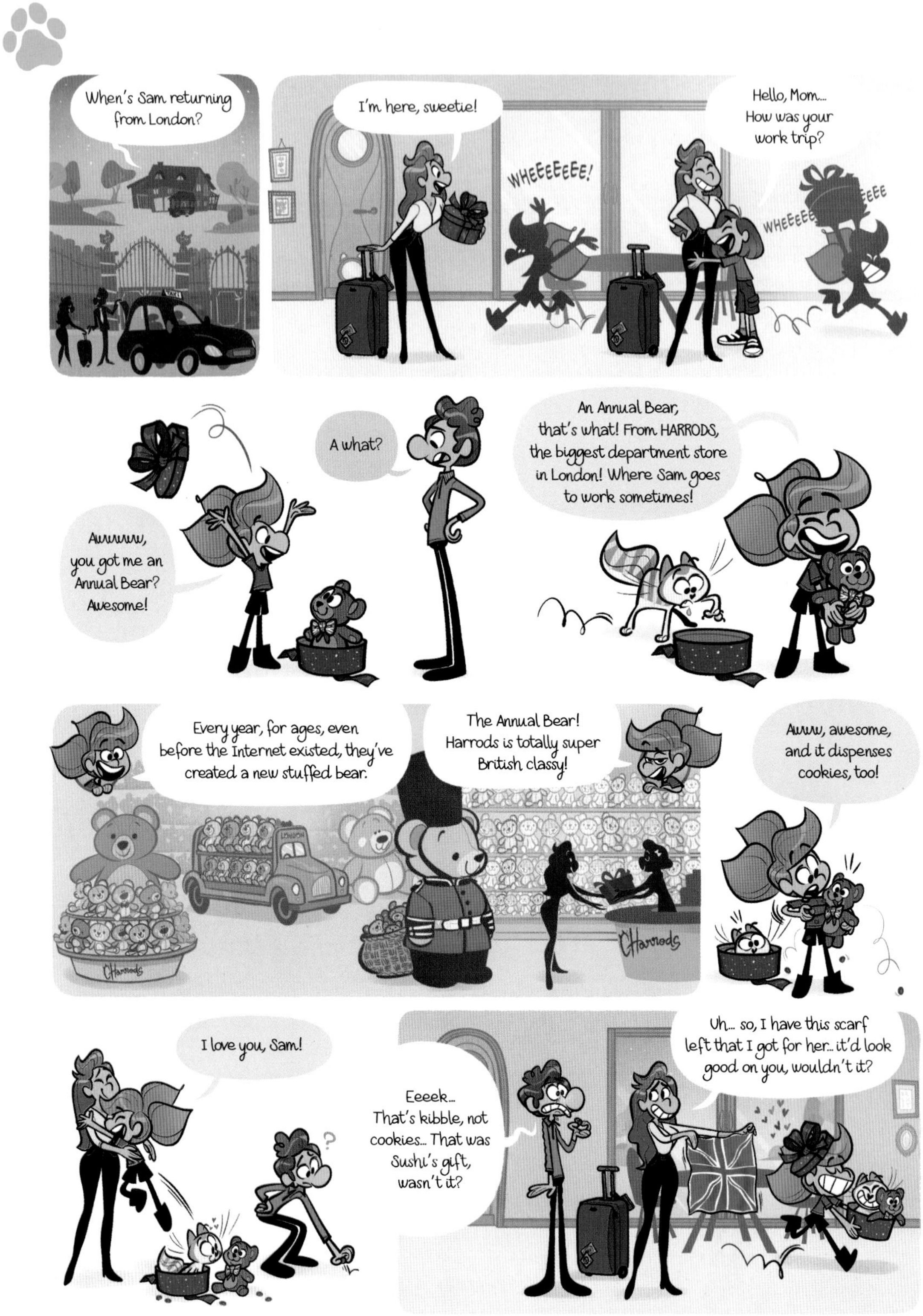

When's Sam returning from London?
I'm here, sweetie!
WHEEEEEEE!
Hello, Mom... How was your work trip?
WHEEEEEEEE
A what?
Auuuuu, you got me an Annual Bear? Awesome!
An Annual Bear, that's what! From HARRODS, the biggest department store in London! Where Sam goes to work sometimes!
Every year, for ages, even before the Internet existed, they've created a new stuffed bear.
The Annual Bear! Harrods is totally super British classy!
Auuu, awesome, and it dispenses cookies, too!
Harrods
Harrods
I love you, Sam!
Eeeek... That's kibble, not cookies... That was Sushi's gift, wasn't it?
Uh... so, I have this scarf left that I got for her... it'd look good on you, wouldn't it?

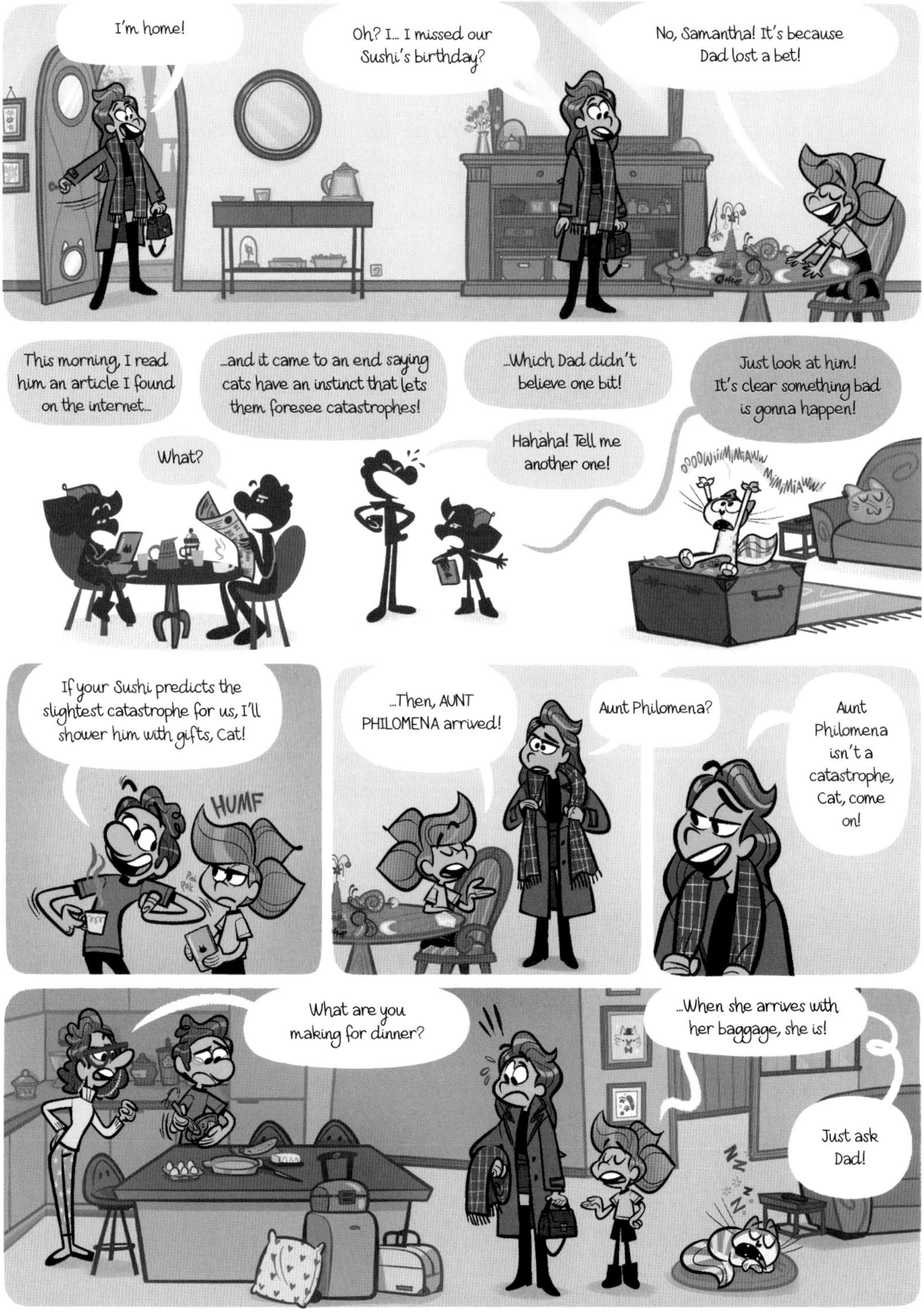
I'm home!
Oh? I... I missed our Sushi's birthday?
No, Samantha! It's because Dad lost a bet!
This morning, I read him an article I found on the internet...
What?
...and it came to an end saying cats have an instinct that lets them foresee catastrophes!
...Which Dad didn't believe one bit!
Hahaha! Tell me another one!
Just look at him! It's clear something bad is gonna happen!
oOOOWiiiMiMiAWW
MiMiMiAWW!
If your Sushi predicts the slightest catastrophe for us, I'll shower him with gifts, Cat!
HUMF
...Then, AUNT PHILOMENA arrived!
Aunt Philomena?
Aunt Philomena isn't a catastrophe, Cat, come on!
What are you making for dinner?
...When she arrives with her baggage, she is!
Just ask Dad!

What are you doing, kids?

We're playing HARRY CATTER. We're recreating exactly what happens to our heroes in the awesome novel that Sam brought back from London!

Novel? This is more a comicbook, isn't it?

Harry Catter is Sushi, obviously. Virgil, with his huge beard, is RUBIKUB HANGRYD, and I'm HERMANY GRUNGE.

Yes, like the movie!

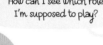

Do you want to play with us?

How can I see which role I'm supposed to play?

What am I supposed to do then?

Easy-peasy! Everything is in the comicbook!

Read the lines from the guy in black.

But hey now, this guy is the--

Well, yeah! He's the bad guy in the story.

We're going to turn you into a gargoyle, VOLDEMORGUE!

Hogsmageddon!

MEEOOOWGOOYLE

EEEEEE!

Well... didn't you want me to take you to the comicbook store, Cat?

Yes, of course!

Today's the day the new issue of the Harry Catter comicbook is coming out! Sushi and I wanted to go there in costumes, like the drawings!

That's a rather showy outfit for going into town!

SUSHLISIUS COMICNAXT KCZ

Hello!

Hello... wow!

Young lady, you and your cat's costumes are awesome! I feel like I'm looking at the real Harry Catter and Hermany Grunge!

Of course, we are the real ones!

Meow!

Tss, those kids, now...

I'll give you the comic for your effort!

Really?!

R--really?

Me, I'll take this copy!

How will you be paying?

HE'S HAD IT UP TO HIS WHISKERS!
CATMAN! ROAR
NEW ISSUE!

COMIC

55

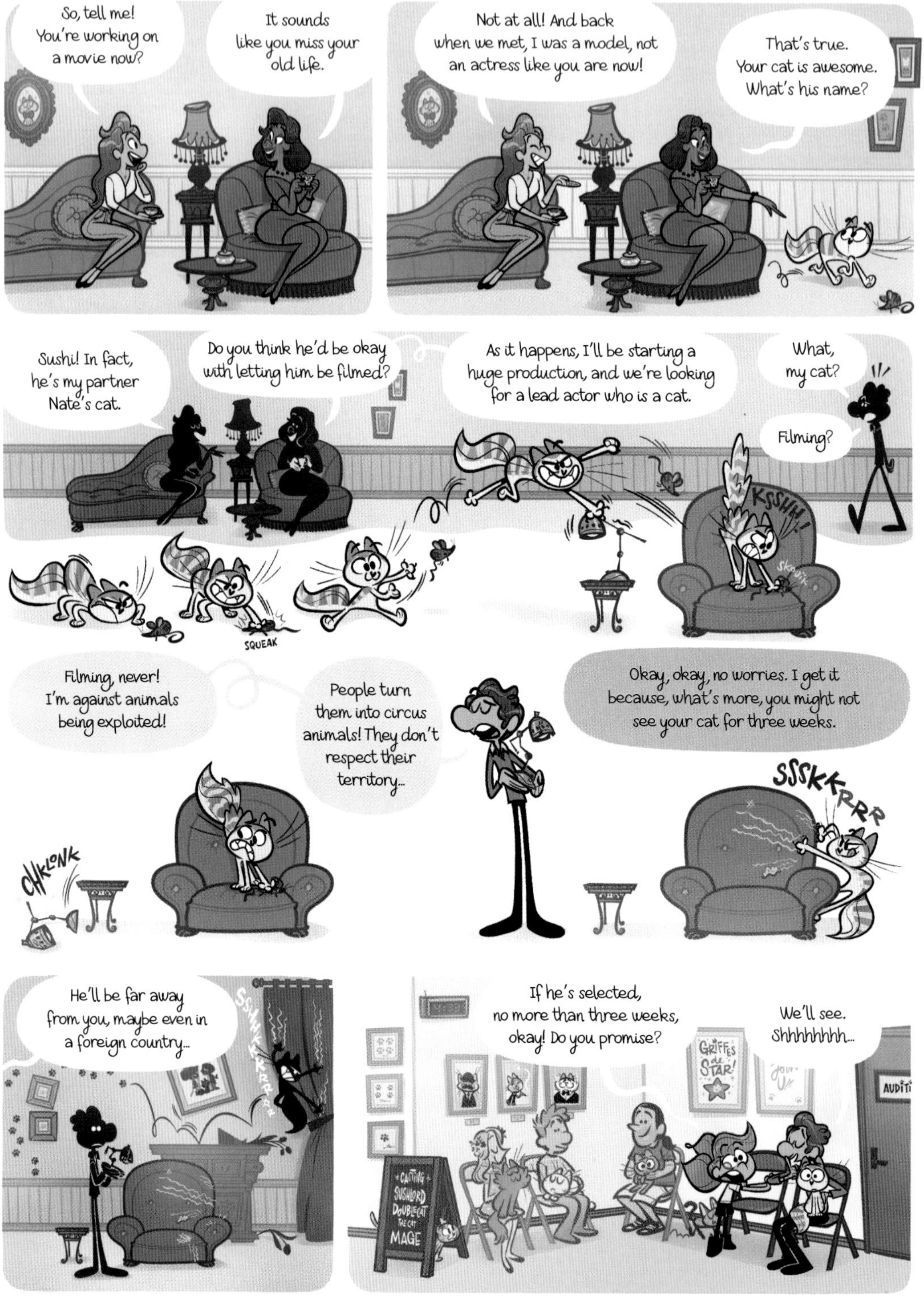

So, tell me! You're working on a movie now?
It sounds like you miss your old life.
Not at all! And back when we met, I was a model, not an actress like you are now!
That's true. Your cat is awesome. What's his name?
Sushi! In fact, he's my partner Nate's cat.
Do you think he'd be okay with letting him be filmed?
As it happens, I'll be starting a huge production, and we're looking for a lead actor who is a cat.
What, my cat?
Filming?
SQUEAK
KSSHH!
Filming, never! I'm against animals being exploited!
People turn them into circus animals! They don't respect their territory...
Okay, okay, no worries. I get it because, what's more, you might not see your cat for three weeks.
CHKLONK
SSSKKRRR
He'll be far away from you, maybe even in a foreign country...
If he's selected, no more than three weeks, okay! Do you promise?
We'll see. Shhhhhhhh...

Sushi? What dumb thing have you done now?

¿Arhhh!¿ You wicked cat!

What? What?! Did Sushi eat the TV remote again?

Way worse than that, Dad!

Nooooo? Not the movie script?

Yes...

Ripped up?

Totally...

That blasted tomcat has torn his chances of being a movie star to shreds! What a CATastrophe!

Especially since the director is supposed to come by this evening to see what we thought of the story.

Even if we tell him we liked what we read, he won't believe us once he sees what condition it's in.

Okay... besides becoming an exile in the NORTH POLE, I don't see what else we can do.

What if we put it back together, Dad?

Between the two of us, we'll be able to remember the story. We just have to put the pages back in order and glue together all the pieces.

Good idea, Cat! We'll pull up our sleeves and stay positive!

Glue! Scissors! Stapler! Coffee!

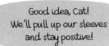

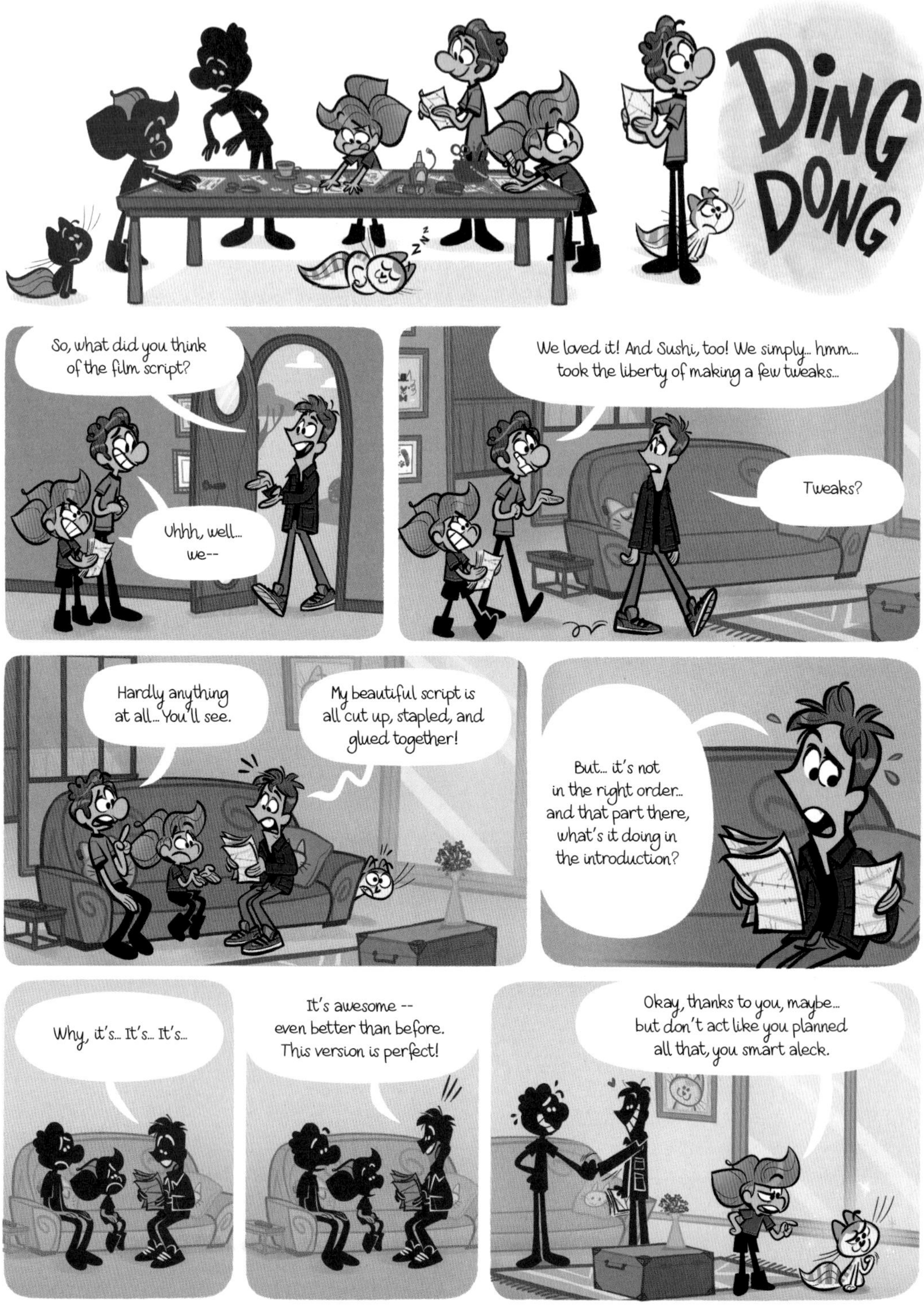
DING DONG
So, what did you think of the film script?
Uhhh, well... we--
We loved it! And Sushi, too! We simply... hmm... took the liberty of making a few tweaks...
Tweaks?
Hardly anything at all... You'll see.
My beautiful script is all cut up, stapled, and glued together!
But... it's not in the right order... and that part there, what's it doing in the introduction?
Why, it's... It's... It's...
It's awesome -- even better than before. This version is perfect!
Okay, thanks to you, maybe... but don't act like you planned all that, you smart aleck.

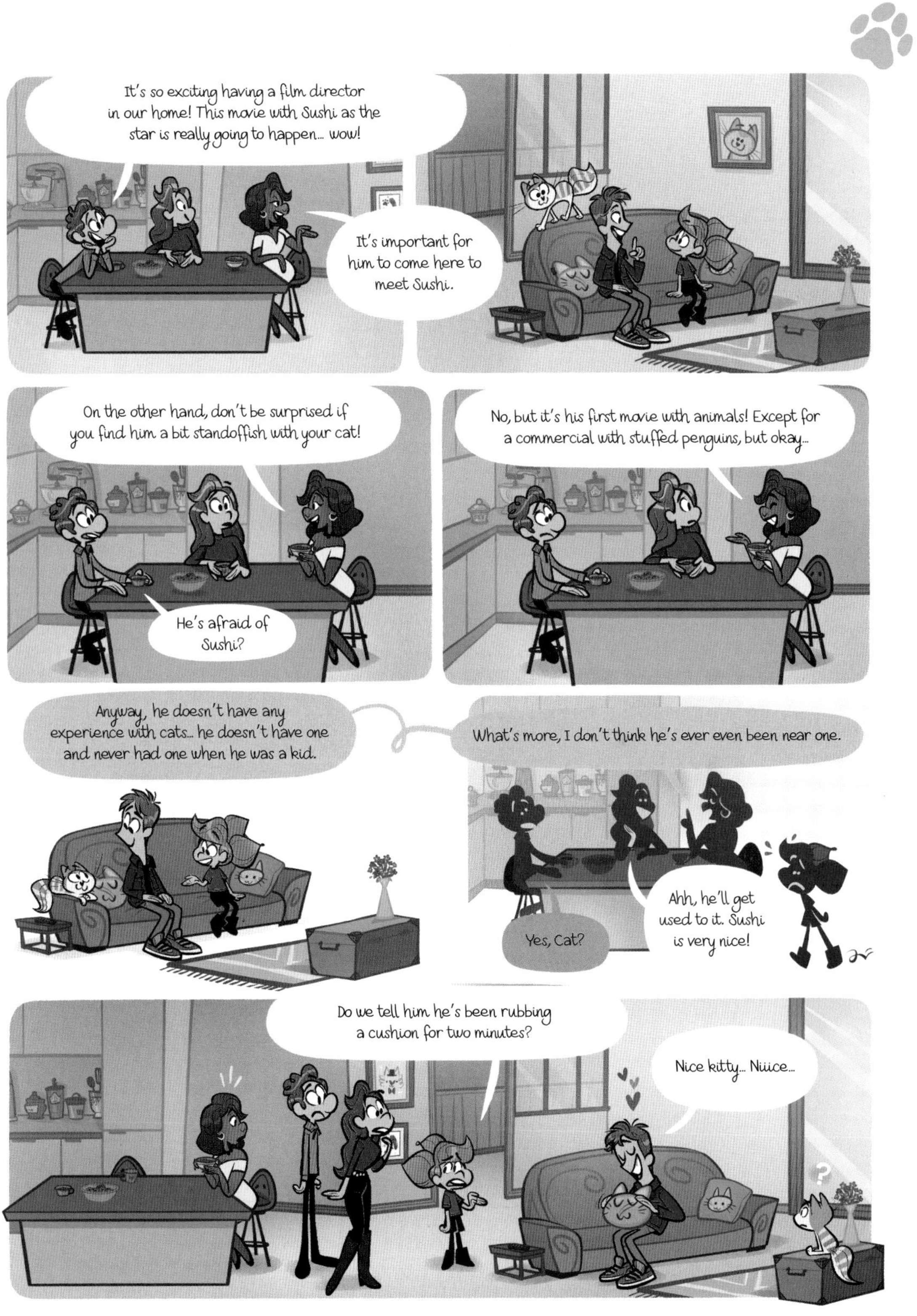
It's so exciting having a film director in our home! This movie with Sushi as the star is really going to happen... wow!
It's important for him to come here to meet Sushi.
On the other hand, don't be surprised if you find him a bit standoffish with your cat!
He's afraid of Sushi?
No, but it's his first movie with animals! Except for a commercial with stuffed penguins, but okay...
Anyway, he doesn't have any experience with cats... he doesn't have one and never had one when he was a kid.
What's more, I don't think he's ever even been near one.
Yes, Cat?
Ahh, he'll get used to it. Sushi is very nice!
Do we tell him he's been rubbing a cushion for two minutes?
Nice kitty... Niiice...

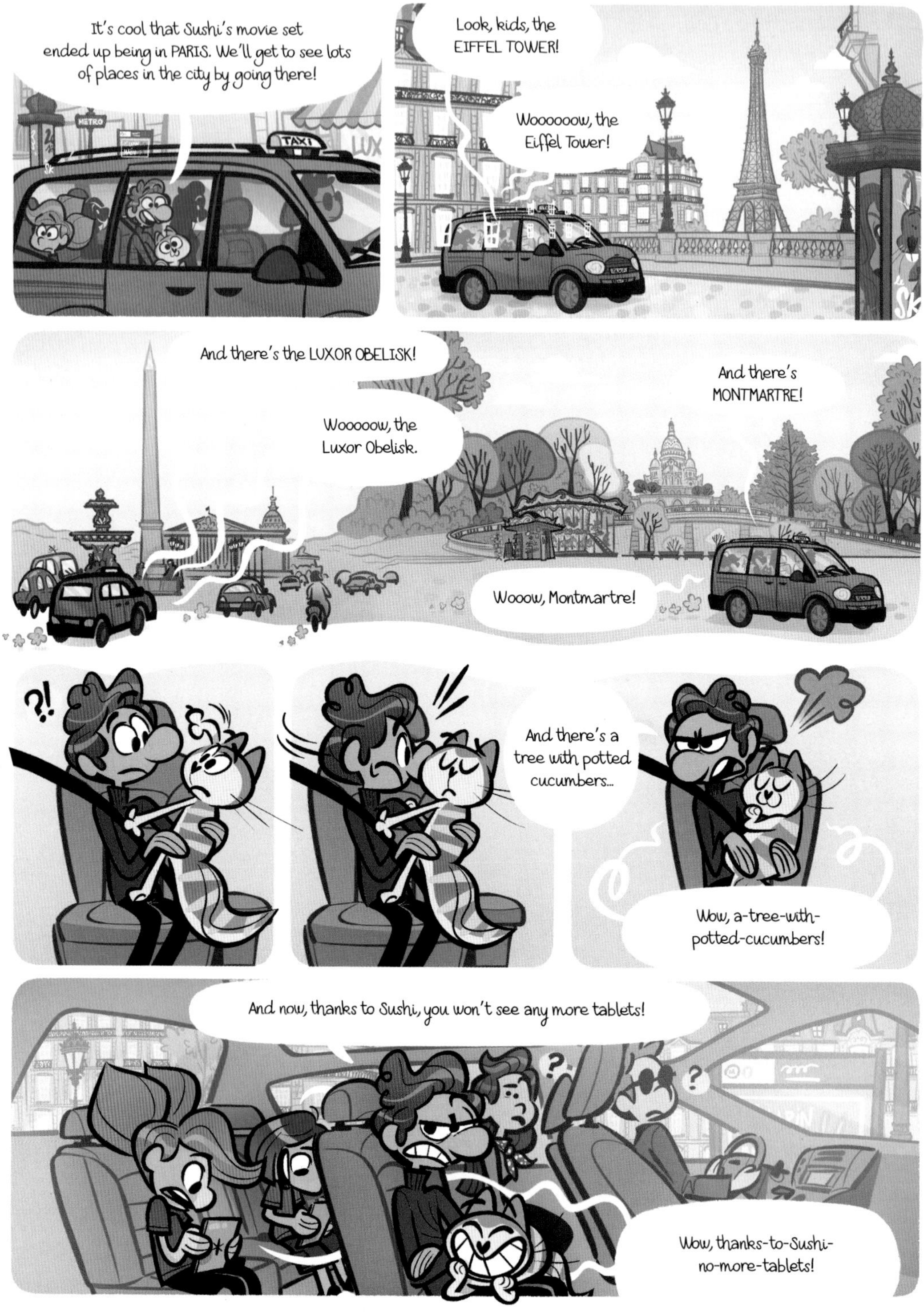
It's cool that Sushi's movie set ended up being in PARIS. We'll get to see lots of places in the city by going there!
TAXI
METRO
Look, kids, the EIFFEL TOWER!
Woooooow, the Eiffel Tower!
And there's the LUXOR OBELISK!
Wooooow, the Luxor Obelisk.
And there's MONTMARTRE!
Wooow, Montmartre!
?!
And there's a tree with potted cucumbers...
Wow, a-tree-with-potted-cucumbers!
And now, thanks to Sushi, you won't see any more tablets!
?
?
Wow, thanks-to-Sushi-no-more-tablets!

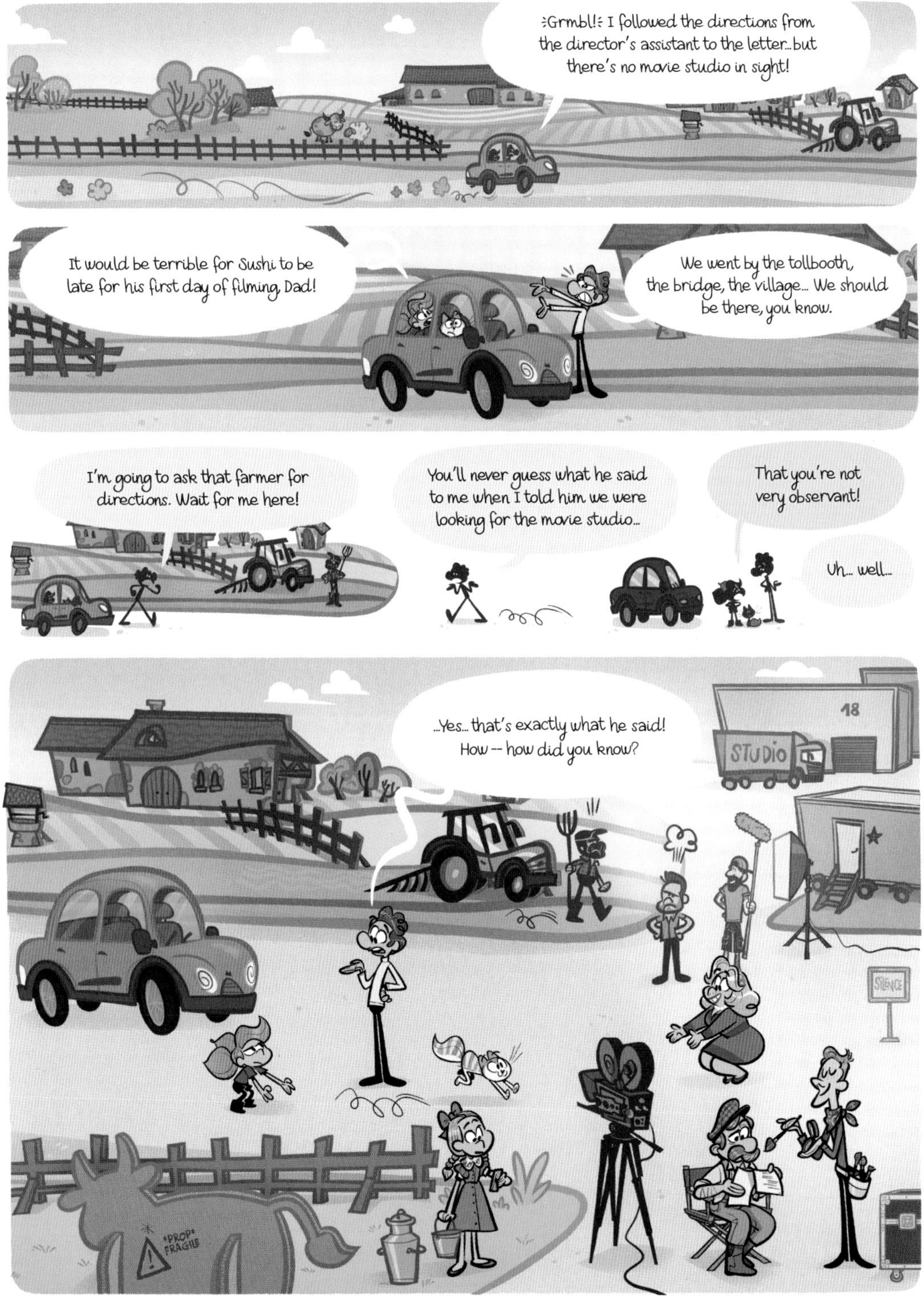

⁝Grmbl!⁝ I followed the directions from the director's assistant to the letter... but there's no movie studio in sight!
It would be terrible for Sushi to be late for his first day of filming, Dad!
We went by the tollbooth, the bridge, the village... We should be there, you know.
I'm going to ask that farmer for directions. Wait for me here!
You'll never guess what he said to me when I told him we were looking for the movie studio...
That you're not very observant!
Uh... well...
...Yes... that's exactly what he said! How -- how did you know?
18
STUDIO
SILENCE
PROP
FRAGILE

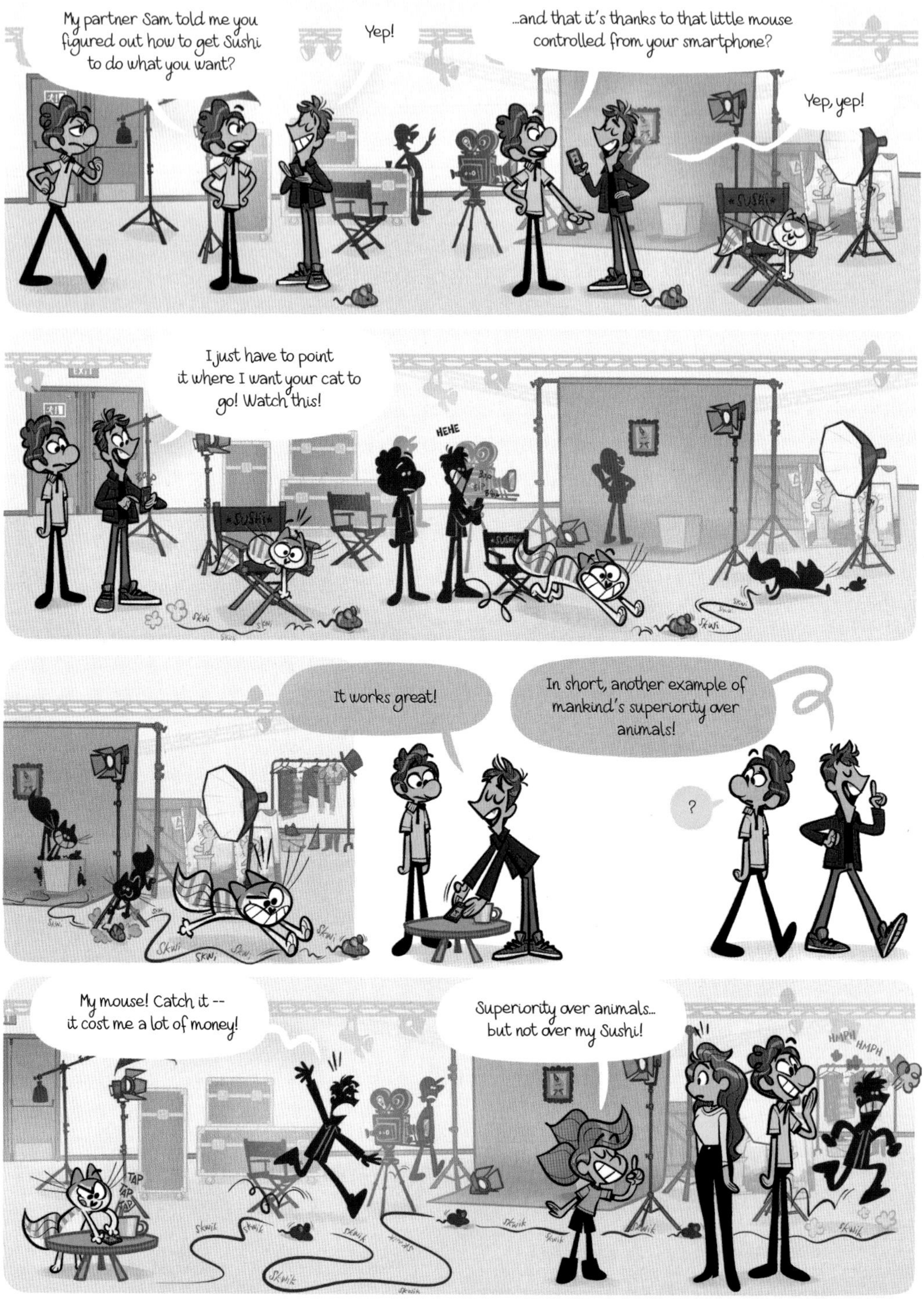
My partner Sam told me you figured out how to get Sushi to do what you want?
Yep!
...and that it's thanks to that little mouse controlled from your smartphone?
Yep, yep!
I just have to point it where I want your cat to go! Watch this!
HEHE
It works great!
In short, another example of mankind's superiority over animals!
?
My mouse! Catch it -- it cost me a lot of money!
Superiority over animals... but not over my Sushi!
TAP
HMPH
HMPH

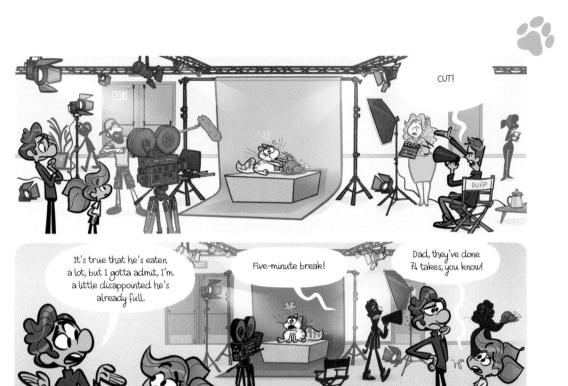

CUT!

It's true that he's eaten a lot, but I gotta admit, I'm a little disappointed he's already full.

Five-minute break!

Dad, they've done 74 takes, you know!

Since when has that stopped our Sushi? Normally, he's a stomach on paws!

But okay, something must be done or else they'll never manage to film this scene.

Seeing that he's stuffed, I'd advise you to use fake plastic food from here on. Otherwise, my cat will explode, and you'll end up never finishing this scene!

POOOweeDITTT

It was plastic right from the start...*

Your Sushi isn't a cat, he's an ogre.

*NEVER FEED YOUR CAT PLASTIC!

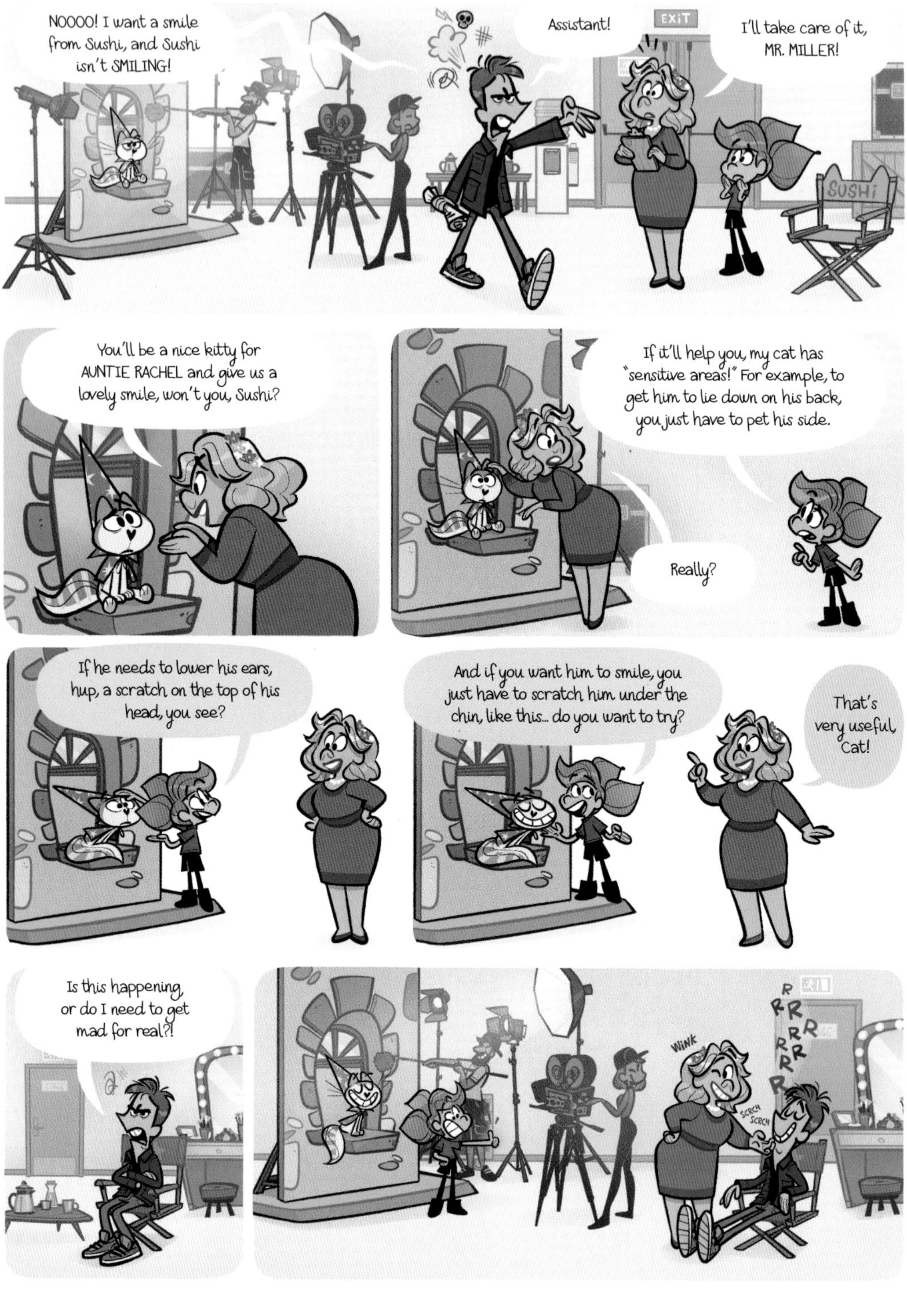
NOOOO! I want a smile from Sushi, and Sushi isn't SMILING!
EXIT
Assistant!
I'll take care of it, MR. MILLER!
SUSHi
You'll be a nice kitty for AUNTIE RACHEL and give us a lovely smile, won't you, Sushi?
If it'll help you, my cat has "sensitive areas!" For example, to get him to lie down on his back, you just have to pet his side.
Really?
If he needs to lower his ears, hup, a scratch on the top of his head, you see?
And if you want him to smile, you just have to scratch him under the chin, like this... do you want to try?
That's very useful, Cat!
Is this happening, or do I need to get mad for real?!
WiNK
RRRRRRRR
SCRCH SCRCH

Your attention, please! Before filming, I'll read you the script for this scene.

It's the love-at-first-sight scene of SUSHILORD DOUBLECAT and PRINCESS CATBADDA of PERSIA.

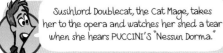

We're in the Victorian era. Sushilord Doublecat, the CAT MAGE, at the foot of BIG BEN, falls in love at first sight with the Persian princess who's descending from her richly adorned carriage.

The princess notices him, and our cat magician causes a bunny rabbit to appear to charm her.

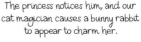

Susihlord Doublecat, the Cat Mage, takes her to the opera and watches her shed a tear when she hears PUCCINI'S "Nessun Dorma."

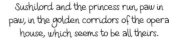

Sushilord and the princess run, paw in paw, in the golden corridors of the opera house, which seems to be all theirs.

And love works its magic...

And when will you film that scene?

‡Pfff‡ once they've healed.

GRUMPH

65

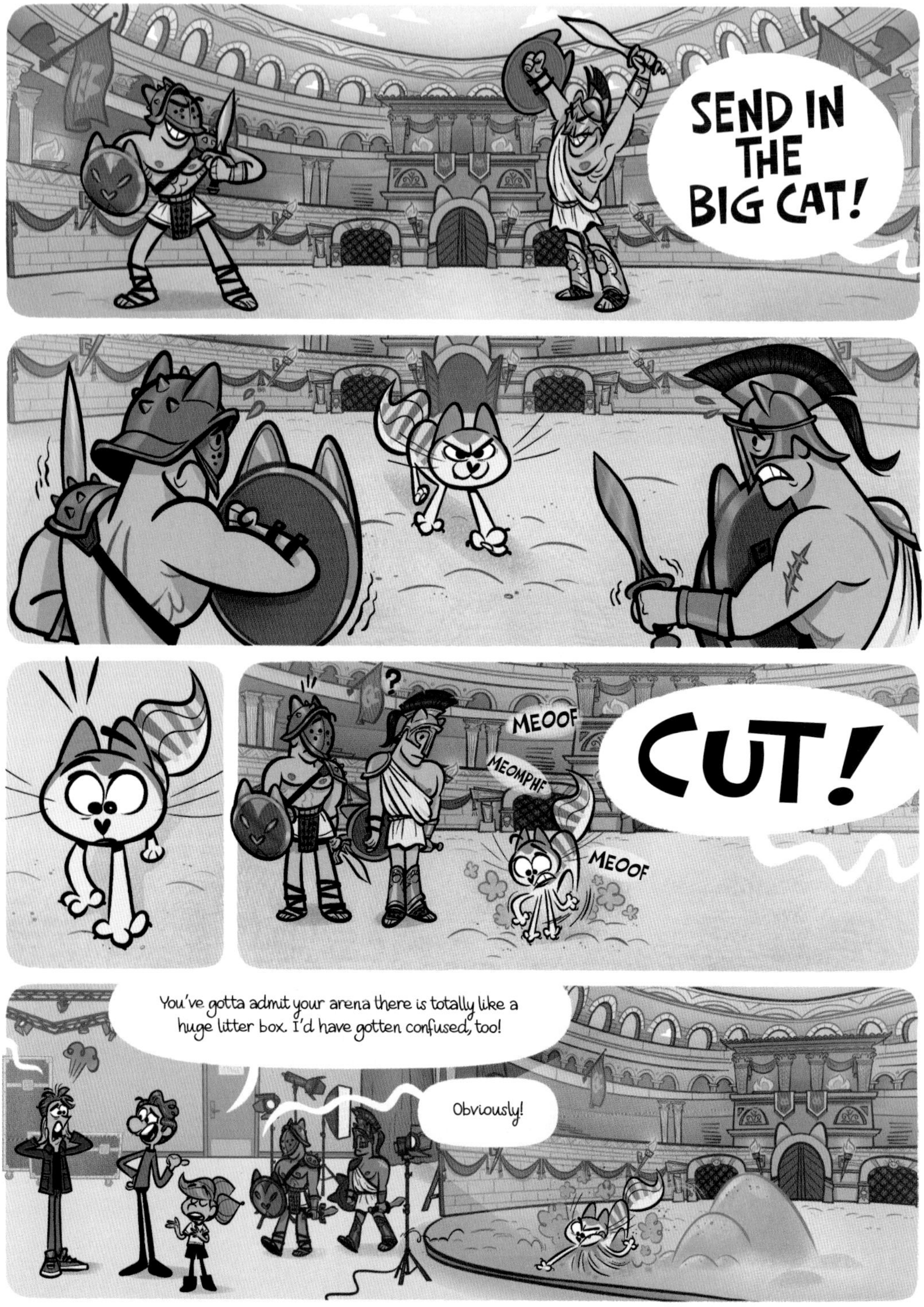
SEND IN THE BIG CAT!
MEOOF
MEOMPHF
MEOOF
CUT!
You've gotta admit your arena there is totally like a huge litter box. I'd have gotten confused, too!
Obviously!

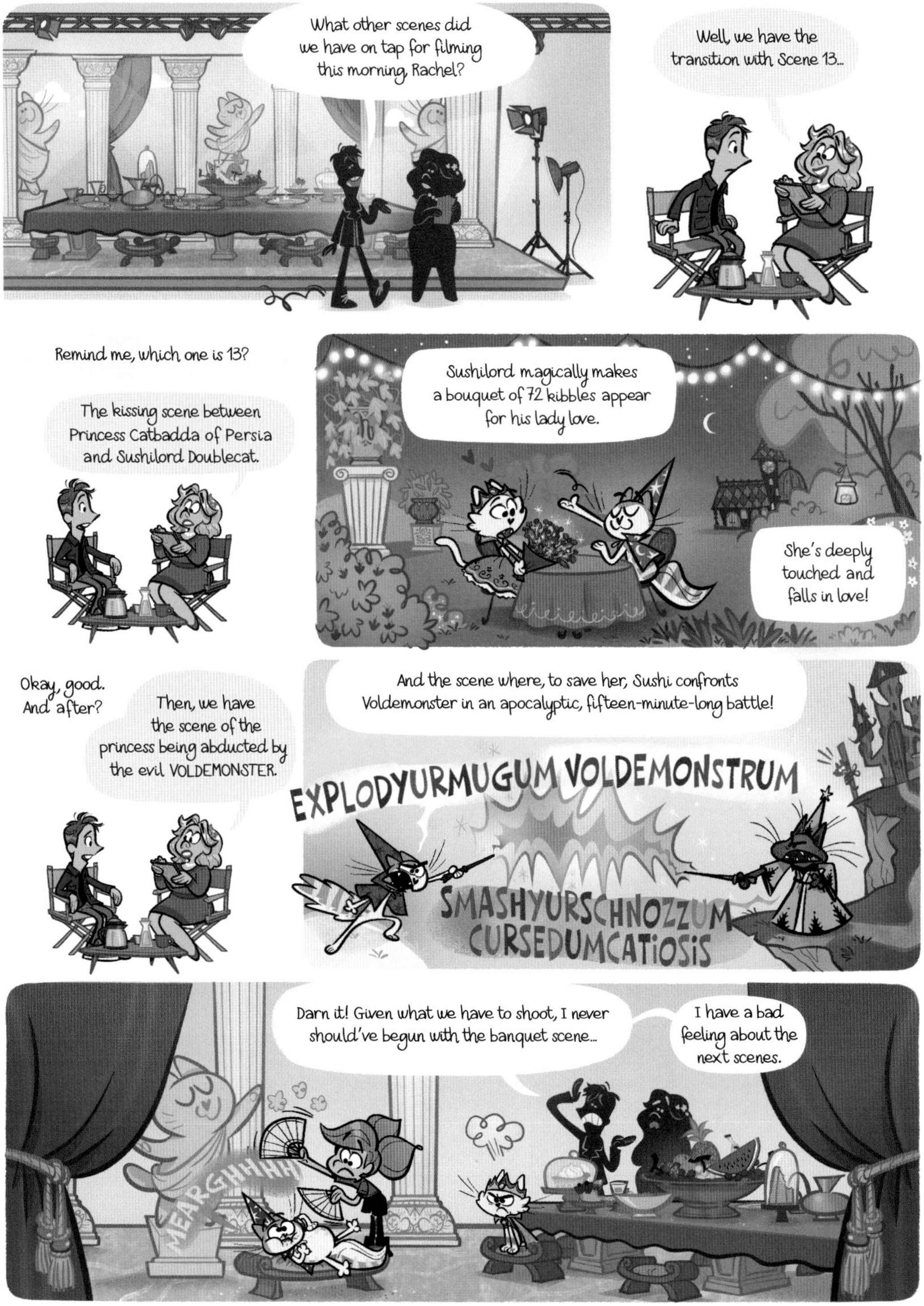
What other scenes did we have on tap for filming this morning, Rachel?
Well, we have the transition with Scene 13...
Remind me, which one is 13?
The kissing scene between Princess Catbadda of Persia and Sushilord Doublecat.
Sushilord magically makes a bouquet of 72 kibbles appear for his lady love.
She's deeply touched and falls in love!
Okay, good. And after?
Then, we have the scene of the princess being abducted by the evil VOLDEMONSTER.
And the scene where, to save her, Sushi confronts Voldemonster in an apocalyptic, fifteen-minute-long battle!
EXPLODYURMUGUM VOLDEMONSTRUM
SMASHYURSCHNOZZUM CURSEDUMCATIOSIS
Darn it! Given what we have to shoot, I never should've begun with the banquet scene...
I have a bad feeling about the next scenes.
MEARGHHHH

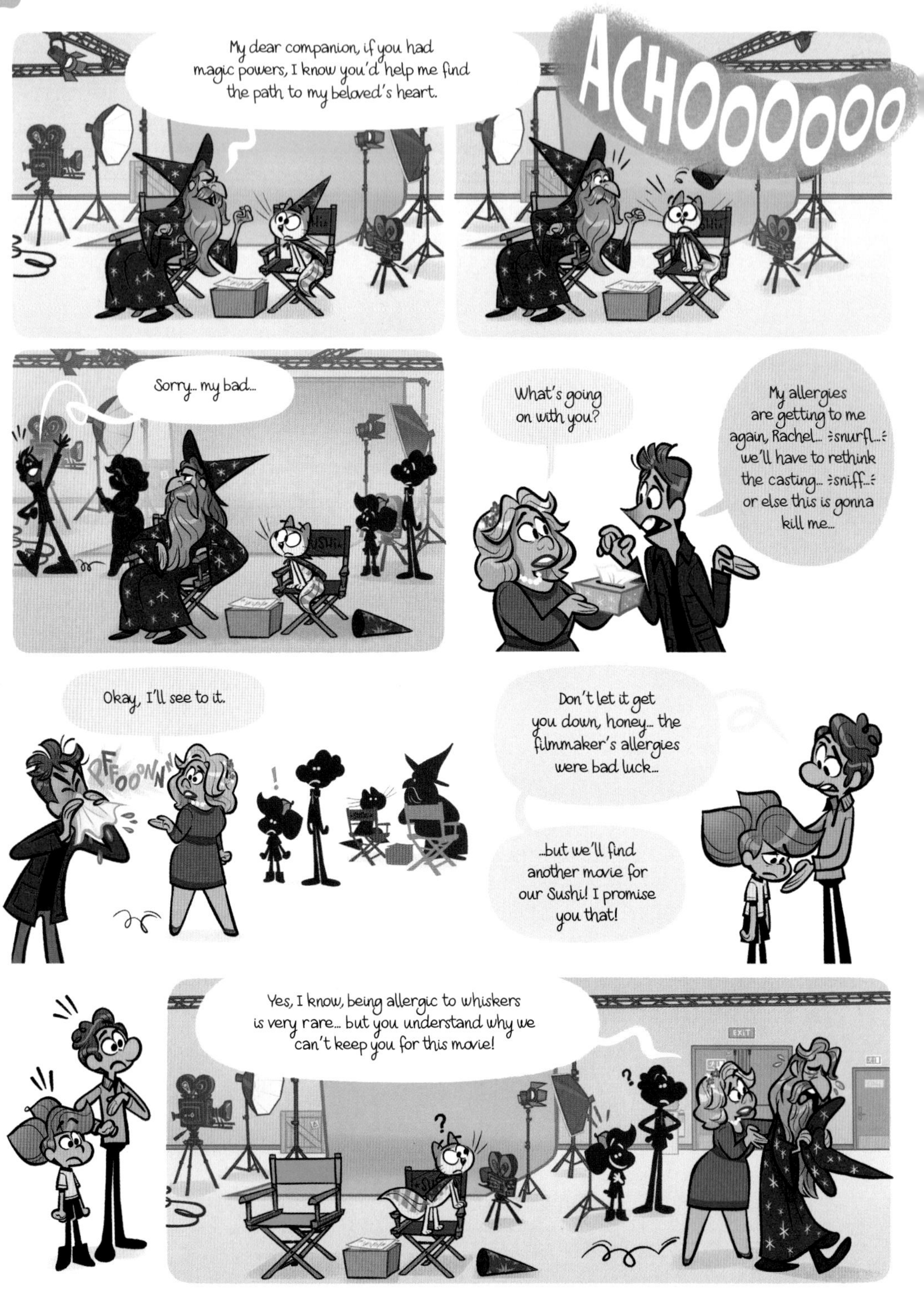
My dear companion, if you had magic powers, I know you'd help me find the path to my beloved's heart.
ACHOOOOOOO
Sorry... my bad...
What's going on with you?
My allergies are getting to me again, Rachel... ⁝snurfl...⁝ we'll have to rethink the casting... ⁝sniff...⁝ or else this is gonna kill me...
Okay, I'll see to it.
PFFOONN
Don't let it get you down, honey... the filmmaker's allergies were bad luck...
...but we'll find another movie for our Sushi! I promise you that!
Yes, I know, being allergic to whiskers is very rare... but you understand why we can't keep you for this movie!
EXIT

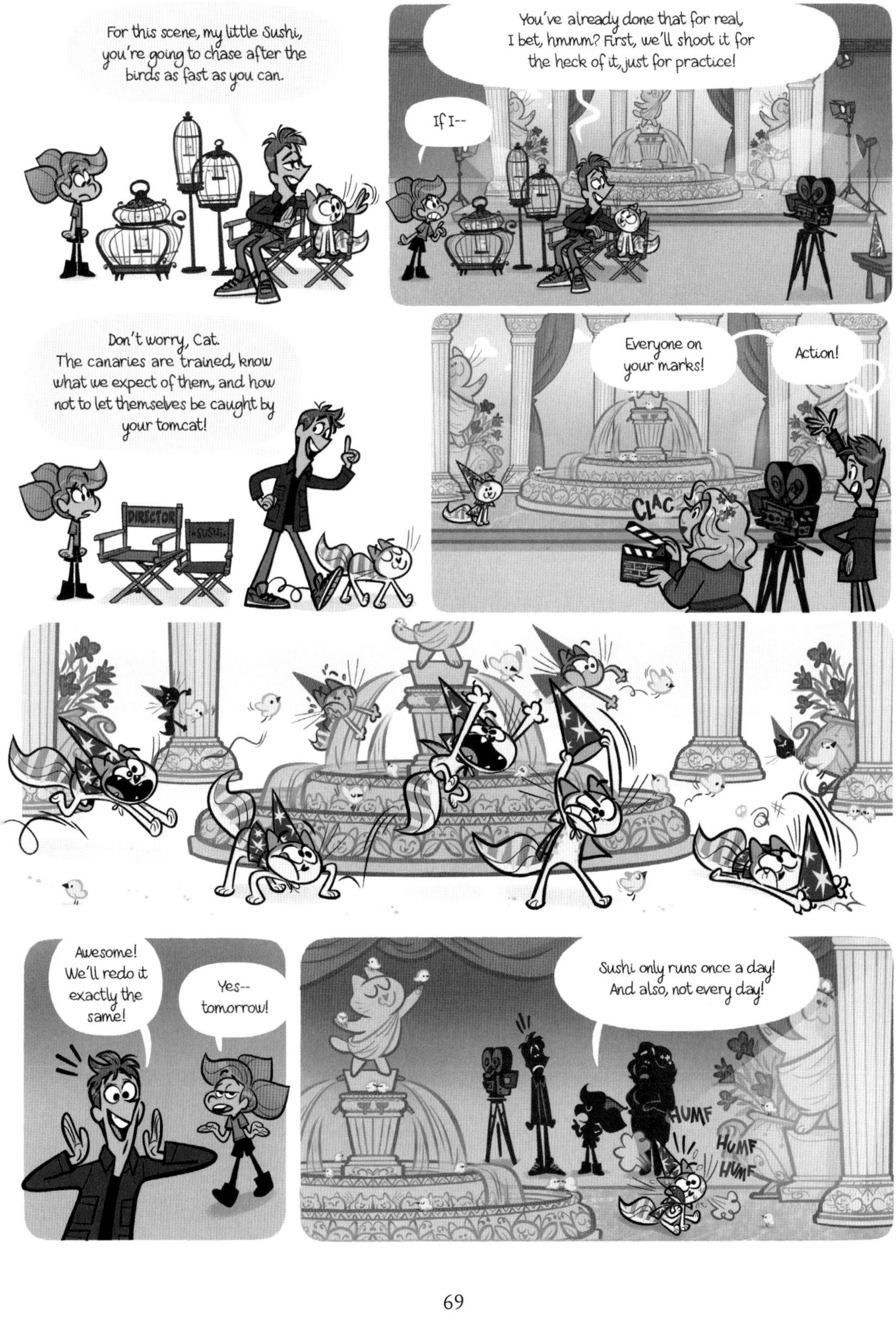
For this scene, my little Sushi, you're going to chase after the birds as fast as you can.
You've already done that for real, I bet, hmmm? First, we'll shoot it for the heck of it, just for practice!
If I--
Don't worry, Cat. The canaries are trained, know what we expect of them, and how not to let themselves be caught by your tomcat!
DIRECTOR
SUSHI
Everyone on your marks!
Action!
CLAC
Awesome! We'll redo it exactly the same!
Yes-- tomorrow!
Sushi only runs once a day! And also, not every day!
HUMF
HUMF
HUMF

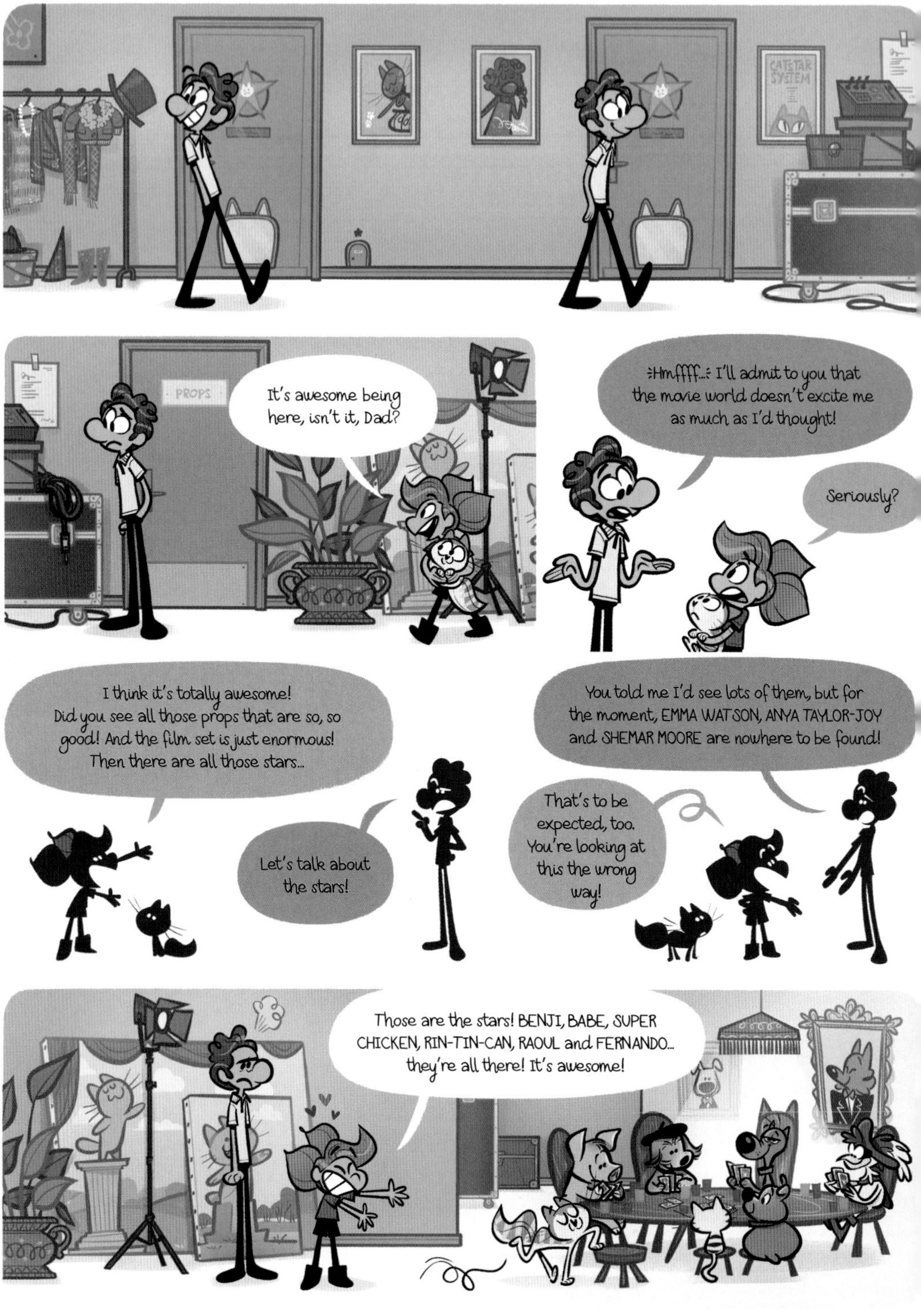
It's awesome being here, isn't it, Dad?
Hmffff... I'll admit to you that the movie world doesn't excite me as much as I'd thought!
Seriously?
I think it's totally awesome! Did you see all those props that are so, so good! And the film set is just enormous! Then there are all those stars...
Let's talk about the stars!
You told me I'd see lots of them, but for the moment, EMMA WATSON, ANYA TAYLOR-JOY and SHEMAR MOORE are nowhere to be found!
That's to be expected, too. You're looking at this the wrong way!
Those are the stars! BENJI, BABE, SUPER CHICKEN, RIN-TIN-CAN, RAOUL and FERNANDO... they're all there! It's awesome!

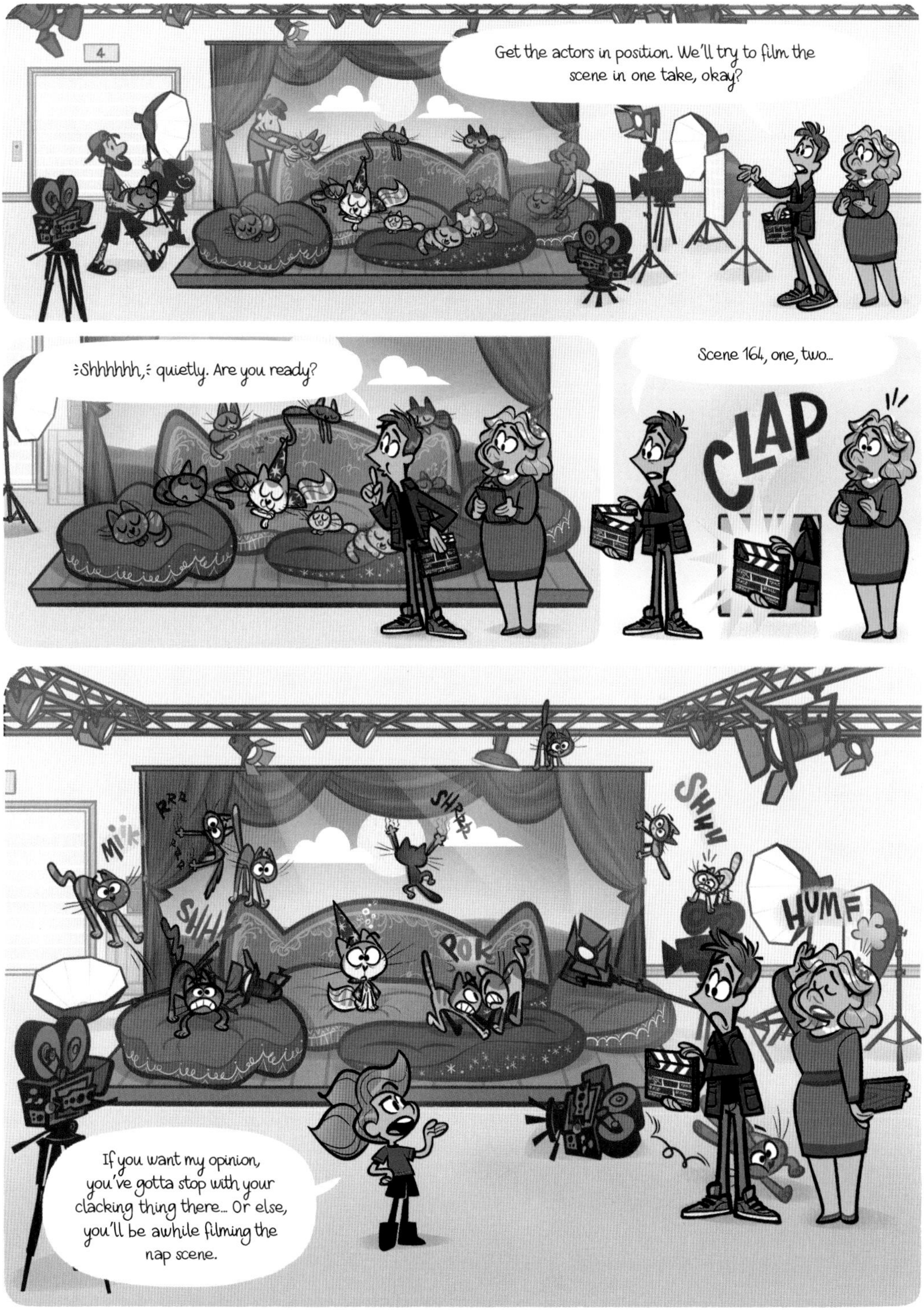
Get the actors in position. We'll try to film the scene in one take, okay?
Shhhhhh, quietly. Are you ready?
Scene 164, one, two...
CLAP
HUMF
If you want my opinion, you've gotta stop with your clacking thing there... Or else, you'll be awhile filming the nap scene.

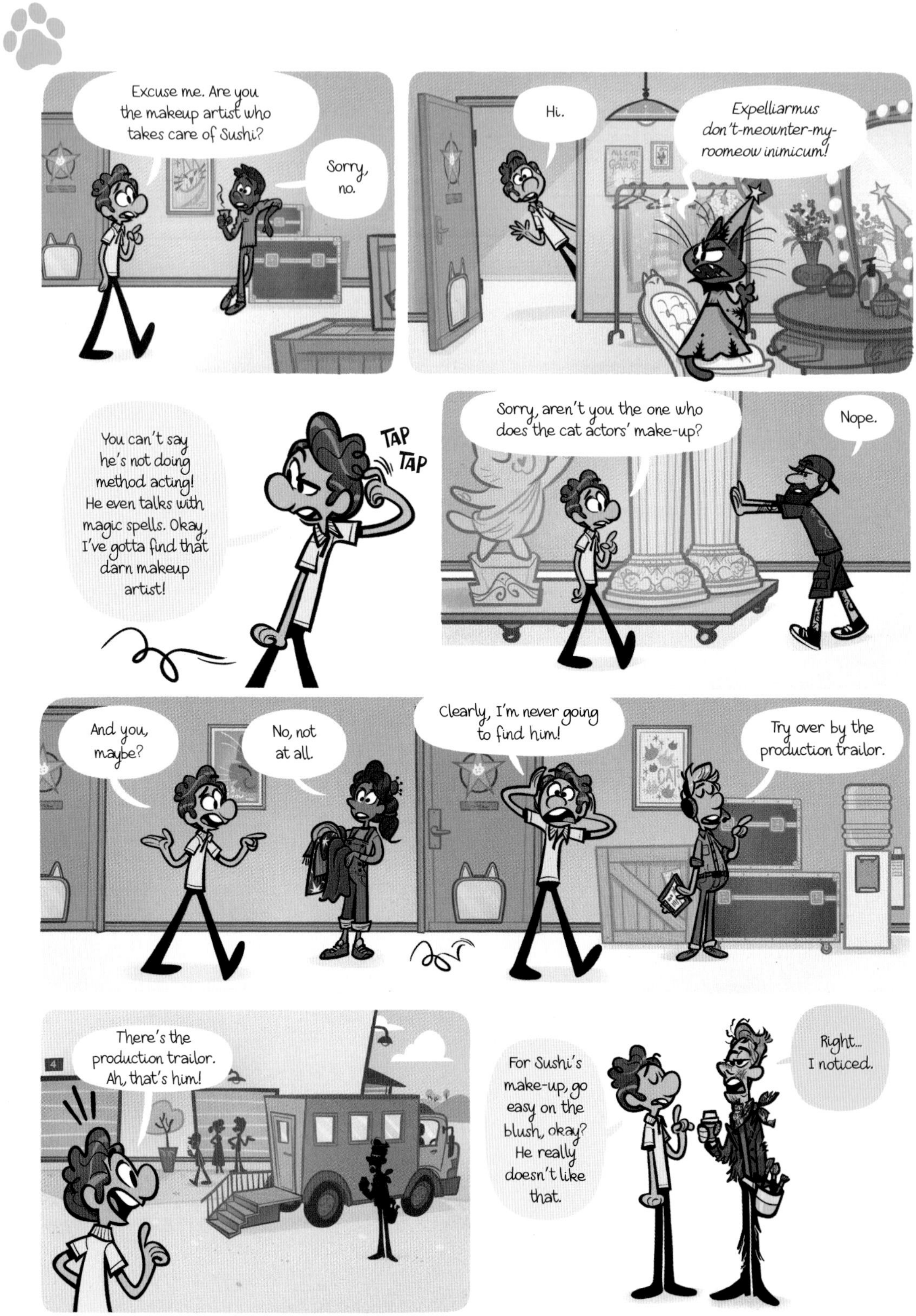
Excuse me. Are you the makeup artist who takes care of Sushi?
Sorry, no.
Hi.
Expelliarmus don't-meownter-my-roomeow inimicum!
You can't say he's not doing method acting! He even talks with magic spells. Okay, I've gotta find that darn makeup artist!
TAP TAP
Sorry, aren't you the one who does the cat actors' make-up?
Nope.
And you, maybe?
No, not at all.
Clearly, I'm never going to find him!
Try over by the production trailor.
There's the production trailor. Ah, that's him!
For Sushi's make-up, go easy on the blush, okay? He really doesn't like that.
Right... I noticed.

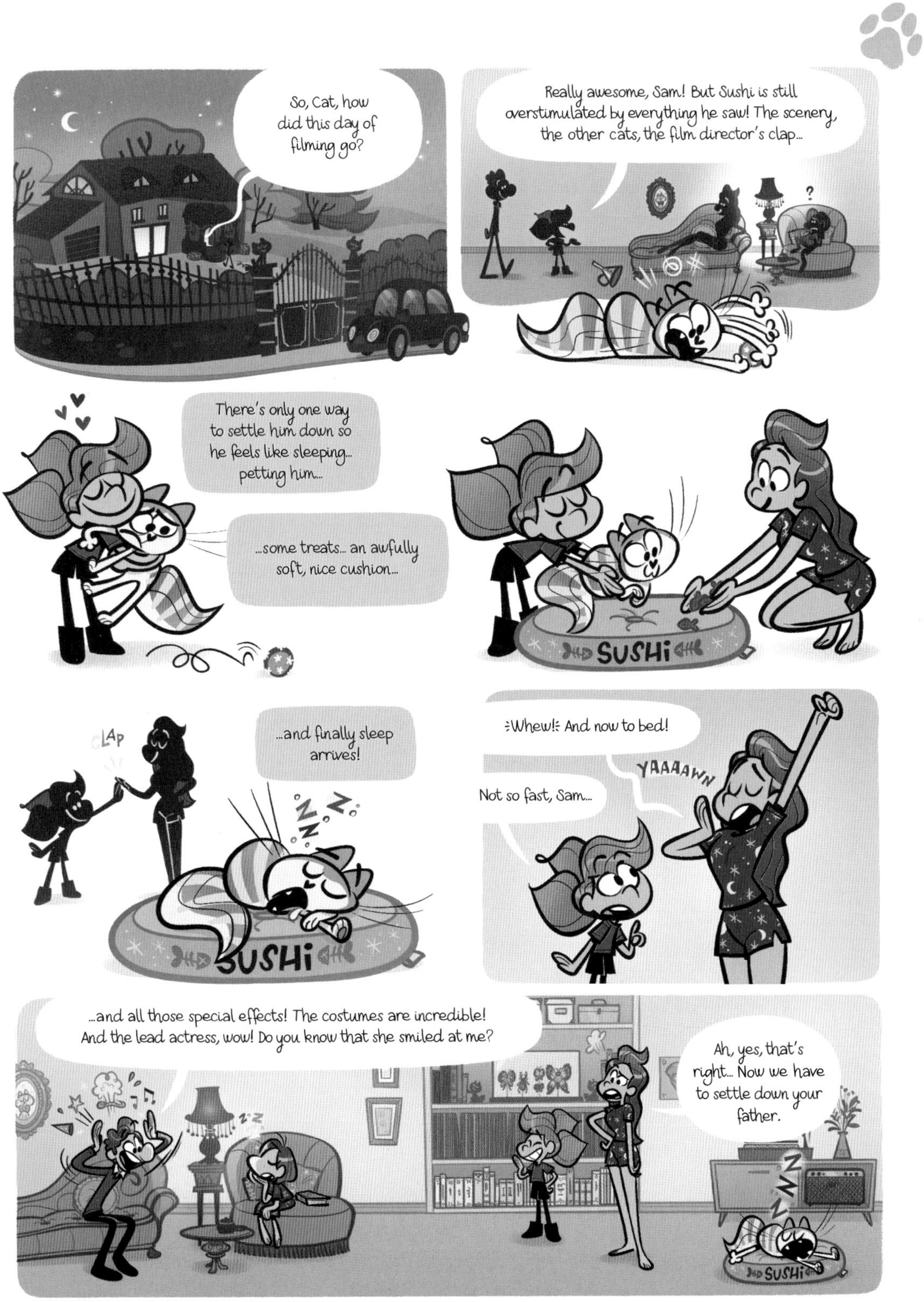
So, Cat, how did this day of filming go?
Really awesome, Sam! But Sushi is still overstimulated by everything he saw! The scenery, the other cats, the film director's clap...
?
There's only one way to settle him down so he feels like sleeping... petting him...
...some treats... an awfully soft, nice cushion...
SUSHI
CLAP
...and finally sleep arrives!
Z Z Z Z
SUSHI
Whew! And now to bed!
YAAAAWN
Not so fast, Sam...
...and all those special effects! The costumes are incredible! And the lead actress, wow! Do you know that she smiled at me?
Ah, yes, that's right... Now we have to settle down your father.
SUSHI

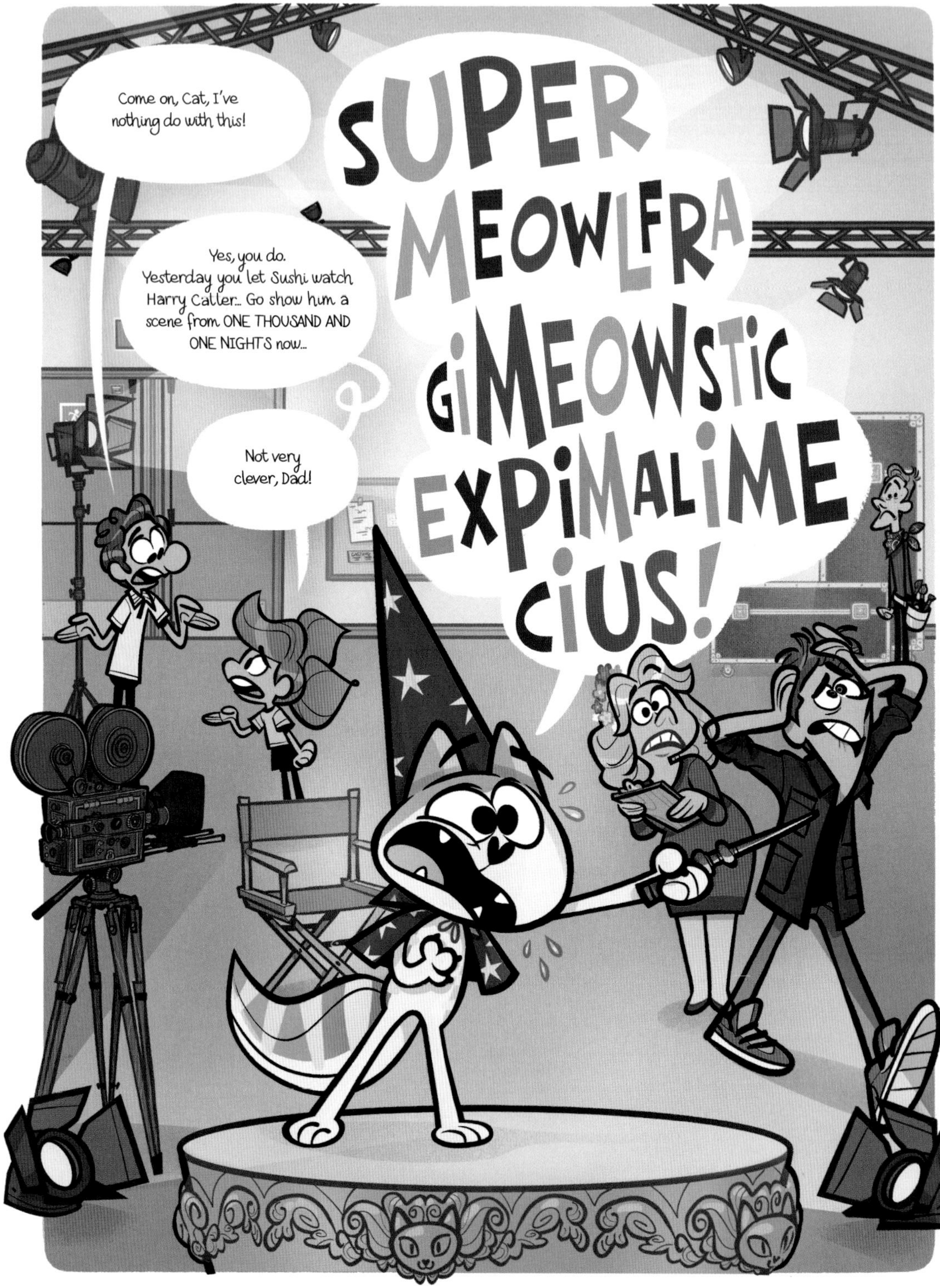
Come on, Cat, I've nothing do with this!
Yes, you do. Yesterday you let Sushi watch Harry Catter... Go show him a scene from ONE THOUSAND AND ONE NIGHTS now...
Not very clever, Dad!
SUPER MEOWLFRA GIMEOWSTIC EXPIMALIME CIUS!

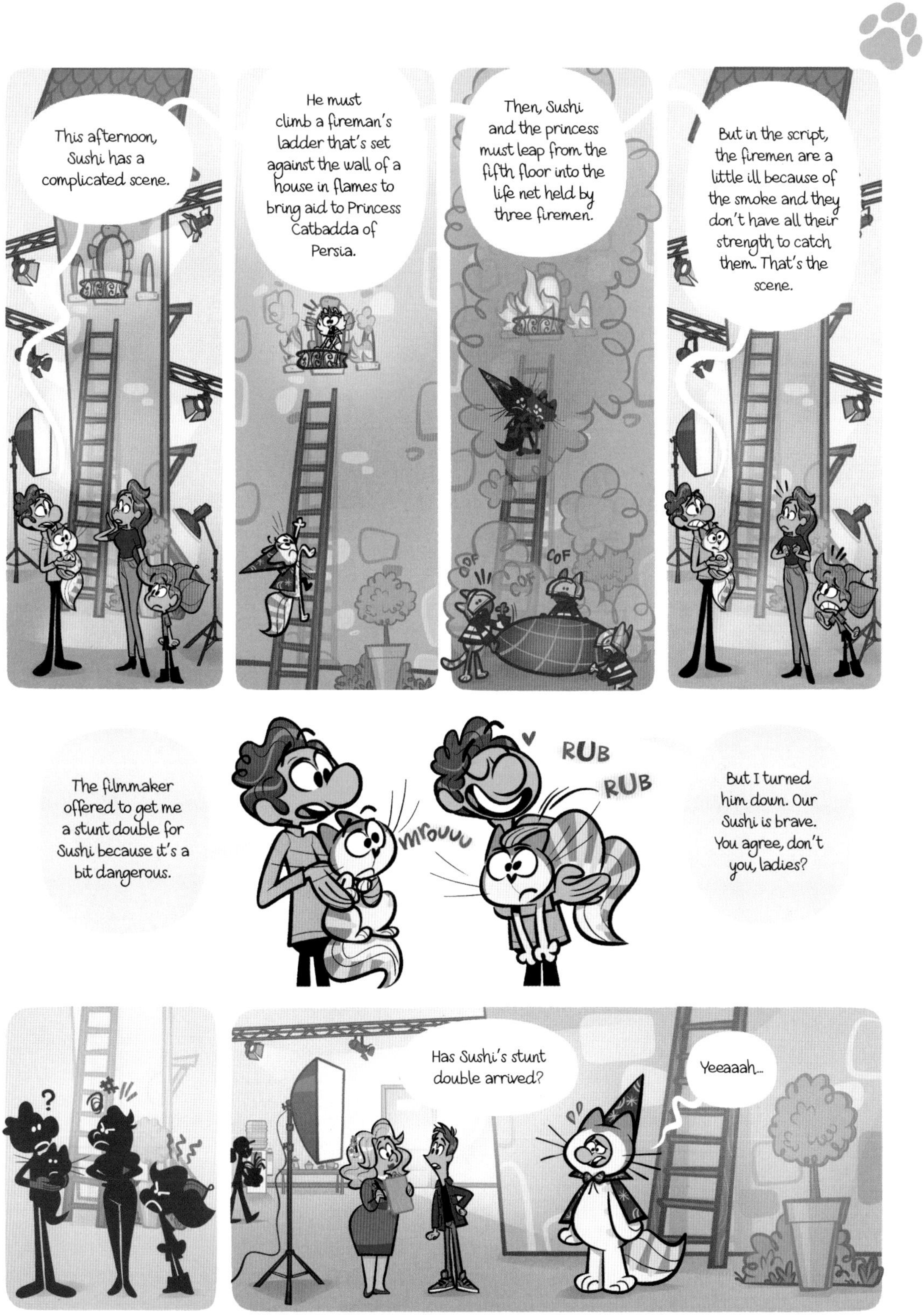
This afternoon, Sushi has a complicated scene.
He must climb a fireman's ladder that's set against the wall of a house in flames to bring aid to Princess Catbadda of Persia.
Then, Sushi and the princess must leap from the fifth floor into the life net held by three firemen.
COF
COF
COF
But in the script, the firemen are a little ill because of the smoke and they don't have all their strength to catch them. That's the scene.
The filmmaker offered to get me a stunt double for Sushi because it's a bit dangerous.
Mrouuu
RUB
RUB
But I turned him down. Our Sushi is brave. You agree, don't you, ladies?
?
Has Sushi's stunt double arrived?
Yeeaaah...

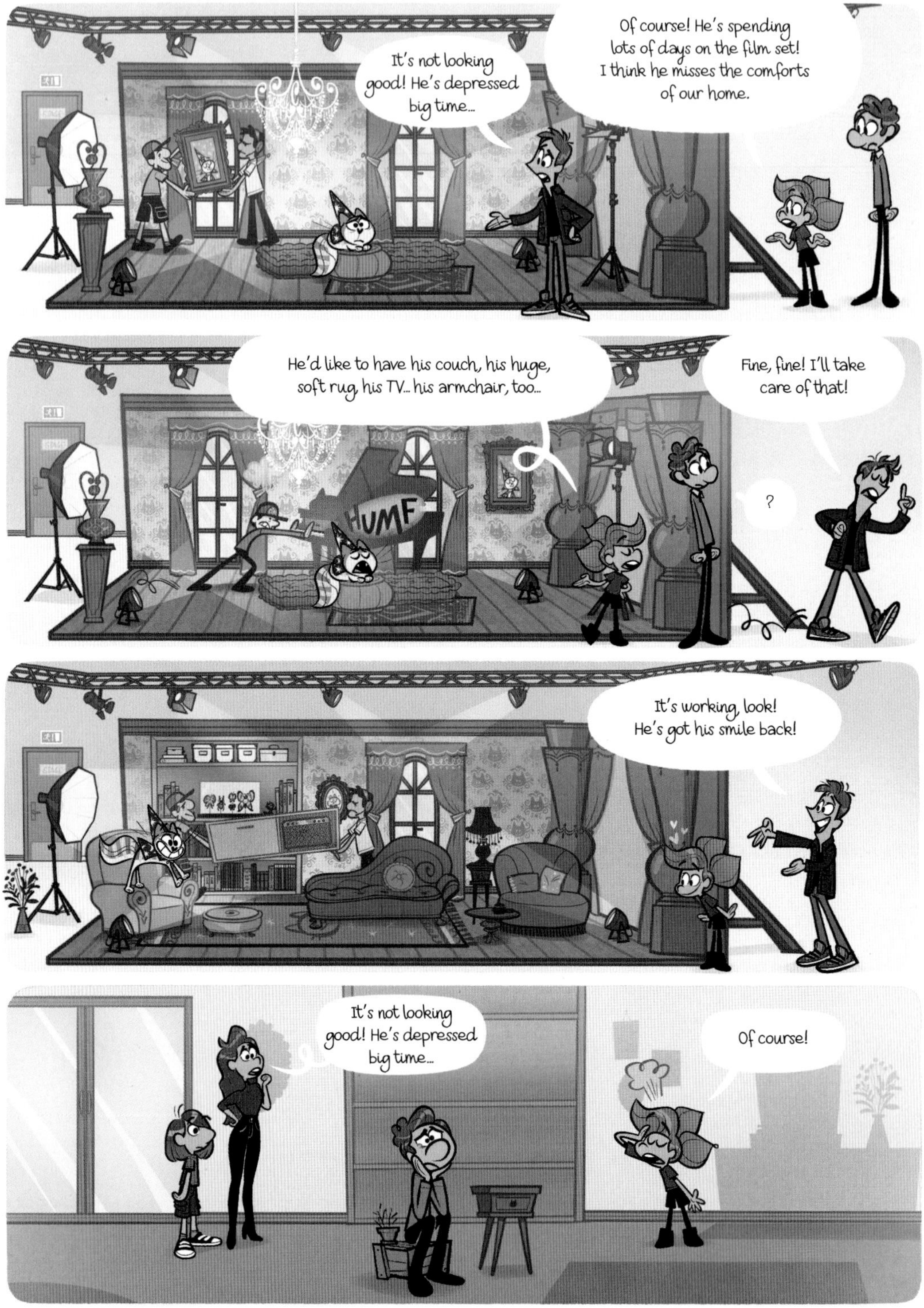
It's not looking good! He's depressed big time...
Of course! He's spending lots of days on the film set! I think he misses the comforts of our home.
He'd like to have his couch, his huge, soft rug, his TV... his armchair, too...
HUMF
Fine, fine! I'll take care of that!
?
It's working, look! He's got his smile back!
It's not looking good! He's depressed big time...
Of course!

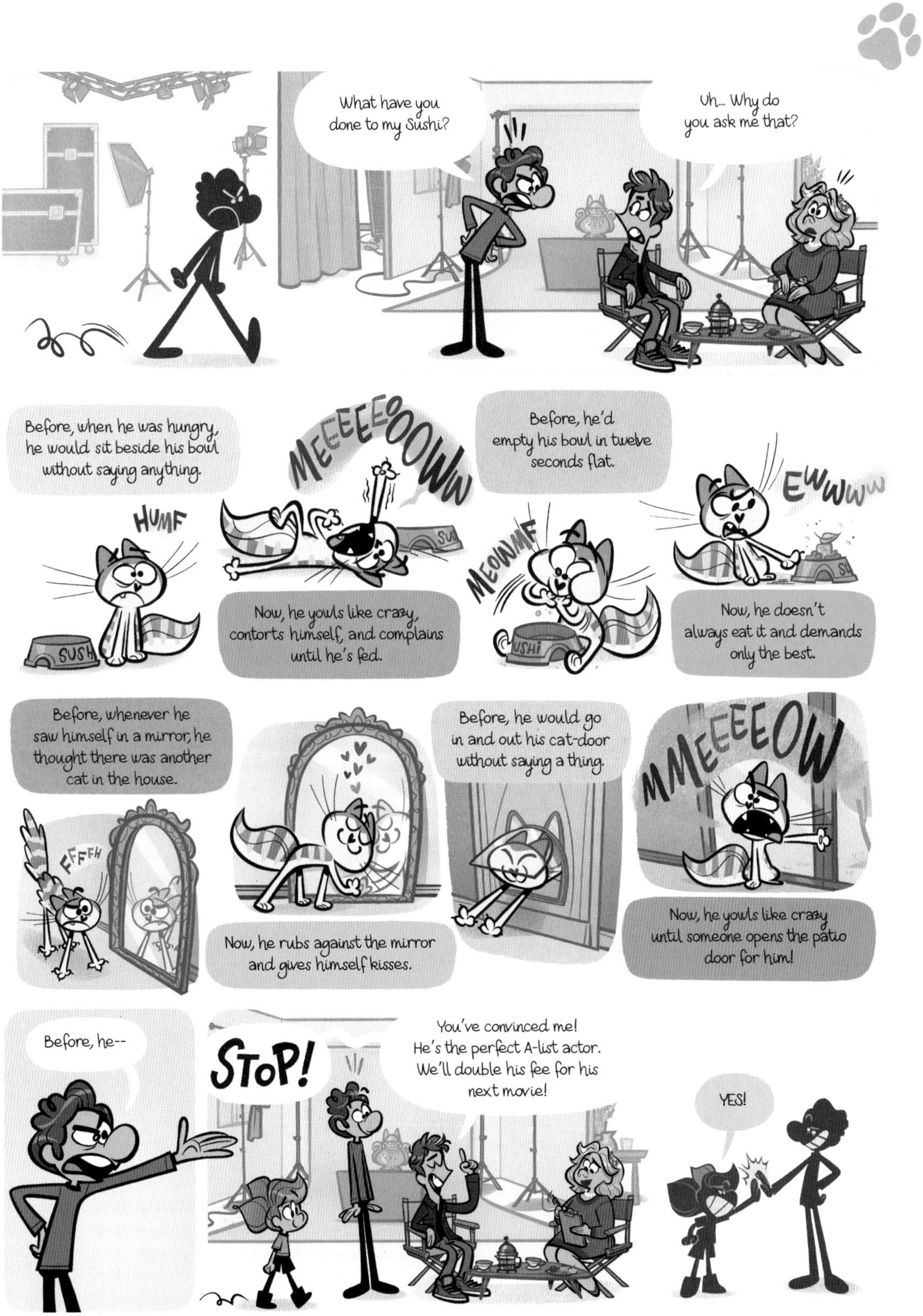
What have you done to my Sushi?
Uh... Why do you ask me that?
Before, when he was hungry, he would sit beside his bowl without saying anything.
HUMF
MEEEEEOOOWW
Now, he yowls like crazy, contorts himself, and complains until he's fed.
Before, he'd empty his bowl in twelve seconds flat.
MEOWMF
EWWWW
Now, he doesn't always eat it and demands only the best.
Before, whenever he saw himself in a mirror, he thought there was another cat in the house.
FFFFH
Now, he rubs against the mirror and gives himself kisses.
Before, he would go in and out his cat-door without saying a thing.
MMEEEEEOW
Now, he yowls like crazy until someone opens the patio door for him!
Before, he--
STOP!
You've convinced me! He's the perfect A-list actor. We'll double his fee for his next movie!
YES!

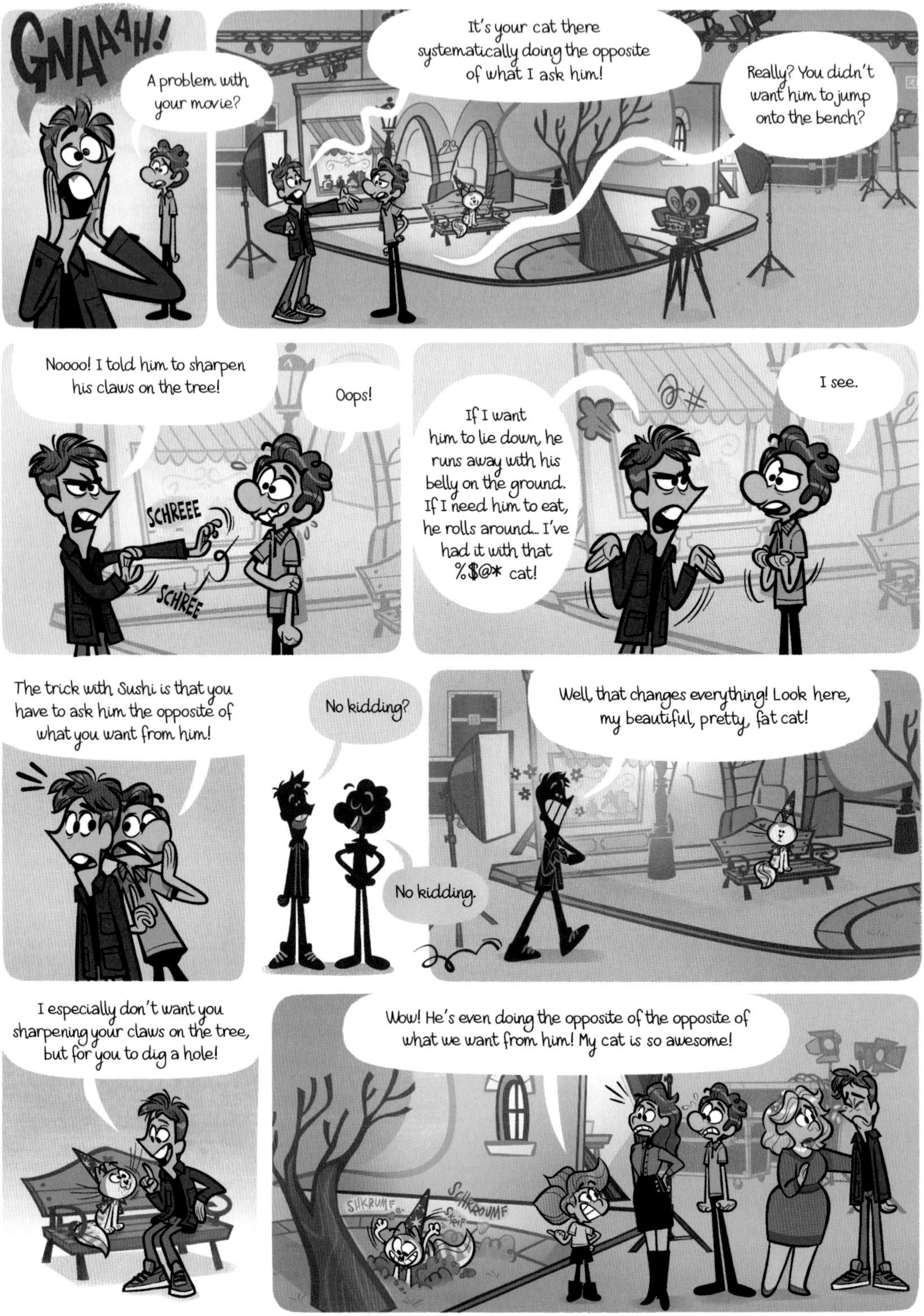
GNAAAH!
A problem with your movie?
It's your cat there systematically doing the opposite of what I ask him!
Really? You didn't want him to jump onto the bench?
Noooo! I told him to sharpen his claws on the tree!
Oops!
SCHREEE
SCHREE
If I want him to lie down, he runs away with his belly on the ground. If I need him to eat, he rolls around... I've had it with that %$@* cat!
I see.
The trick with Sushi is that you have to ask him the opposite of what you want from him!
No kidding?
No kidding.
Well, that changes everything! Look here, my beautiful, pretty, fat cat!
I especially don't want you sharpening your claws on the tree, but for you to dig a hole!
Wow! He's even doing the opposite of the opposite of what we want from him! My cat is so awesome!
SHKRUMF
SCHROUMF

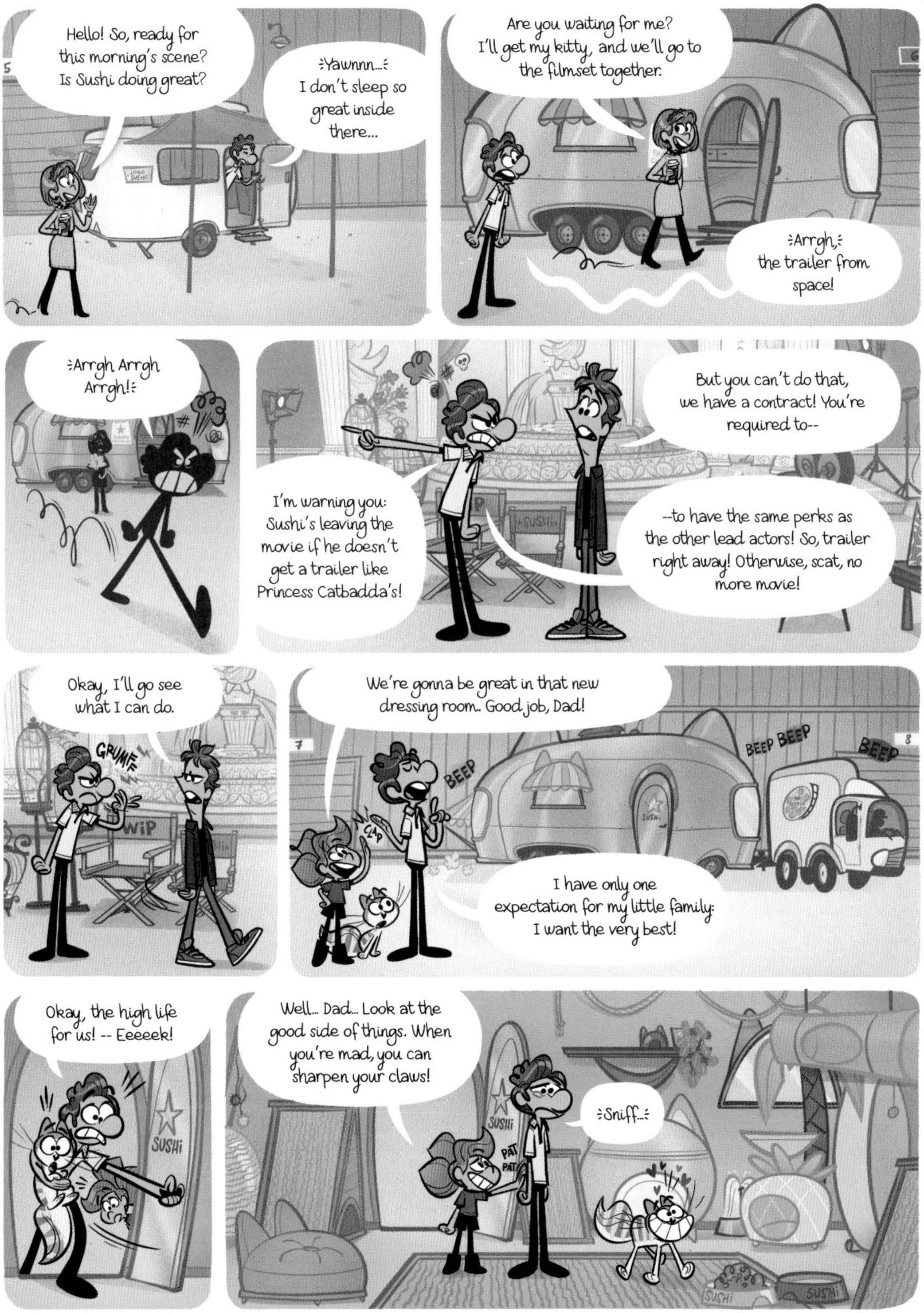
Hello! So, ready for this morning's scene? Is Sushi doing great?
:Yawnnn...: I don't sleep so great inside there...
Are you waiting for me? I'll get my kitty, and we'll go to the filmset together.
:Arrgh,: the trailer from space!
:Arrgh Arrgh Arrgh!:
But you can't do that, we have a contract! You're required to--
I'm warning you: Sushi's leaving the movie if he doesn't get a trailer like Princess Catbadda's!
--to have the same perks as the other lead actors! So, trailer right away! Otherwise, scat, no more movie!
Okay, I'll go see what I can do.
GRUMFF
We're gonna be great in that new dressing room. Good job, Dad!
CLAP
BEEP
BEEP BEEP
BEEP
I have only one expectation for my little family: I want the very best!
Okay, the high life for us! -- Eeeeek!
SUSHI
Well... Dad... Look at the good side of things. When you're mad, you can sharpen your claws!
:Sniff...:
PAT PAT

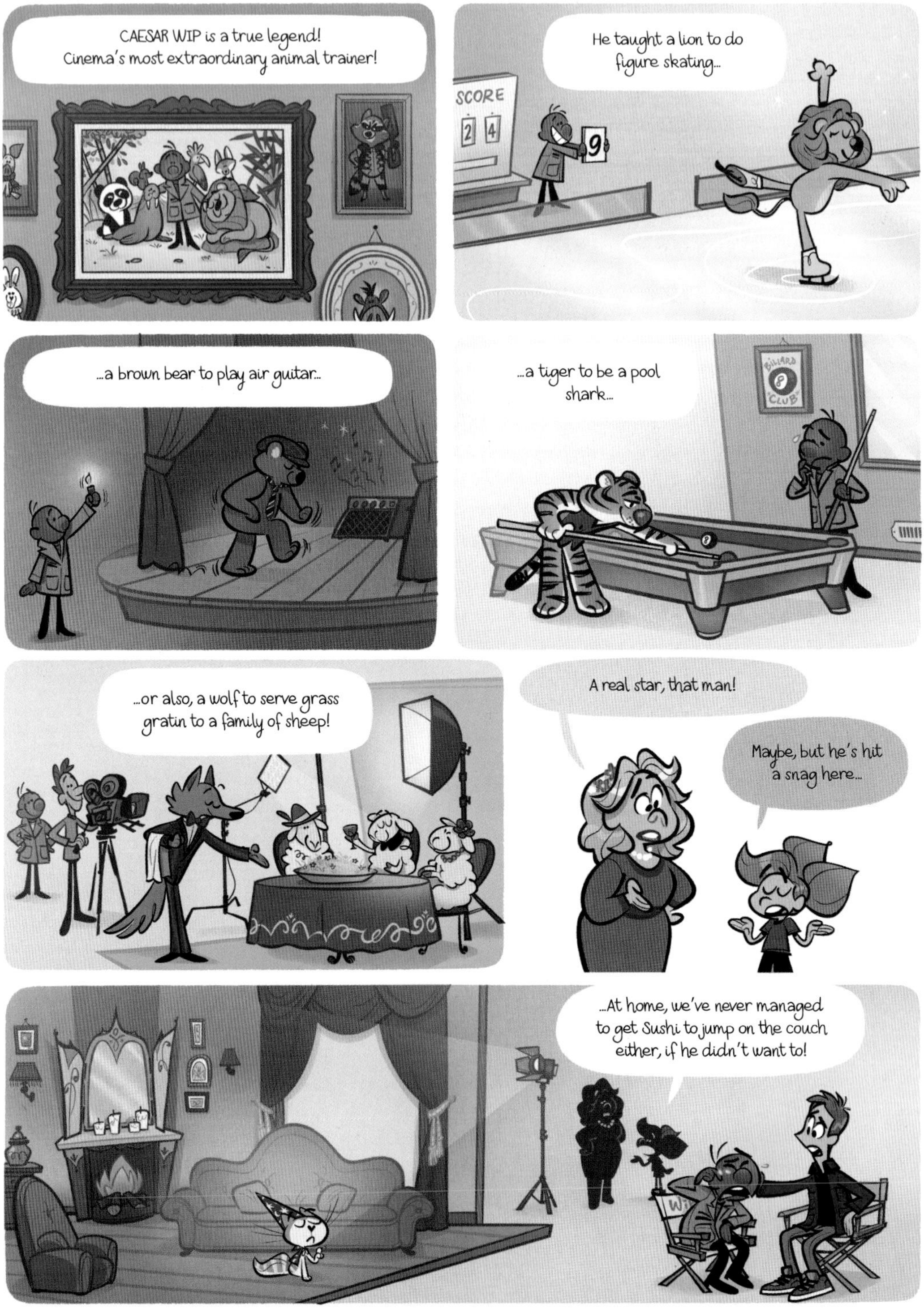
CAESAR WIP is a true legend!
Cinema's most extraordinary animal trainer!
He taught a lion to do figure skating...
SCORE
2 4
9
...a brown bear to play air guitar...
...a tiger to be a pool shark...
BILLARD CLUB
...or also, a wolf to serve grass gratin to a family of sheep!
A real star, that man!
Maybe, but he's hit a snag here...
...At home, we've never managed to get Sushi to jump on the couch either, if he didn't want to!

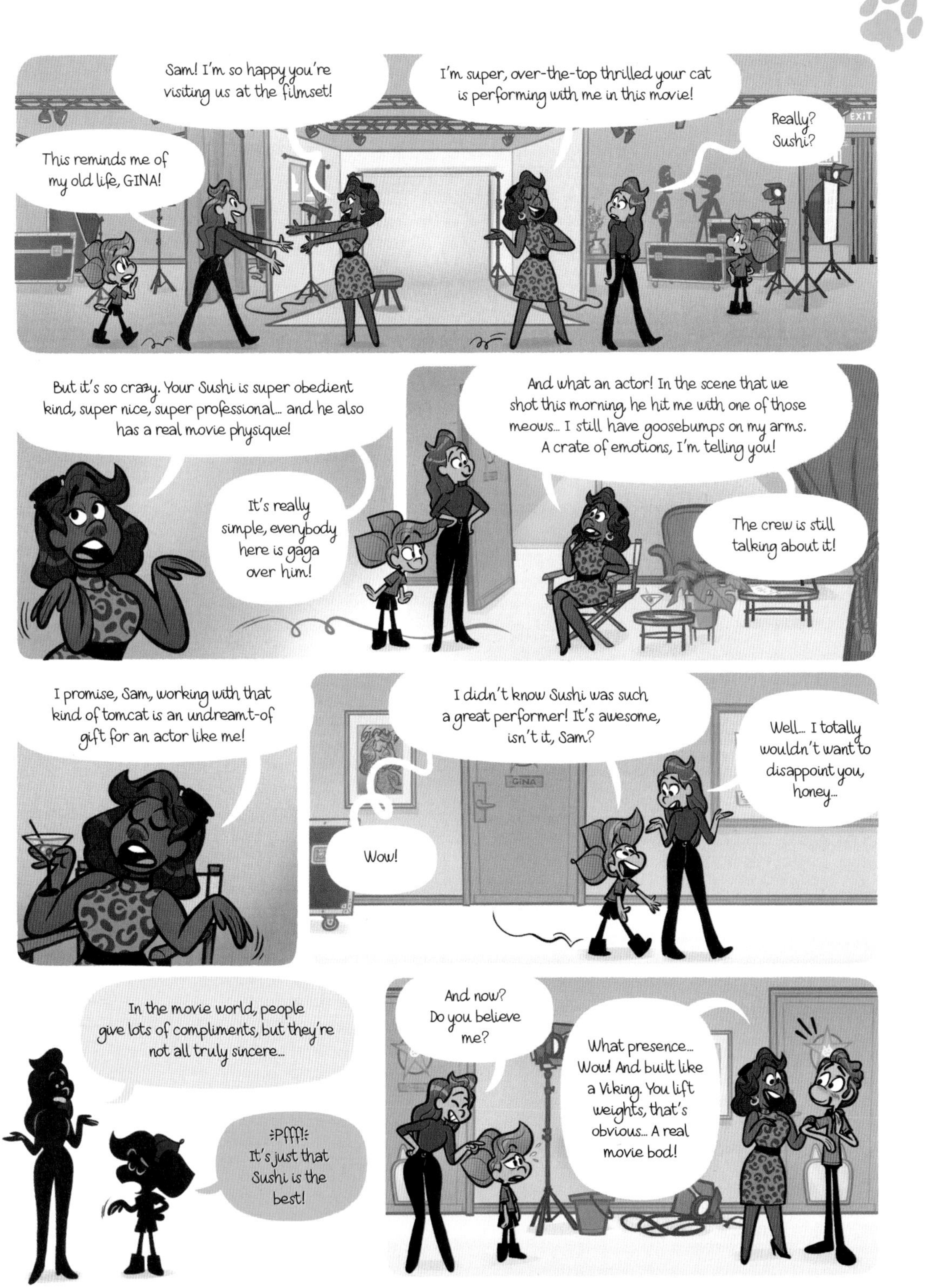
This reminds me of my old life, GINA!
Sam! I'm so happy you're visiting us at the filmset!
I'm super, over-the-top thrilled your cat is performing with me in this movie!
Really? Sushi?
EXIT
But it's so crazy. Your Sushi is super obedient kind, super nice, super professional... and he also has a real movie physique!
It's really simple, everybody here is gaga over him!
And what an actor! In the scene that we shot this morning, he hit me with one of those meows... I still have goosebumps on my arms. A crate of emotions, I'm telling you!
The crew is still talking about it!
I promise, Sam, working with that kind of tomcat is an undreamt-of gift for an actor like me!
I didn't know Sushi was such a great performer! It's awesome, isn't it, Sam?
Wow!
Well... I totally wouldn't want to disappoint you, honey...
GINA
In the movie world, people give lots of compliments, but they're not all truly sincere...
Pfff! It's just that Sushi is the best!
And now? Do you believe me?
What presence... Wow! And built like a Viking. You lift weights, that's obvious... A real movie bod!

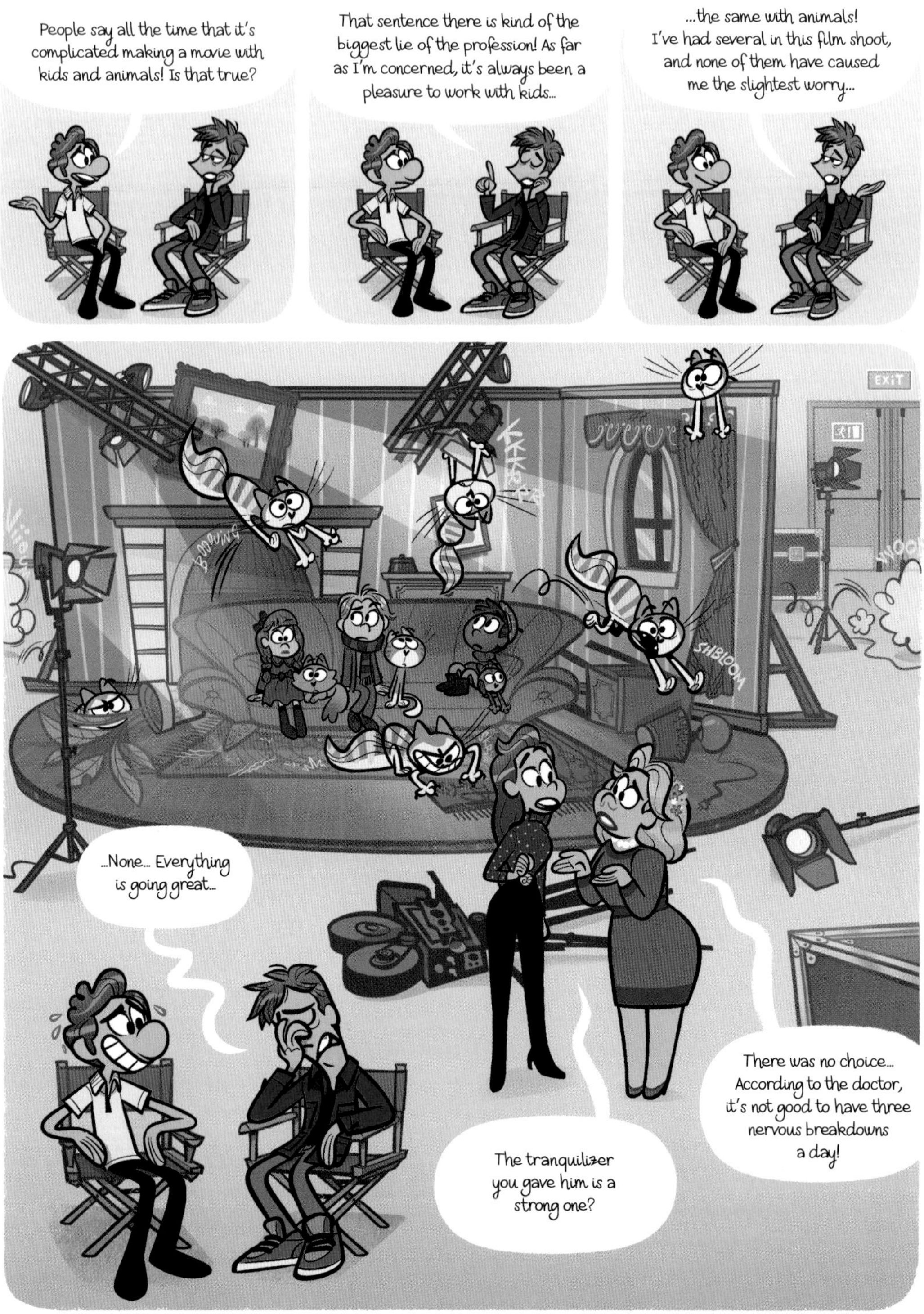
People say all the time that it's complicated making a movie with kids and animals! Is that true?
That sentence there is kind of the biggest lie of the profession! As far as I'm concerned, it's always been a pleasure to work with kids...
...the same with animals! I've had several in this film shoot, and none of them have caused me the slightest worry...
EXIT
BOOOING
SHBLOOM
...None... Everything is going great...
The tranquilizer you gave him is a strong one?
There was no choice... According to the doctor, it's not good to have three nervous breakdowns a day!

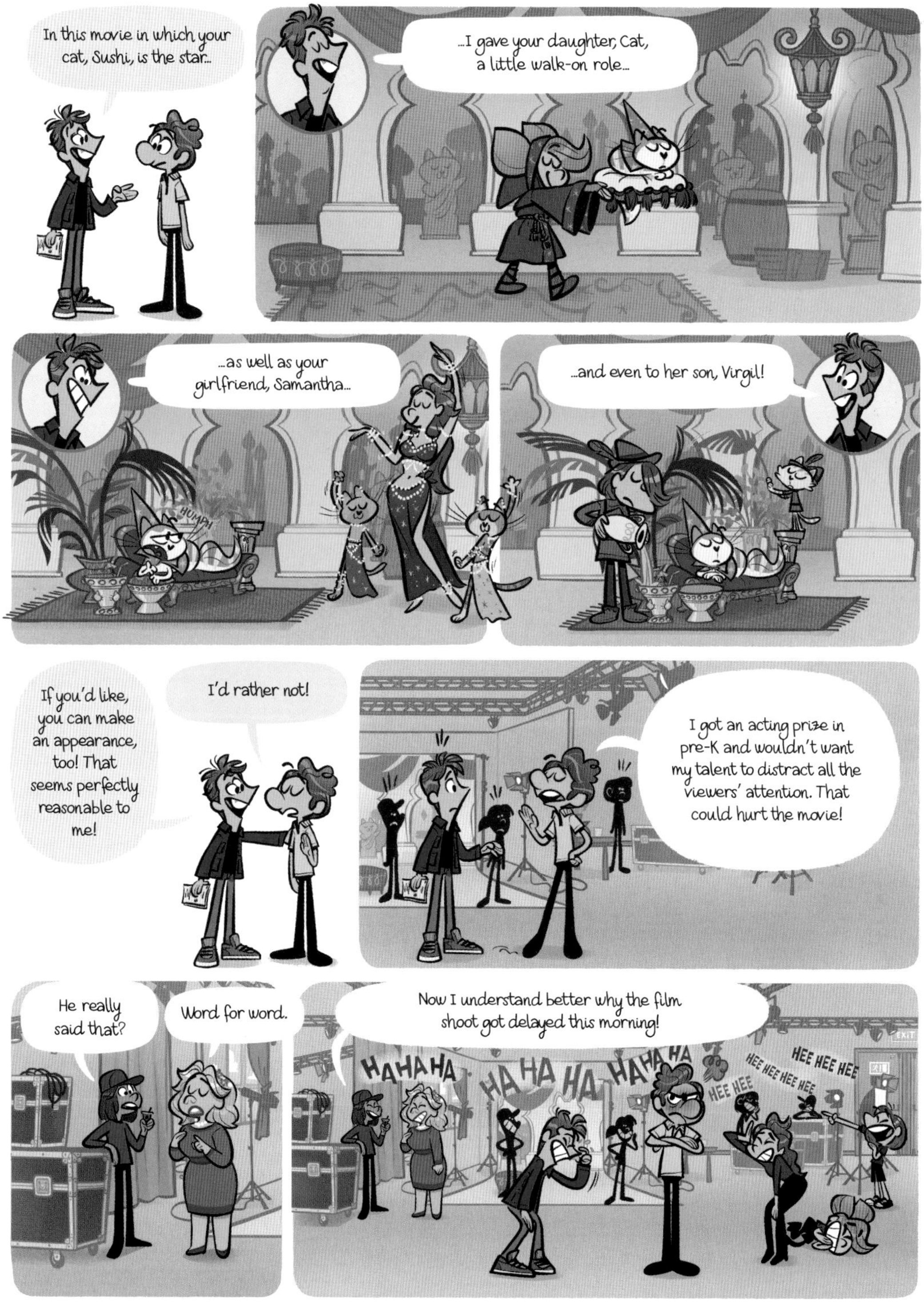
In this movie in which your cat, Sushi, is the star...
...I gave your daughter, Cat, a little walk-on role...
...as well as your girlfriend, Samantha...
HUMPH
...and even to her son, Virgil!
If you'd like, you can make an appearance, too! That seems perfectly reasonable to me!
I'd rather not!
I got an acting prize in pre-K and wouldn't want my talent to distract all the viewers' attention. That could hurt the movie!
He really said that?
Word for word.
Now I understand better why the film shoot got delayed this morning!
HAHAHA HA HA HA HAHAHA
HEE HEE
HEE HEE HEE HEE
HEE HEE HEE

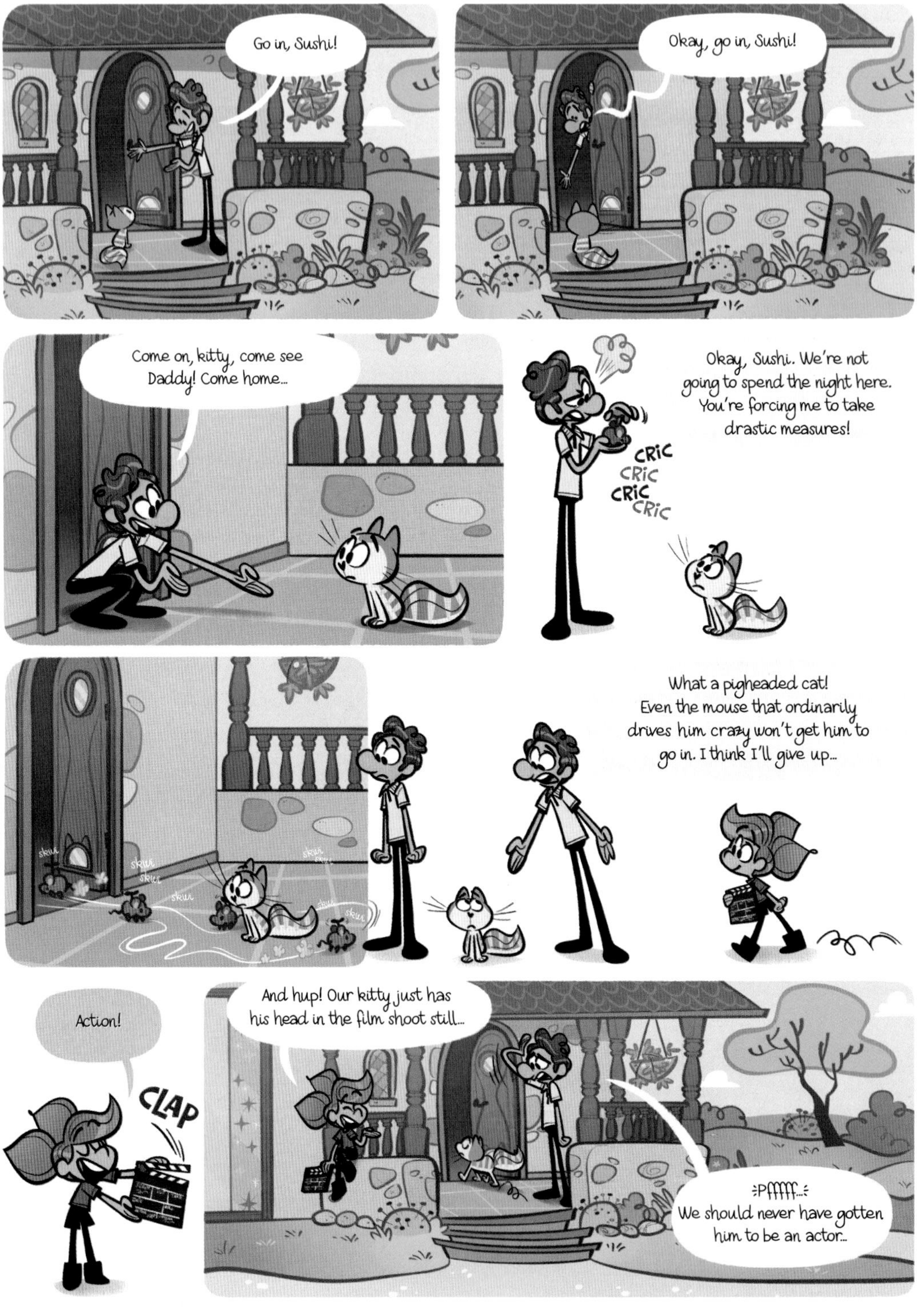

Go in, Sushi!
Okay, go in, Sushi!
Come on, kitty, come see Daddy! Come home...
Okay, Sushi. We're not going to spend the night here. You're forcing me to take drastic measures!
CRIC CRIC CRIC CRIC
What a pigheaded cat! Even the mouse that ordinarily drives him crazy won't get him to go in. I think I'll give up...
Action!
CLAP
And hup! Our kitty just has his head in the film shoot still...
PFFFFF...
We should never have gotten him to be an actor...

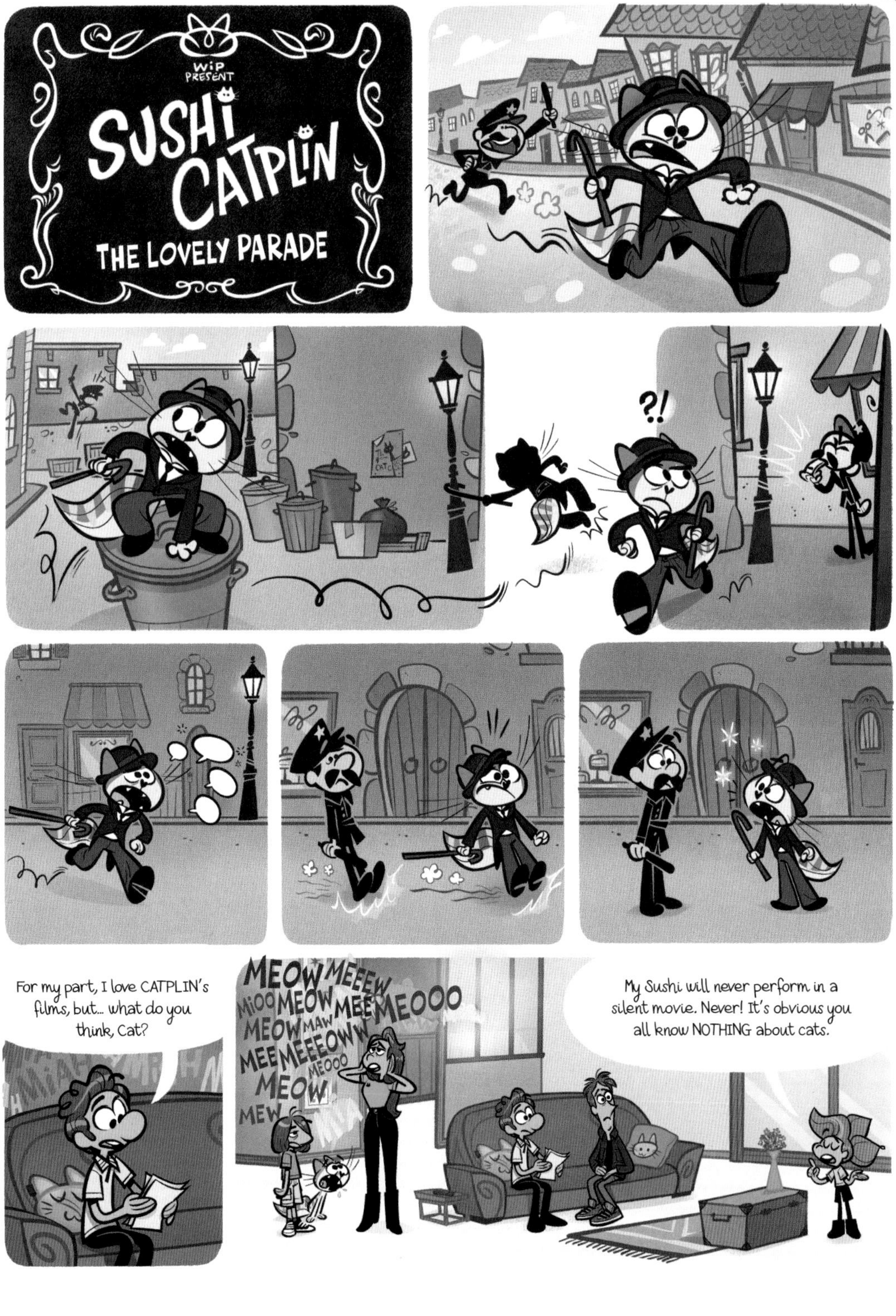
WIP
PRESENT
SUSHI CATPLIN
THE LOVELY PARADE
?!
For my part, I love CATPLIN's films, but... what do you think, Cat?
MEOW MEEEW MIOO MEOW MEE MEOOO MEOW MAW MEEEOWW MEE MEOOO MEOW MEW
My Sushi will never perform in a silent movie. Never! It's obvious you all know NOTHING about cats.

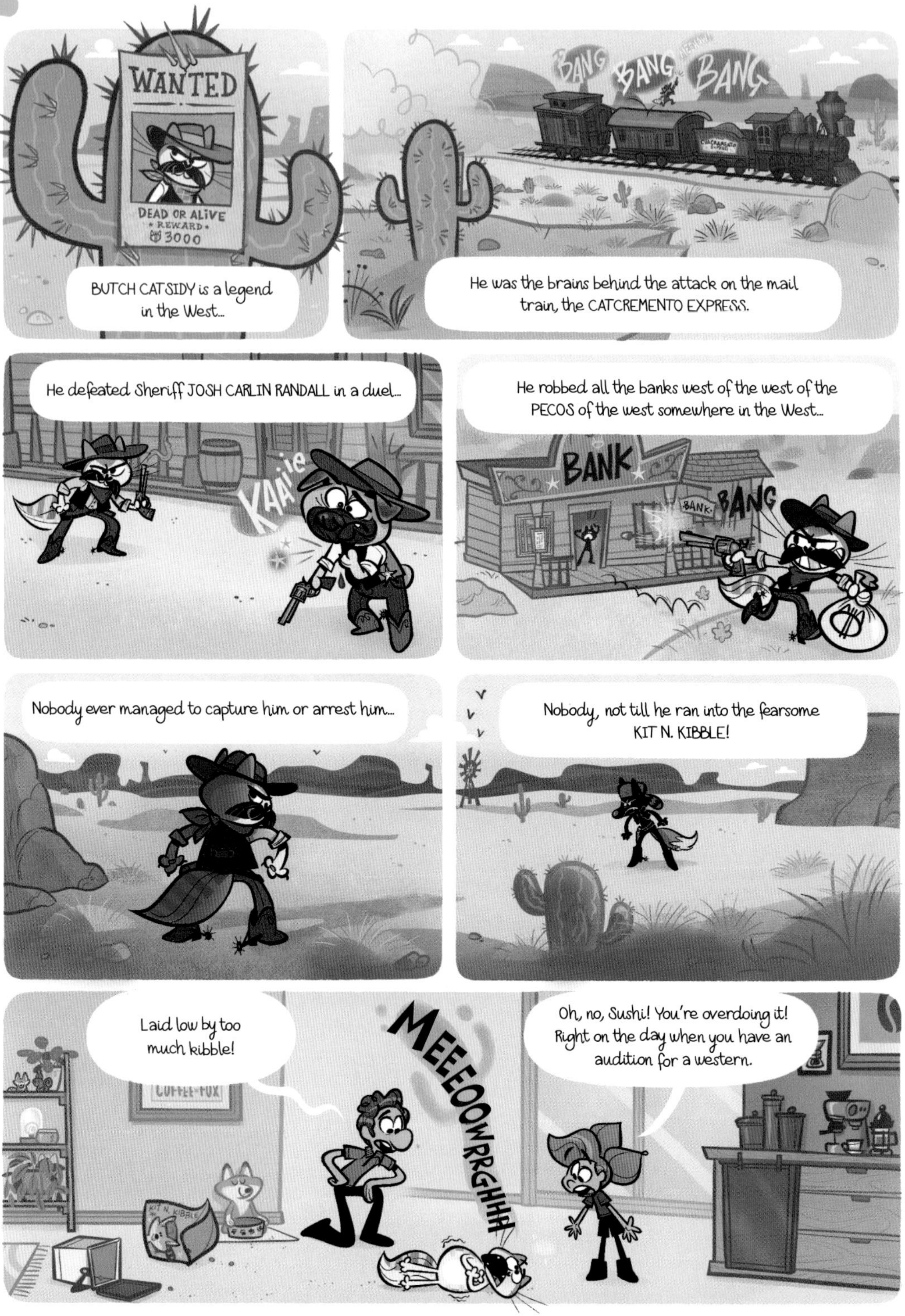
WANTED
DEAD OR ALIVE
REWARD
3000
BUTCH CATSIDY is a legend in the West...
BANG BANG BANG
He was the brains behind the attack on the mail train, the CATCREMENTO EXPRESS.
He defeated Sheriff JOSH CARLIN RANDALL in a duel...
KAAIIE
He robbed all the banks west of the west of the PECOS of the west somewhere in the West...
BANK
BANK
BANG
Nobody ever managed to capture him or arrest him...
Nobody, not till he ran into the fearsome KIT N. KIBBLE!
Laid low by too much kibble!
MEEEOOWRRGHHH
Oh, no, Sushi! You're overdoing it! Right on the day when you have an audition for a western.
COFFEE-FOX
KIT N. KIBBLE

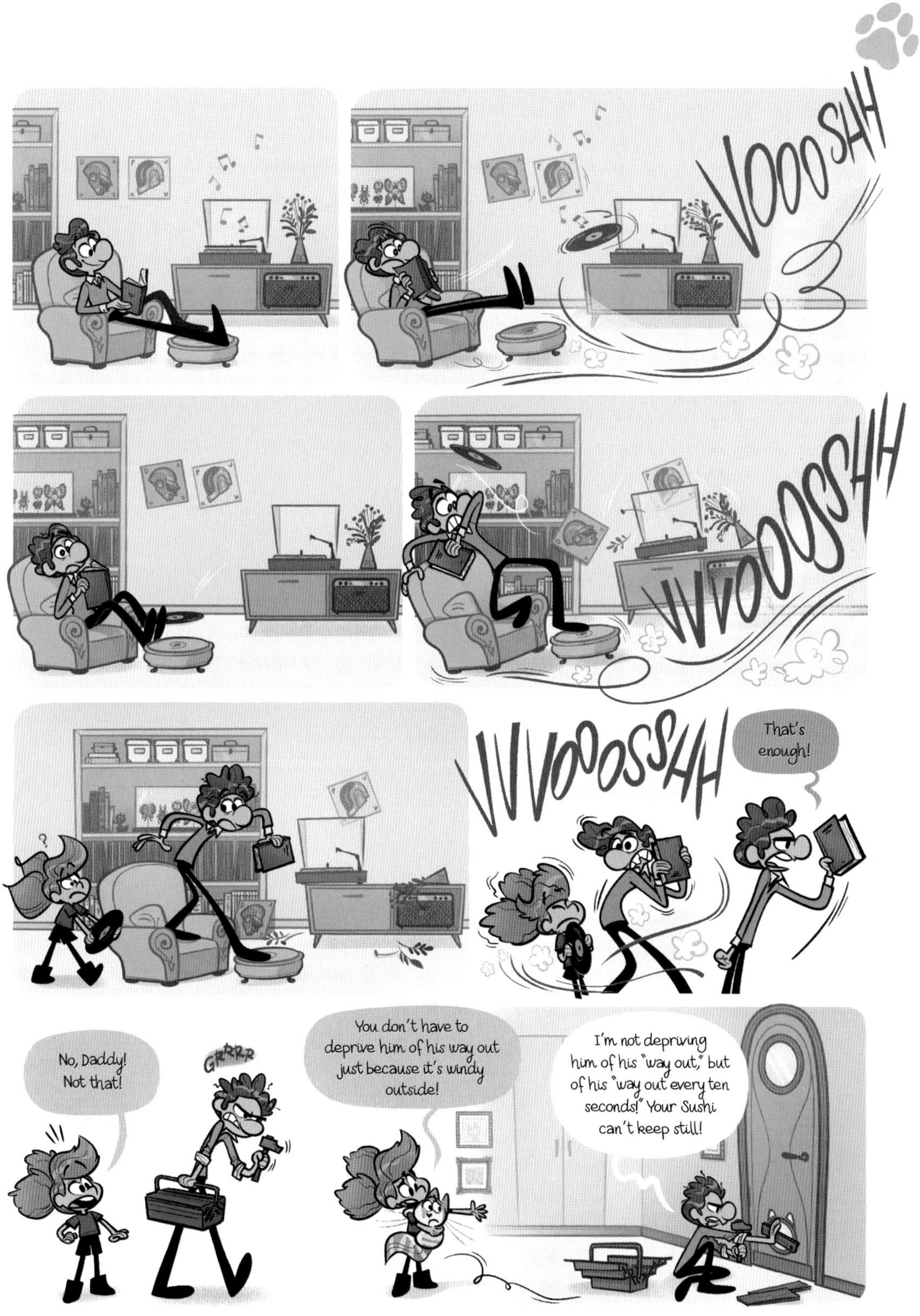
VOOOSHH
VVVOOOSSHH
VVVOOOSSHH
That's enough!
No, Daddy! Not that!
GRRRR
You don't have to deprive him of his way out just because it's windy outside!
I'm not depriving him of his "way out," but of his "way out every ten seconds!" Your Sushi can't keep still!

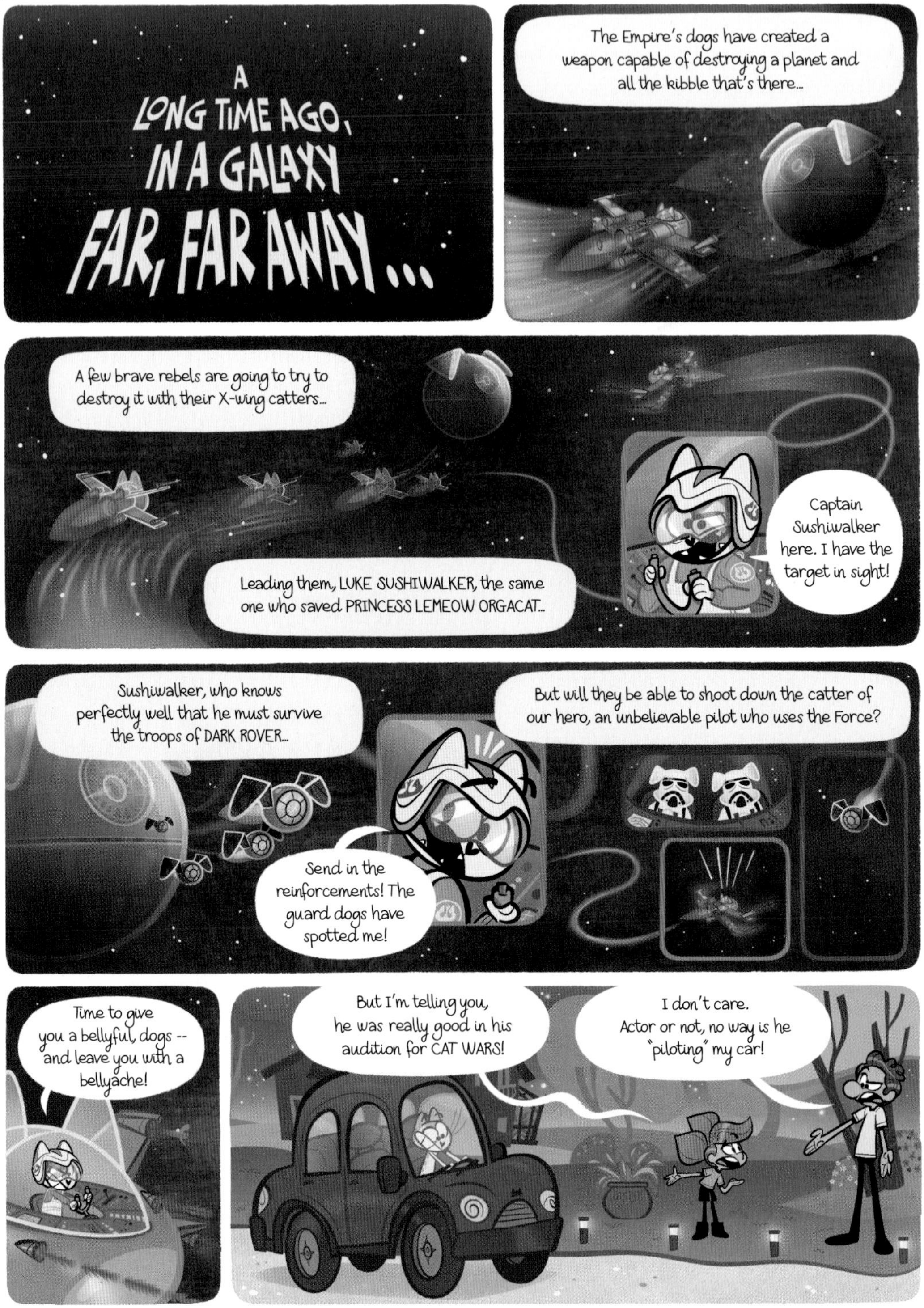

A LONG TIME AGO, IN A GALAXY FAR, FAR AWAY...
The Empire's dogs have created a weapon capable of destroying a planet and all the kibble that's there...
A few brave rebels are going to try to destroy it with their X-wing catters...
Leading them, LUKE SUSHIWALKER, the same one who saved PRINCESS LEMEOW ORGACAT...
Captain Sushiwalker here. I have the target in sight!
Sushiwalker, who knows perfectly well that he must survive the troops of DARK ROVER...
But will they be able to shoot down the catter of our hero, an unbelievable pilot who uses the Force?
Send in the reinforcements! The guard dogs have spotted me!
Time to give you a bellyful, dogs -- and leave you with a bellyache!
But I'm telling you, he was really good in his audition for CAT WARS!
I don't care. Actor or not, no way is he "piloting" my car!

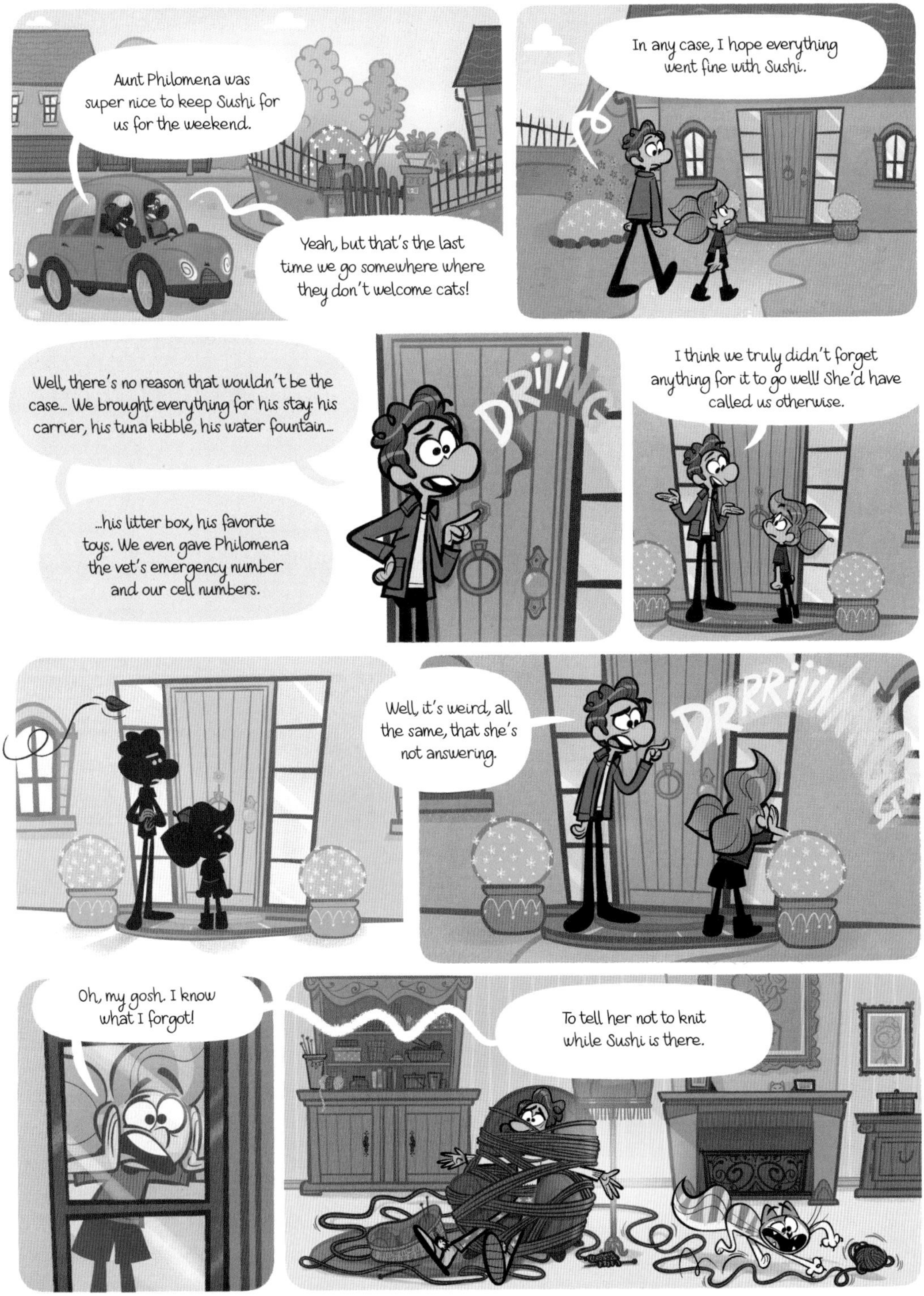
Aunt Philomena was super nice to keep Sushi for us for the weekend.
Yeah, but that's the last time we go somewhere where they don't welcome cats!
In any case, I hope everything went fine with Sushi.
Well, there's no reason that wouldn't be the case... We brought everything for his stay: his carrier, his tuna kibble, his water fountain...
...his litter box, his favorite toys. We even gave Philomena the vet's emergency number and our cell numbers.
DRIIING
I think we truly didn't forget anything for it to go well! She'd have called us otherwise.
Well, it's weird, all the same, that she's not answering.
DRRRIIINNNG
Oh, my gosh. I know what I forgot!
To tell her not to knit while Sushi is there.

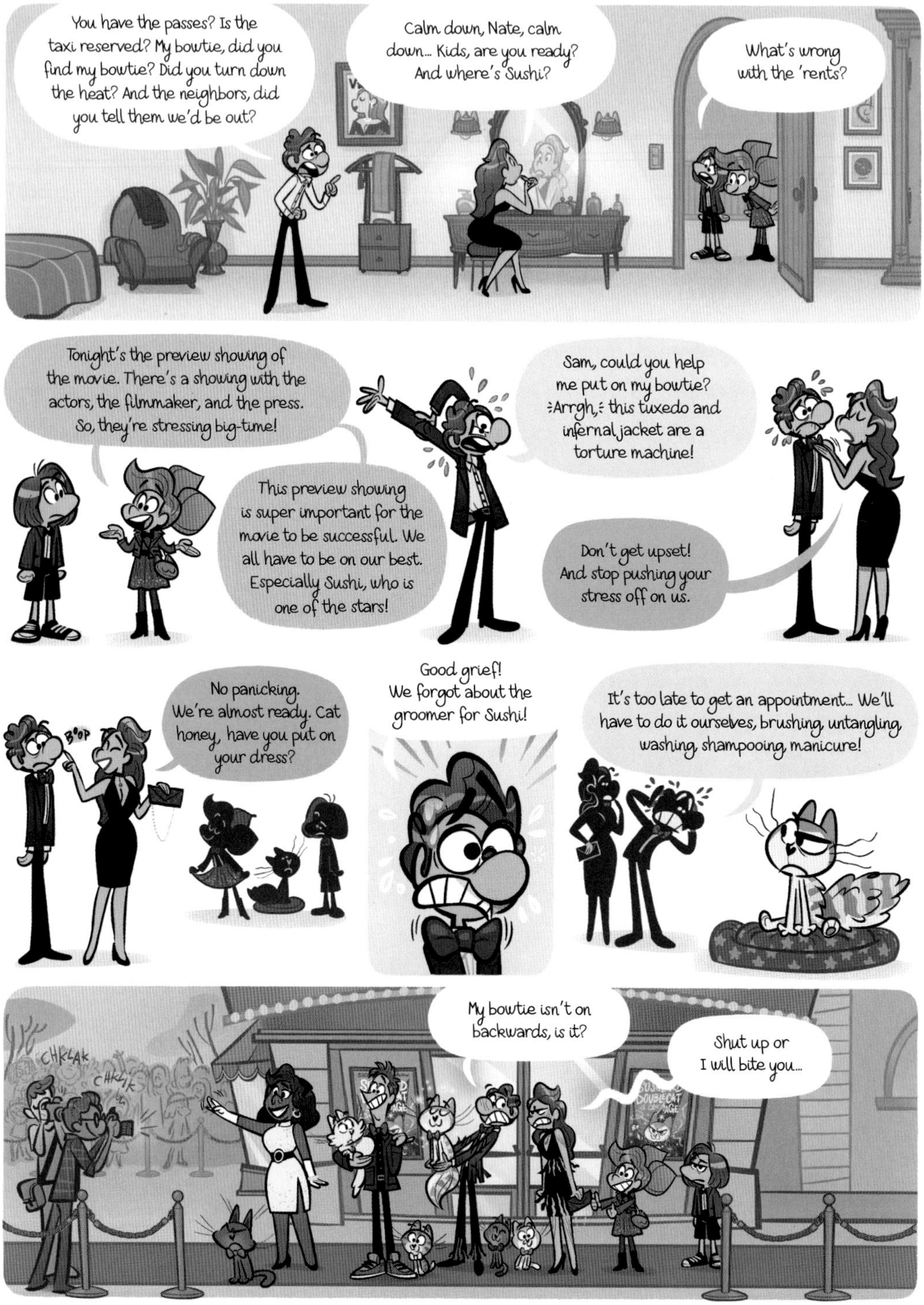

You have the passes? Is the taxi reserved? My bowtie, did you find my bowtie? Did you turn down the heat? And the neighbors, did you tell them we'd be out?
Calm down, Nate, calm down... Kids, are you ready? And where's Sushi?
What's wrong with the 'rents?
Tonight's the preview showing of the movie. There's a showing with the actors, the filmmaker, and the press. So, they're stressing big-time!
This preview showing is super important for the movie to be successful. We all have to be on our best. Especially Sushi, who is one of the stars!
Sam, could you help me put on my bowtie? Arrgh, this tuxedo and infernal jacket are a torture machine!
Don't get upset! And stop pushing your stress off on us.
BOOP
No panicking. We're almost ready. Cat honey, have you put on your dress?
Good grief! We forgot about the groomer for Sushi!
It's too late to get an appointment... We'll have to do it ourselves, brushing, untangling, washing, shampooing, manicure!
CHKLAK
CHKLIK
My bowtie isn't on backwards, is it?
Shut up or I will bite you...

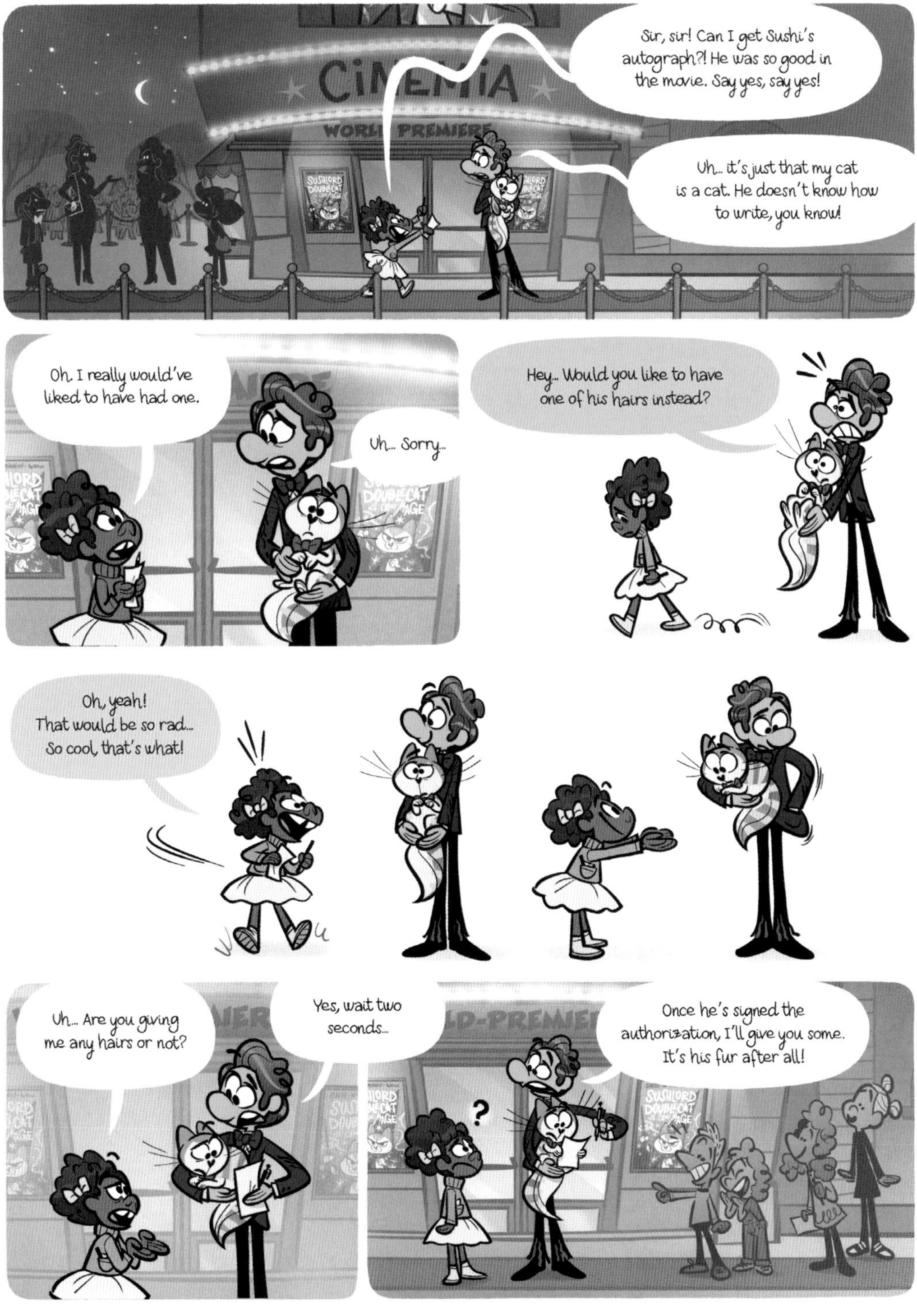
CiNEMiA
WORLD PREMIERE
Sir, sir! Can I get Sushi's autograph?! He was so good in the movie. Say yes, say yes!
Uh... it's just that my cat is a cat. He doesn't know how to write, you know!
Oh. I really would've liked to have had one.
Uh... Sorry...
Hey... Would you like to have one of his hairs instead?
Oh, yeah! That would be so rad... So cool, that's what!
Uh... Are you giving me any hairs or not?
Yes, wait two seconds...
Once he's signed the authorization, I'll give you some. It's his fur after all!

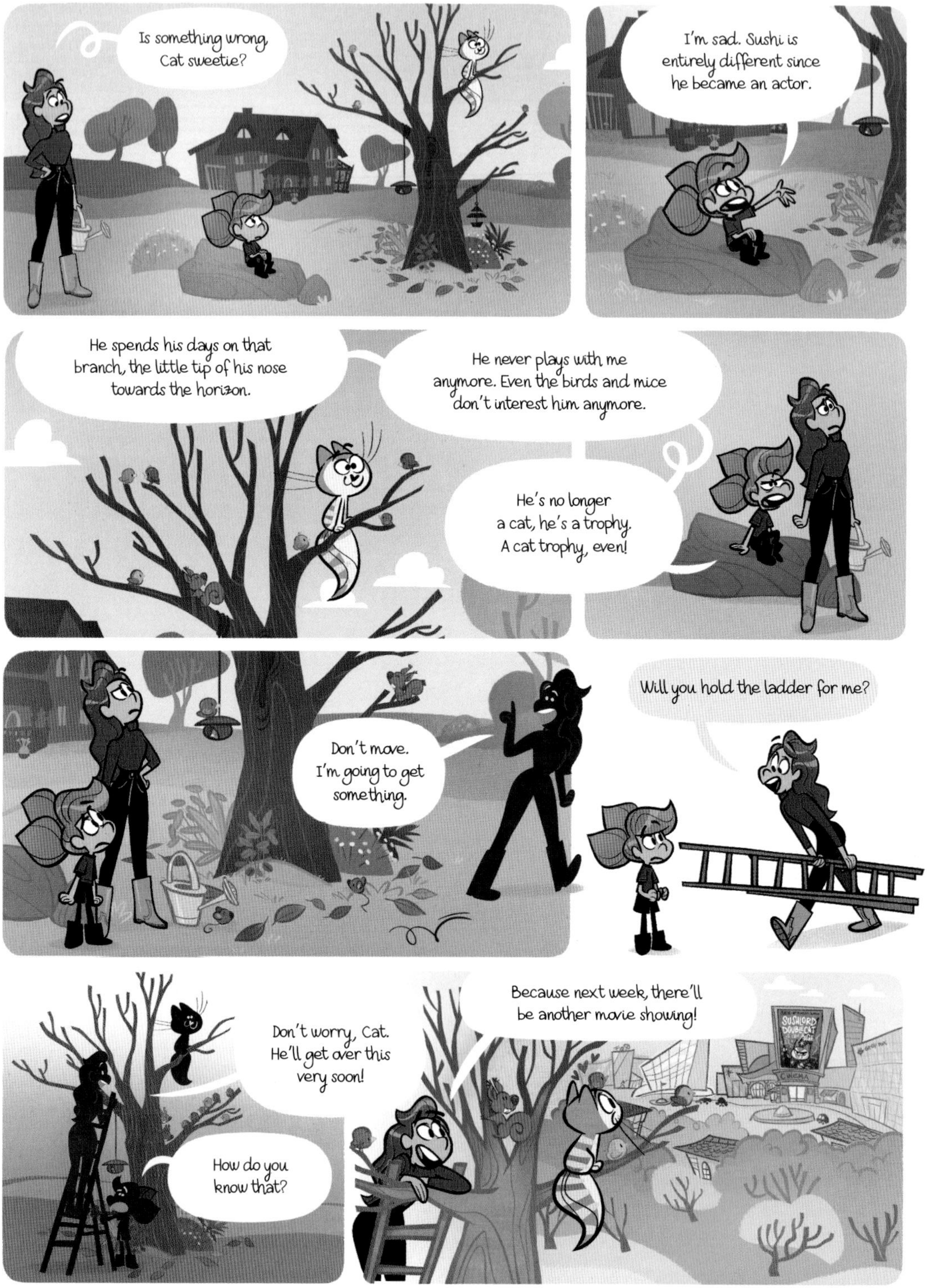
Is something wrong, Cat sweetie?
I'm sad. Sushi is entirely different since he became an actor.
He spends his days on that branch, the little tip of his nose towards the horizon.
He never plays with me anymore. Even the birds and mice don't interest him anymore.
He's no longer a cat, he's a trophy. A cat trophy, even!
Don't move. I'm going to get something.
Will you hold the ladder for me?
Don't worry, Cat. He'll get over this very soon!
How do you know that?
Because next week, there'll be another movie showing!
CINEMA

WATCH OUT FOR

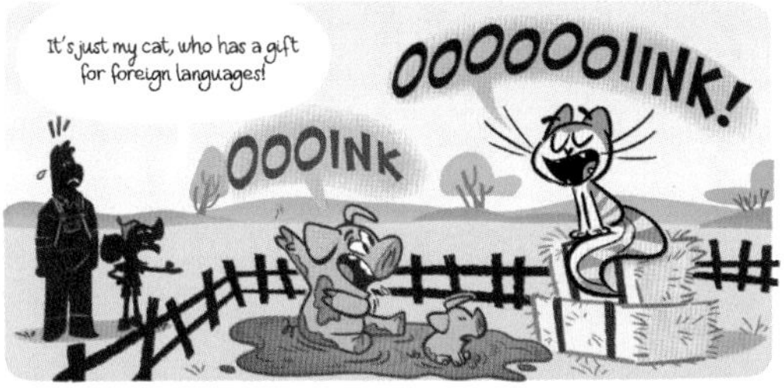
It's just my cat, who has a gift for foreign languages!
OOOOOOIINK!
OOOINK

Welcome to the fifth fabulous furry CAT & CAT graphic novel by Christophe Cazenove and Hervé Richez, writers, and Yrgane Ramon, artist, brought to you by Papercutz, those feline-adoring folks dedicated to publishing great graphic novels for all ages. I'm Jim Salicrup, the Editor-in-Chief and Cartoon Cat Caretaker here to reflect a bit on how Papercutz brings you great comics from around the world...

But first, let me share one of my few regrets with you. My parents were born in the United States, but my mother's parents were from Poland and Hungary, and my father's parents were from Spain and Puerto Rico. My parents grew up in New York City amongst many other immigrants, all trying to assimilate and become "American." They didn't want their children to be seen as other, so we were raised speaking only English. In school, I had taken a couple of Foreign Language classes—French and Spanish—and I was just awful at it. I just wasn't focused enough. I was too busy just trying to get through the school day so I could get home and enjoy TV, comics, music, toys, etc. As an adult, I regretted that I didn't try harder to learn other languages.

One of the comics I enjoyed appeared in a magazine called *Children's Digest* (sort of the kid's version of *Reader's Digest*, a very popular magazine at the time). The comic was *Tintin* by Hergé. There was also an animated version of *Tintin* on TV back then that was on every weekday early in the morning (these 60s cartoons are easily found on YouTube now). I also remember that there were also these larger (and more expensive) than regular comicbooks comics that featured *Tintin* available at my local Woolworth's store in their Children's Books section. I couldn't afford these graphic novels back then, and had to make do with the serialized, two-color version in *Children's Digest* and the cartoon show.

Back then, I didn't fully realize that comics weren't exclusively produced in the USA, I just knew I loved comics and could never get enough of them. I knew that cartoons such as *Speed Racer*, *Gigantor*, 8th Man, and others were probably made in Japan, but I had no idea that Japan had a huge comics industry.

When I started working at Marvel, I was still a teenager, and my first professional comics editing job was converting Marvel's full-color monthly comics into black and white weekly comics such as THE MIGHTY WORLD OF MARVEL and SPIDER-MAN COMICS WEEKLY. The idea was to approximate the style and feel of Britain's weekly comics. I'd have to divide up the original Marvel Comics stories into multiple parts and create new first pages (called splash pages), and "translate" the stories from American English into British English—me, a kid from the Bronx! Changing words such as color to "colour," for example. Years later, when I was editing the American Marvel comics, I had the opportunity to do the opposite of what I had been doing editing those British titles—I got to edit the produced-in-Marvel's-British-offices *Doctor Who* comics for publication in Marvel's American comics.

The longer I was working in comics, the more I realized that there were incredible comics being produced all over the world. While some, such as *Tintin* were being published in English in America, most were unavailable to me. And even if I could get my hands on them, the only ones I could read were from England. How could I ever be able to enjoy all those incredible comics being created in France, Belgium, Spain, Italy, Brazil, and the rest of the world?

Well, who would've guessed I'd wind up co-founding Papercutz with Terry Nantier, one of the pioneers of bringing European graphic novels to America through his company NBM? My whole life has been one dream coming true after another—first my childhood dream of working at Marvel Comics and then through Papercutz, a way to read such classic comics such as THE SMURFS and ASTERIX. It's as if I have my very own company to translate the comics I want to read most from around the world—and I get to share them all with you. How great is that?

At Papercutz we've been fortunate to have such great translators as Jeff Whitman, Elizabeth Tieri, and, in the case of CAT & CAT (and so many other Papercutz titles), Joe Johnson. Or to use his formal title, from his *other* job: Dr. E. Joe Johnson, Professor of French and Spanish, Interim Assistant Dean, College of Arts & Sciences at Clayton State University. How he manages to translate as many pages of comics for Papercutz, I'll never know. But he always does an excellent job. Our intentions are always to be as faithful to the original authors' work, while also making the material as understandable as possible to an American audience.

While I'm thrilled to be able to enjoy all these great comics, a part of me still wishes I can enjoy the comics in their original languages. The good thing is that you have options now. So much material from around the world is being presented in English for the American market from not just Papercutz and NBM, but many other graphic novel publishers as well. So, the choice is yours—learn other languages and enjoy these comics as they were originally created or simply appreciate the translated versions. The choice is yours!

And speaking of comics from around the world, check out the preview of ASTRO MOUSE AND LIGHTBULB #3 on the following pages. After experiencing a cat on a farm and in Hollywood, seems like seeing a mouse (and an intelligent light bulb) in space is that crazy. Besides, we publish so many cat comics at Papercutz (or should we call ourselves Papercatz?) it seems only fair to provide equal time to mice (Such as ASTRO MOUSE and GERONIMO STILTON REPORTER). ASTRO MOUSE was created in Spain by Fermín Solís (and translated by Jeff Whitman) and is available now at booksellers and libraries everywhere.

Au revoir,

JIM

STAY IN TOUCH!

EMAIL: salicrup@papercutz.com
WEB: www.papercutz.com
TWITTER: @papercutzgn
INSTAGRAM: @papercutzgn
FACEBOOK: PAPERCUTZGRAPHICNOVELS

Go to papercutz.com & sign up for the free Papercutz e-newsletter!

Special Preview of

FERMÍN SOLÍS

ASTRO MOUSE AND LIGHT BULB

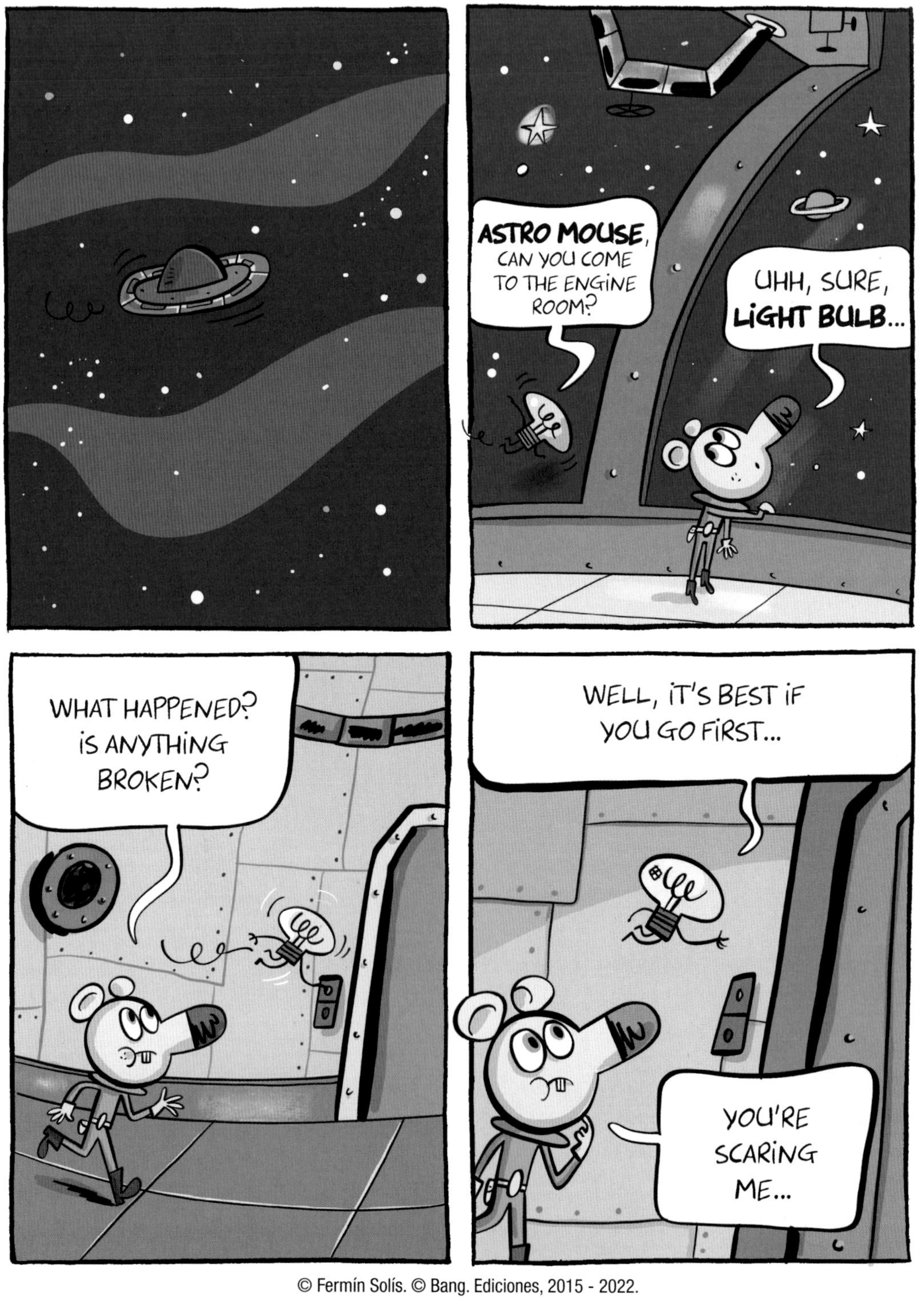

ASTRO MOUSE, CAN YOU COME TO THE ENGINE ROOM?
UHH, SURE, LIGHT BULB...
WHAT HAPPENED? IS ANYTHING BROKEN?
WELL, IT'S BEST IF YOU GO FIRST...
YOU'RE SCARING ME...

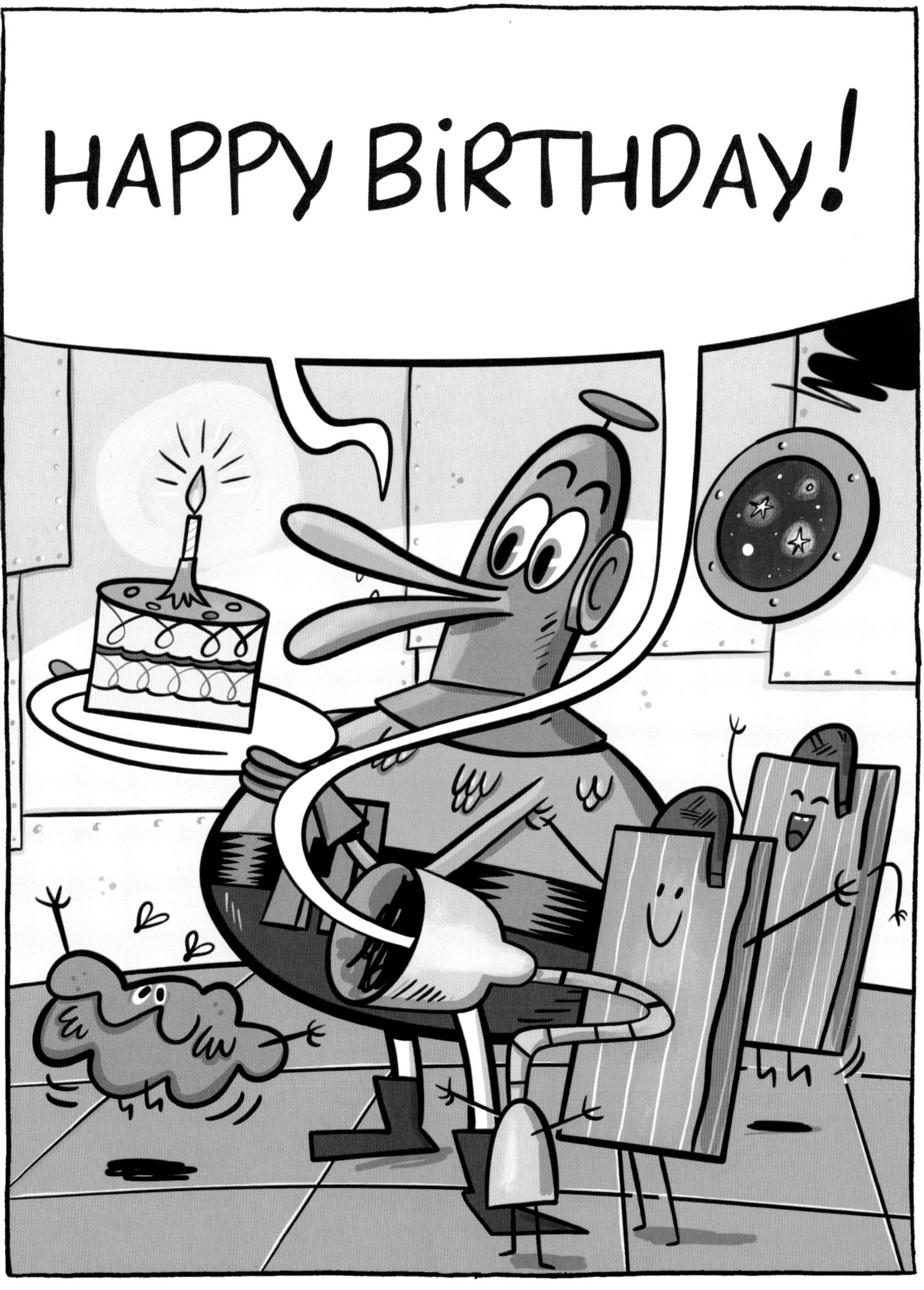
HAPPY BiRTHDAY!